THE TROPHY WIFE

SUNDAY TOMASSETTI

COVER DESIGN: Shasti O'Leary Soudant

DEVELOPMENTAL EDITOR: Ashley Cestra

LINE EDITOR: Kelley Harvey at Next Level Line Edits, Coaching, and Critiquing

COPY EDITOR/PROOFREADER: Wendy Chan, The Passionate Proofreader

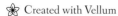 Created with Vellum

"It's easier to fool people than to convince them they've been fooled." – Unknown

DESCRIPTION

What are friends for?

Wallflower Cate Cabot has always been content to keep the world at arms' length, particularly from behind the register at the upscale Floridian boutique where she's worked for the last nine years. Her days are filled with old-moneyed locals and nouveau-riche tourists, most of them paying her no mind as she rings up their lavish hauls.

Until Odessa DuVernay.

At first glance, she's just another picture-perfect Palm Shores trophy wife—until she proves herself personable, humble, and unassuming. She even goes so far as to take a genuine interest in Cate, inviting her for lunch dates, matinees, and girl talk—a refreshing change of pace for the woman who never quite mastered the art of making (and keeping) friends.

But what begins as an unlikely friendship detours into the unthinkable when Odessa leaves Cate a panicked voicemail asking to meet—and then ghosts her. And worse—when Cate attempts to find her, it's as if the enigmatic Mrs. DuVernay never existed at all...

Consumed, Cate refuses to stop searching. But the truth won't come easy.

In fact, it just might cost her everything.

1

CATE

"THEY SAY it's bad luck to buy yourself an opal." My first customer of the day brushes a strand of silky-blonde hair from her ageless face and gifts me with a lip-bitten smile from the other side of the glass counter. "But I'm feeling lucky today and that piece is to die for. Would you mind?"

With a polished nail the color of a ballet slipper, she points to a vintage Blanchard-Moet cocktail ring, an unapologetic gold number with an oversized opal in the center and a halo of glistening diamonds.

"Of course." I remove the key from the satin ribbon on my wrist and retrieve the bauble, careful to place it on a pale pink square of velvet as if it were worth a million dollars and not five hundred—shop owner's rule. I keep close as she examines it under the store lights with the kind of enthusiasm that belongs in another world, another time. It's almost as if she's never seen anything so magnificent as this ring, childlike oohs and aahs, a whole production. "This is off the record, but allegedly this piece once belonged to Wallis Simpson. A gift from her *first* husband—before she married King Edward VIII."

The woman diverts her gaze—the bluest I've ever seen—to me. "You're kidding."

I lift a palm in protest. "That's what our seller told us, though I will say we haven't been able to verify that."

The woman slips it over her right ring finger, taking in the shimmering view from all angles as she exhales with the purest of sighs. It fits as if it were made for her, and it looks as though it were too. I suppose when your hand is slender and delicate, you can pull off anything from gaudy cocktail rings to chunky diamond eternity bands to the unapologetic rock on her left ring finger.

Everyone is married in Palm Shores. Everyone but me, that is. But technically I only work in Palm Shores. I live in her western, less glamorous sister city, the one with more people, more crime, less money, and houses without sweeping views of the rolling Atlantic. Most people don't vacation to *West* Palm Shores.

Not that I'm complaining.

I'm quite content with my life exactly the way it is.

Honest.

I wouldn't change a thing.

Folding my hands together in front of my hips, I place my stunted, thickset digits out of sight, though I can still hear my mother's voice tsk-ing away at the sorry fact that I inherited the unfortunate *Cabot Fingers.*

"Even if the Wallis Simpson story isn't true, I love the idea of it, don't you?" She bounces on the balls of her feet once, an excited woman-child. "Makes it a little more than something pretty. Gives it meaning. A story that lives on forever."

"This place is full of stories," I say. And it's true. Smith + Rose is Palm Shores' most popular high-end consignment boutique, drawing in fastidious shoppers of a certain breed from all over the world as well as bored vacationers ambling away from their resorts, money so Florida-hot it's burning holes in their pockets.

"That silk scarf." I point to a mannequin in the front window display. "Once belonged to Jackie O. in the seventies."

"Allegedly?"

"Verifiably. Her great niece's sister-in-law brought it in last month, along with a picture and a notarized document."

The leggy blonde, still wearing the opal ring, departs from the glass case to check out the vintage scarf.

I check the time on my watch, jonesing for my next break. I can almost taste the nicotine sting on the tip of my tongue. Smoking at work is always a whole thing—a paper-thin PVC jacket to keep the stink from leaching into my clothes, gloves to protect my fingers from staining, peppermint gum. I tried the whole patch thing once without luck. My doctor wrote me some pills last year that were supposed to help, but they only gave me nightmares. It's a dirty, disgusting habit, but for now it owns me.

"It isn't my style, but my God is it beautiful," she says.

She's right. It isn't her style at all. She's sleek and modern, dressed in head-to-toe black with hair so pale it's almost white—not a hint of brass. If she's a local, I imagine she goes to one of those upmarket hair salons on Caraway Avenue, where the stylists are so busy they have assistants—and some of their assistants are so busy *they* have assistants.

"My mother would just adore this," she says, her fingertips light along the patterned fabric. "Though we're a long way from Christmas, and her birthday isn't until October. I'll keep this in mind."

"Of course." Although I earn a small commission on all of my transactions, we're under strict orders not to pressure shoppers or oversell products. The owners of Smith + Rose feel any high-pressure tactics cheapen the shop's experience.

"You know ..." she says, returning, her fingers toying with the opal ring. "I have a few things I'm looking to sell, but I haven't the slightest idea where to begin."

"What kinds of things?"

"Nice things," she glances around, peering through fringes of jet-black lashes as soft as gossamer. "Heirloom quality pieces. Vintage. Rare. Designer."

"You'll want to make an appointment with the owners. They personally handpick everything. If you have receipts, documents, appraisals, anything to help show the value of your item, you'll have the best chance at being accepted. Here." I retrieve a business card from behind the register and hand it over.

She tucks the card into a cognac-hued Balworth bag, a purse that—if I'm not mistaken—costs a whopping twelve grand retail and requires an eighteen-month stint on a wait list. The wooden handle boasts a black silk scarf tied into a flouncy bow—a little pop of feminine whimsy against the backdrop of a perfectly chic ensemble.

"Thank you so much. I'll definitely reach out to them."

A rumble comes from outside, and the sky has darkened from just a few moments ago. Angry clouds usher in a tropical thunderstorm. It'll likely last twenty minutes or so, and anyone strolling by will seek refuge in my store until it passes.

Tourists always forget umbrellas.

They don't know Palm Shores isn't always sunshine and blue skies.

"Just so you know, they're never here on Mondays or Tuesdays." Not that she's asked why they aren't here today, but I feel compelled to share that information should she stop in another time. "But you can almost always find them Wednesday through Friday."

"Must be nice to only have to work three days a week …" she says with a wink. "How long have you worked here?"

"Almost nine years." I've only been asked this question twice since working here. The first time the woman had asked me as an insult when she attempted to imply that my age at the time correlated to unprofessionalism and inexperience. This was after she marched in to demand a refund on a non-returnable necklace. When that didn't work, she claimed the piece was a fake, going so far as to have a fake letter drafted up on fake letterhead from some fake insurance agency.

This woman in front of me is nothing like that miserable lady who never set foot in here again after that shit show.

This woman is anything but miserable. I swear there's an aura about her, vibrant beams of sunlight splaying out from her like an angelic being in an oil painting. "She has good vibes," as one of my old friends would've said. She was always judging people by their "vibes."

I guess after three years of friendship, she decided she didn't like mine anymore because the fruitcake ghosted me without reason or warning.

"You must love it then," she says. "I think I would too, being surrounded by beautiful things, meeting new people all day."

I crack a semblance of a smile. She isn't wrong. I love my job. My bosses, while typically sour-faced or shit-faced, depending on the time of day, are decent to me, and it beats the hell out of sitting behind gray cubicle walls forty hours a week. Or following in my mother's professional footsteps and managing the housekeeping department at Le Bleu Meridien Hotel for decades on end.

Not only that, but I've always had an affinity for the genuine.

In a self-absorbed society with a narcissism epidemic, everyone values image perception over reality. No one cares about being real anymore.

But all of the items in this shop? They're as real as it gets.

None of them are trying to be anything they're not.

They don't care about what came before them or what came after.

They don't care that they were replaced by newer, better things.

They're original.

True.

Authentic.

"Yes, it's a wonderful place to work. So what are we thinking with the ring?" I change the subject. "It really does suit you. And I've never heard that about opals being bad luck ... it must be an old wives' tale."

She laughs under her breath. "I'm sure. It's crazy how these stories come to be, isn't it? Are there a bunch of bored housewives sitting around a coffee table making up ridiculous rules about jewelry to entertain themselves? Surely they have better things to do with their time ..."

Probably not.

This town is full of old wives (though you'd never guess any of their ages), most of them bored, bronzed, gossipy little drama magnets trying to one-up one another. It's its own culture and, honestly, I find it fascinating.

I take the opportunity to get a closer look at her. Glassy forehead. Not a single crinkle around her eyes or between her brows. She could be thirty or she could be a fifty-year-old science experiment—Lord knows, Palm Shores has some of the best plastic surgeons in the country, if not the world.

"All right," she exhales, clasping her elegant hands over her heart. "I'm sold. It's too beautiful to pass up."

"Wonderful. I can take that for you." I place my hand out, palm facing up. She slips it off her ring finger and places it carefully in my hand, like it's the most precious thing she's ever touched. I retrieve a wooden box made of unstained, matte white oak and a white satin ribbon. "I'll wrap this and meet you at the register—unless you'd like to keep shopping?"

I steal another glimpse of the sky, which is now a deeper shade of blue, blanketed in malignant clouds. I'm guessing she has five minutes tops before that rain destroys her pristine blow-out.

The woman checks the glinting diamond-and-white-gold timepiece on her wrist, releasing a quiet hum. I take another gander at her ring, the stone having fallen to one side with its weight. I'm guessing it's five, six carats tops—excessive, yet more tasteful than the postage-stamp-sized hunks of carbon many of our shoppers wield.

"I'm supposed to meet my husband for lunch at that new place on Sapphire Shore Drive in a few ..." she says. "Though I could spend all day in here."

"No worries. We're here seven days a week." I carry the box to the register closest to the front door. She follows on the opposite side of the counter, heels clicking against the marble floor with each step. "You'll just have to come back and pick up where you left off another time."

"Absolutely." Her tone wholeheartedly convinces me.

"Five hundred sixty-four dollars and eleven cents," I say a short minute later.

I swipe her card, setting it down while it processes. Then I help my curious self to a one-second peek at the name on the bottom.

Odessa DuVernay.

Palm Shores is a magnet for celebrities, billionaires, and Golden Age-old money types—but I don't recognize the name. It's possible she's a transplant. We get a lot of New Yorkers down this way, though I didn't catch an accent. She could be anyone from anywhere.

The card reader beeps before expelling a paper receipt, which I slide across the glass countertop along with a blue-inked fountain pen etched with the Smith + Rose logo. Despite the fact that they're imported from Switzerland and twenty dollars a pop and are always being "accidentally stolen," my employers refuse to consider more economical alternatives, considering them tax write-offs well spent.

It's all about the complete Smith + Rose experience. Every detail, from the fig and cassis scent being diffused from strategic sections of the space to the helpful-but-not-too-personal staff on the sales floor to the smooth flick of the fountain pens as they sign their receipts has all been carefully orchestrated by long-time best friends, high-end retail aficionados, and sun-bronzed Betties: Elinor Smith and Margaret Rose.

The sky releases a groan and little specks of rain pelt the sidewalk. Odessa doesn't notice or, if she does notice, she doesn't care ... it seems she's too focused on me.

"Thank you so much, *really*. You've been so kind and

helpful." Her voice is airy and laced in profound apprecia-
tion—which almost distracts me from calculating my fifty-
dollar commission from the sale of this ring.

"You're so welcome." I smile so big my cheeks hurt.

"I don't believe I caught your name?" She lifts
one brow.

The owners have never required nametags, claiming
they're just another formality that downgrades the high-end
shopping experience. We're supposed to assist the
customers, not get personal with them. According to
Margaret and Elinor, most of these people don't want to be
bothered with friendly banter and exchanging names is a
gateway to that.

"Cate." I come around from behind the register to hand-
deliver her purchase. "Receipt's in the bag. I do hope you'll
come again soon."

Odessa DuVernay glances over her shoulder on her way
out the door, her voluminous blonde hair bouncing with
each click of her aqua-bottomed heels. "I absolutely will.
Take care, Cate."

Just like that, the sky opens and the kindest Palm Shores
trophy wife I've ever met disappears into a tropical thunderstorm sans designer umbrella.

I lock the front door, flip the "Be Right Back" sign, and
head out back for my two-minute smoke break and a quick
sip from my can of Royal Crown cola in the breakroom. For
a moment, I consider the patrons stuck in the downpour
and a twinge of guilt slices through my middle, but it's
quickly replaced by the restless nicotine craving screaming
through my blood.

In my PVC jacket a minute later, fingers gloved, I stand
beneath an overhang, back against the brick. I light a

menthol Newport, and while the rain pools in the pitted blacktop pockets of the parking lot, I take my first drag.

I was a crisp eighteen when I started smoking, and for the dumbest reason. Some kids buy a pack of cigs on their eighteenth birthday because they can. Me? The nostalgia practically called to me by name. The packaging was almost straight out of the eighties—which was the last time I saw my father. And the brand name—Newport—had this East Coast, old money feel to it: also reminiscent of my father, seeing how he and his "real" family hailed from Newport, Rhode Island and the Cabots were Golden Age legends alongside the Astors and Morgans and Rockefellers.

I take another drag and stub out my half-finished stick on the wall before jamming it back into the pack, and then I head inside to peel out of my coat and gloves and pop a stick of gum.

The rain lets up by the time I unlock the front door.

The trophy wife is long gone, of course, but if I'm lucky, maybe I'll see her again sometime.

I don't say this about a lot of people, but she seemed authentic. Genuine. And I've spent my entire life learning the difference between real and fake.

2

ZSOFIA

IT'S QUITE LATE, and Mrs. DuVernay is in a mood again.

She steps out of her heels as if they disgust her, kicking them askew as she makes her way to her dressing room on the other side of her bedroom. I scramble to grab her shoes, waiting for her to peel out of the day's clothes and emerge in her favorite silk robe with her initials monogrammed over the right breast.

She's taking longer than usual to undress today, nothing but huffs and sighs coming from the other side of the doorway. If I had to guess, she's gained a few pounds. That always seems to send her into a quiet fit when she's changing. I imagine her examining her tall, thin body from the three angles of her mirror, hugging the shoes against my chest as I wait to go in.

Mrs. DuVernay sighs when she finally comes out a minute later, bare feet covered in red markings from the day spent out and about in killer heels. Markings, I'm convinced, she no longer feels. I tried them on once, when she wasn't looking—her favorite pair of shoes, the black ones with the teal bottoms. In less than ten steps, I swear I had a blister forming on the back of one of my heels.

"My drink, Zsofia," she says, hands on her hips as she peers around her bedroom with raised eyebrows and flattened lips.

I nod toward her vanity, where her usual—a dry white wine with a splash of organic pineapple juice—rests on a vintage coaster made of rhinoceros ivory.

Mrs. DuVernay swipes her drink off the table, taking it with her into the master *en suite*. I carry her shoes into the closet, praying I can locate the correct place for them before she yells for me to fetch her a heated facial towel from the warmer in the spa.

This past Friday, she had two professionals come and sort through her closet—a stylist and an organizer. One helped her create toss/sell/donate piles and the other reconfigured the rest of her things to the point where I can't find half of what she sends me to retrieve now.

An empty red shoebox with its top misaligned is situated in the middle of the closet. Dropping to my knees, I place the heels neatly inside, fasten the lid, and find the proper spot for it amongst the others along her expansive wall of designer shoes.

"Zsofia," she calls from the next room, her tone flat and void of emotion.

I leave the closet to find her at the vanity, the day washed off of her face and a thick mask of rosehip stem cells and sea kelp on her face, sinking into her pore-less, ageless, glass-like complexion.

"I'll be right back with a towel." I head to the spa room at the end of the hall.

Mrs. DuVernay prefers to have her facialists, masseuses, and manicurists come to the house so she can beautify in private, though I believe it has more to do with the falling-out she had with her group of friends a few years back. They always used to schedule their pampering appointments together. After the squabble, Mrs. DuVernay couldn't bear to be seen alone and friendless in her favorite beauty haunts, so she persuaded Charles to turn one of the spare bedrooms into a home spa. Not that it took much convincing—Mrs. DuVernay controls the purse strings around here, as much as she prefers to flit around like a Palm Shores trophy wife.

It's just another act of hers.

Like everything else.

I tiptoe down the hall to the spa room, retrieving a couple of damp wash cloths from the towel warmer on the back counter, and I bring them to her, stepping a few feet back as she breathes in the soft, lavender-scented steam and wipes away the exotic remains of her skincare routine.

When she's finished, she hands them off, reaches for her wine, and shuffles to her bed, her snow-colored silk robe billowing behind her with every leggy step.

"That's all for tonight, Zsofia." She waves me off as she climbs beneath a mountain of high-thread count bed coverings. "Oh. One more thing. Tell Charles it's time to come to bed on your way out."

"Yes, Mrs. DuVernay." I shut the door behind me without making a sound so as not to wake Aviana down the hall. Lord knows teenagers need their rest, and she can be a bit of a bear to deal with in the morning. As her human alarm clock, I prefer that she not be overly tired come six AM. It certainly makes my job a lot easier.

I run my palm along the polished banister on my way down, careful not to make a sound this time of night, when the house has quieted and settled and every footstep or cleared throat reverberates. Once I arrive on the main floor, I head for Mr. DuVernay's study—a room placed in the farthest reaches of the house, so Charles can play his jazz music and strum on his prized collection of rare guitars without disturbing his headache-prone wife.

Rapping on the outside of the door, I wait for him to answer.

The other side is quiet tonight. No jazz records. No clumsy, six-string chords.

I knock once more, holding my breath as I wait in silence.

Perhaps he isn't in there?

Twisting the door knob, I crack the door a few inches to check. "Mr. DuVernay?"

With no response, I push the door wider, peeking my entire head in to look around. The room is dark save for the floor lamp in the corner, and the curtains are open, show-casing a view of the water from the floor-to-ceiling windows on his east-facing wall. Boat lights sparkle, their reflections swaying in the distance on the buoying Atlantic. I've always thought it seemed dangerous to boat late at night. Then again, I've never boated in my life. What would I know?

Peering around the room one last time, I draw in a sharp breath when my gaze comes to him lying on the sofa, still as a statue, fast asleep. Peaceful because he's anywhere but here.

Padding across the room without a sound, I make my

way to him, a slow smile bending my mouth as I watch him sleep.

Charles is an impossibly handsome man; generous brown hair with salt-and-peppered temples, chiseled chin, sun-kissed complexion, runner's body much younger than his physical age. When he isn't having an 'off' day, he's a force to be reckoned with, a personality much larger than the room Mrs. DuVernay keeps him confined to most of the time. Charles' smile alone has turned some of my worst days into some of my brightest, and I live for his eyes—ocean blue on the outside with a ring of hazel in the middle—like they can't decide what they want to be.

A man like this is wasted on Mrs. DuVernay.

He deserves better.

She deserves worse.

"Mr. DuVernay," I say his name on the breath of a whisper before placing my fingertips on his shoulder, giving him three light taps. "Mrs. DuVernay would like you to come to bed."

His dark lashes flutter as his eyes open, and then he squints, focusing on me.

"Ah. It's you," he says, placing his hand over mine, gentle and unrushed. "Is my wife asleep yet?"

I swallow the rigid protuberance that has suddenly found a home in my throat. "No, sir."

Charles pulls himself to a standing position, his gaze never abandoning mine, not for one second. "Well, that's a shame, isn't it?"

Our eyes hold for a moment, and I stifle the knowing smile that threatens to curl my lips. He and I both know that the DuVernay household is a serene place when the missus is sleeping—or better yet: off on one of her solo vacations. There are more smiles when she's away. More laughter. Less tension. More living. Less silent suffering.

We're both prisoners of circumstance.

Prisoners with very different privileges.

Prisoners of Mrs. DuVernay.

"Goodnight, Zsofia," he says before striding to the door. "Get some rest."

I wait alone in his study for a beat, and then I shut off his lamp and close the door on my way out. He's gone by the time I reach the hall, leaving nothing but the faintest trail of his posh Italian cologne.

Tiptoeing through the darkened DuVernay residence, I make my way to the apartment above the garage—the only home I've ever known.

Home sweet prison cell.

3

CATE

"WHAT KIND of sham operation are you running here?"
The forty-something blonde standing before me late
Tuesday morning slams her broken locket on the glass
counter. I try not to wince at the thought of it shattering
beneath her palm. "*One time*. I wore this *one time*. And
now look at it."

Her voice is laced in anger with a side of stifled tears as
she attempts—and fails—to keep her cool.

I examine the timeworn gold piece—an 1847
Longcheau piece my colleague, Amada, sold two weeks
back. It wasn't cheap. Over three grand if I remember
correctly—grossly overpriced in my humble opinion.

The necklace was already in delicate condition, which
meant Amada should've gone over the purchase agreement
in detail with this woman, the one that explicitly stated it
was non-refundable and that insurance was highly
recommended.

Some of the items in our shop are meant to be worn and enjoyed—others, like this, are meant to be stored, kept, showcased as if they were in a museum display. They're purchased for their value more than their function, purchased so they can be passed down from generation to generation—not unlike old men who pass down coin collections to grandchildren.

Her ageless eyes flash and the nostrils of her too-perfect nose flare with each deep inhalation. "This is unacceptable. I *demand* a full refund or I *will* involve my attorney."

"May I have your name?"

She chuffs, as if answering my question is an inconvenience. "Annette Townsend."

The Townsend Law Firm commercials come to my mind, the ones advertised on all the billboards on my drive to work, always touting how they can make millionaires of those suffering personal injuries.

I doubt she's bluffing, but a contract is a contract.

"One moment, please." I head to the file cabinet in the back to locate a carbon copy of the original purchase agreement.

She can stomp her designer heels and pout her glossy lips all she wants, but she's not getting a full refund. Of course, if this were *my* business, I wouldn't run things this way. I don't think it's right to sell jewelry that's practically falling apart under any circumstances, but that isn't my call to make. If I were to give this woman a full refund and restock a broken, unsellable locket, it'd be my neck on the line.

I need this job more than this well-coiffed woman needs that three grand, I'm certain.

I return, placing the rectangular sheet of paper on the glass counter and turning it to face her. "Okay. I found the contract you signed. Unfortunately, you did initial off three times regarding the non-refundable nature of the piece."

She scoffs. "Well this is just ridiculous. I'm going to report you to the local business association. Actually ... who's your manager? I'd like to speak to someone in charge. You're *incredibly* unhelpful."

"Ma'am, this isn't my decision. I'm simply not allowed to process returns on non-refundable items," I use the clear, concise, and patient tone I've honed to perfection over the years. My tongue hums for a Newport even though my last was thirty minutes ago. "The shop owners come in tomorrow, if you'd like to speak to one of them in person."

"I'm leaving for St. Thomas tomorrow." She looks me up and down as if I should've known. She prods an almond-shaped, taupe-colored nail against the countertop. "I need to speak to someone *today*. Call them. Get them in here immediately."

The bells on the front door jangle, and I glance over the angry woman's shoulders as a handful of new customers shuffle in—a group of teenage girls with cropped tops, reedy legs in cut-off shorts, and tiny designer bags slung over their tanned shoulders. They bump into one another as they make their way around, turning their noses up as they examine the displays, trying on sunglasses and hats and snapping pictures with their phones, tongues wagging out as they mock our beautiful things.

The woman before me is momentarily distracted by a text message on her phone, her nails clacking against her screen as she forms a series of responses.

The girls grow bored soon enough and waste no time shuffling out, squeezing past another shopper making her way inside. Peeling a pair of cat-eye sunglasses from the bridge of her straight nose, the newest patron greets me with a warm smile and a flittering, five-fingered wave—the kind of thing you'd do with an old friend or acquaintance.

It's the woman from yesterday—Odessa DuVernay.

"*Hello*," the bitter woman before me snaps her fingers in my face, and I'm instantly taken aback—physically and otherwise.

"I'm sorry," I say. "Yes."

Annette Townsend slams her hand on the glass counter. "Are you going to call your manager or not?"

"Excuse me, ma'am, you can't speak to her like that." Odessa charges toward the counter, her manicured brows pointed inward.

"It's ... fine." My attention navigates between the two women who are now facing each other, shoulders squared.

Nine years working at Smith + Rose and I've never seen anything like this.

"No." Odessa speaks to me, but looks at her challenger. "It isn't fine. It's never okay to snap your fingers in someone's face. Do you treat everyone like this? Like they're beneath you? Like they're a *dog*?"

The Townsend woman's mouth forms a hindered snarl. I imagine if her forehead weren't so filled with muscle paralyzing toxins she'd be scowling right now. "I don't know who you think you are, but this is none of your concern."

I'm half riveted, half embarrassed for the two of them, but intervening at this point might be akin to trying to break up a fight between street dogs, and I'm not willing to lose a proverbial finger in this.

"Ms. Townsend, I'd be happy to reach out to our owners, but I'm afraid they're traveling today. They'll be back tomorrow, and I can pass along your information then. They can reach out the moment you're back from St. Thomas," I say with the practiced pleased-to-serve-you cadence of a highly-paid concierge—not that I speak from experience.

Annette sniffs before peering down her nose and shoots one last dirty look Odessa's way.

"Fine." Annette slaps her hand over the locket on the counter, gripping it in her unworked palms and shoving it into her purse pocket. I cringe at the thought of untangling its ultra-fine chain, but I doubt it will come to that. The owners have never made an exception on their return policy, and a lawyer-threatening Palm Shores housewife isn't about to change that. "My number's on the form. I'd like a phone call *next* Friday. Not this Friday. *Next*."

"Of course. I'll relay the message." I smile, holding my breath until she's out the door a few seconds later. With burning lungs, I turn to Odessa. "You didn't have to do that."

She clasps a hand over her chest. "Oh my goodness, Cate. Yes, I did."

I'm speechless for half of a second, though I'm not sure if it has to do with what just happened or the fact that Odessa remembered my name.

"No one deserves to be spoken to that way." She turns toward the door, though the offender is long gone, disappearing beneath a sunny sky amongst the brightly-dressed shoppers. I picture her heels click-clacking against the pitted concrete sidewalk, the chirp-chirp of her car unlocking, the slam of her Bentley's door—all of these assumptions, of course. For all I know, she has a driver. Or she Uber'd. I picture her meeting her husband for dinner later, ordering a double vodka seltzer and giving him an earful about her day while he pretends to listen, nodding in sympathy every few measures to keep her appeased.

"It happens." I shrug.

Odessa clucks her tongue. "But it shouldn't. There are ways of conducting oneself without being nasty. That's just tasteless."

Most of Palm Shores is classy, but we have our share of what my co-worker Amada calls the *rich-n-trashy*. Take away their hair extensions, lip injections, multi-million-dollar oceanfront estates, and oversized egos, and they'd make for perfect Judge Judy guests.

Odessa's lips part, like she's going to add something else, and then she stops herself. Perhaps she was going to say something about the way the "haves" tend to treat the "have-nots" around here, but then that would imply that I'm a "have not" and she seems better mannered than that.

It's better that she saves her breath anyway. My entire life—or at least since my father left us and went back to his other family when I was five—my mother has taken on a whole "us versus them" mentality, angrily obsessed with what she referred to as "a rich man's world." Funny though —the more she lamented the evils of men like my father who could pay to make all their wildest dreams come true and their most wretched of problems disappear, the more preoccupied I became with people like "them."

If my father could have an entire double life—playing house with my mother and I while having a beautiful wife of fifteen years and four happy, healthy kids back in Rhode Island—what other scandals and secrets were people like him hiding?

"So what are we shopping for today?" I change the subject, simultaneously appropriating a peek at her finger. She isn't wearing the opal ring today. I'm not sure why, but I'm kind of disappointed. She seemed so excited about it yesterday.

Odessa lifts a single shoulder, peering around the store

while a moody Chopin number plays from the speaker above us. We're not allowed to play anything contemporary, anything that might remind shoppers of the current year. The backdrop of snappy, synthesized pop music alongside these vintage lovelies makes Elinor want to come out of her skin.

"Nothing in particular. Was in the mood to get out for a bit, do a little window shopping. Plus my visit here was cut short ..." She gives me a wink before heading off to examine a rack of vintage gowns fit for a 1960s First Lady.

Any minute now, Amada should be stopping in to take over and relieve me from the impending monotony of a mid-week afternoon. Tuesdays are my half days, and for that reason Tuesdays are sacred.

"Did you have a nice lunch with your husband?" Maybe I'm overstepping my boundaries. That's the sort of thing you ask a friend. We're hardly acquaintances.

"What's that?" She glances at me with a puzzled expression. "Oh. Right. Yes. We had lunch at that new place on Sapphire ... Tao and Zen. It was remarkable. Highly recommend, though you'll definitely want reservations when you go." Odessa plucks a peacock-blue chiffon number from the rack and holds it toward me. "This is absolutely stunning, isn't it?"

I almost want to tell her it matches her eyes, but I hold my tongue because that would be creepy. Honest, but creepy.

"Would you like to try it on?" I point to a silk-paneled fitting area in the back.

Odessa bites her lower lip, releasing a coy half-chuckle. "I don't know ... if I'm being completely honest, I'm not sure where I'd even wear something like this."

She's being modest—rare for a Palm Shores trophy wife.

"Come on." I come out from behind the counter, motioning for her to follow me to the fitting area. "Never too old to play dress up."

She struts behind me, dress in tow. "Really? Are you sure you don't mind?"

"Not at all." I pull back the curtain, revealing a three-way mirror. "I can grab a few other pieces if you'd like?"

"No, no," she says. "I don't want to be any more of a bother."

I close the curtain behind me and leave her to her devices.

We had this customer years back who used to come in here once every other week. For hours she'd hem and haw over her purchases, as if they were life-and-death decisions. It turned out her husband gave her a monthly allowance—and sometimes it boiled down to a new piece of vintage costume jewelry or a top tier mani-pedi at the uber-chic members-only Paolo Velez Nail Artistry.

Returning to the front of the shop, I check the time.

Amada is late as per usual.

A minute later, the fitting area curtain surges open and Odessa steps out, her dainty hands anchored at the sides of a waist so whittled it would make a 1990s runway model bitter with envy.

"So?" she asks before doing a twirl. The skirt floats up before sailing back to her ankles. "How does it look?"

Holy shit.

"Like it was made for you," I speak the truth, and then I remind myself of our no-pressure-sales rule. "It's an exquisite piece. Henriette LaValle Couture. Circa 1965, if I remember correctly. Originally made for a Rothschild daughter. Only worn once to a governor's ball."

Odessa runs her palms flat along the brilliant blue

chiffon before turning to the mirror and examining herself from all angles.

"I don't want to take it off," she says with a playful pout before doing a little dance in it. "Ever."

"Would you like to wear it out of the store?" It's happened before. A woman stopped in once on her way to some client dinner and wanted to—and I quote—"wow their freaking pants off." And I imagine she did in the slinky, beaded, form-fitting Marilyn Monroe number in which she swanned out of here.

"Oh, no, no, no." Odessa abandons the mirror, gathering the fabric of the skirt. "Like I said, I don't know where I would even wear this. But thank you for letting me try it on, Cate. I appreciate that."

She disappears into the fitting room, pulling the curtain across, and I head back to the front. A quick glance outside reveals Amada, sitting in the front seat of her Jetta looking like she's having an argument with herself, when, in fact, she's probably screaming at her boyfriend via Bluetooth.

"All right." Odessa emerges from the dressing room a minute later, the gown placed perfectly on its hanger. She carries it toward the rack, and I'm silently appreciative as most of our customers leave the fitting rooms a muddle of chaos for us to clean. "Now that that's out of my system ..."

She re-hangs the gown and dusts her hands before turning her back to the display, like it was a quick fix, a little bump to tide her over.

"Are you an earrings girl?" I point to a display in the corner.

Odessa frowns, tugging at her left ear lobe. "I'm not pierced. I have this thing with needles ..."

"Well, you're in luck because I have an entire tray over

here of costume clip-ons," I say, waving her over. "The *good* kind."

She follows me, and I retrieve the tray from the bottom shelf of the display behind the counter.

"We haven't marked these to sell yet, and they're not technically on the floor, but I'll give you an exclusive sneak peek." I give her a wink. I like this chick—and that says a lot because I don't really like anyone.

"You sure?" she asks. "I don't want to get you in trouble …"

"My bosses are out of town." I shake my head like it's no big deal even though it kind of is. The store is covered in cameras that are connected to a remote system my bosses can view from their smart phones 24/7. But as long as I don't sell any of these, I should be fine. I'd hate to let a pair go for eighty dollars when they were supposed to sell for two or three times that. "Here. Try these on."

I hand her a pair of polished lace agate earrings, massive and button-shaped, and then I slide a small mirror on an antique silver pedestal closer to her.

Outside Amada is still fighting with her boyfriend, only now she's slicking on her signature red-orange lipstick using her visor mirror, blotting her lips together before continuing to give him the what-for.

If you ask me, their problems began the day she let him move in with her. I'm not old-fashioned in the slightest, but the second you invite someone into your sacred space, the entirety of your relationship shifts. The dynamic is different. You're now sharing rent and household duties, settling into married-couple routines. And once you start sharing a bathroom, sex is never the same.

These are the things I try to explain to Sean whenever

he goes on one of his kicks about moving in together. He has a habit of putting numbers on things.

"We've been dating almost five years now ..."

"You'd save seven hundred and eighty-five dollars a month ..."

"We should buy a house together ... tax deductions ..."

But his arguments fall on deaf ears.

I'm not ready to live with him, and for some insane reason—love, I suppose—the man stays with me anyway. He's always been a hopeful type. He has enough optimism for the both of us, even if it's slightly misplaced and unwarranted.

If there's one thing I've learned in my thirty-five years, it's that the best things in life are almost always fleeting and impermanent. The sooner a person accepts that, the sooner they can prepare for the inevitable. Nothing wrong with wearing a parachute around your heart. A day will come when the plane's going to tumble from the sky in flames, and I'm going to have to jump—so why not be prepared?

Without warning, the front door flies open, and Amada stamps in, muttering something under her breath in Spanish. Her petite stature and delicate features make it impossible to take her anger seriously some days.

"Everything okay?" I ask, pointing with my eyes toward Odessa so she's aware we have a customer.

Amada catches my drift and stops in her tracks, smoothing her dark glossy hair and clearing her throat.

"I could kill him," she mouths before strangling the air, her hands shaped into claws.

I don't ask her what Alejandro did this time because I don't want to be here for the next forty-five minutes—unpaid. Also, whatever he did, I'm sure it's no different than the thing he did the last time and the last time ... and the time before that.

"You going to be all right?"

She rolls her eyes as if to say, *"I'm here, aren't I?"* But I don't take it personally. I know her frustration is aimed at her one true love ...

"Okay," I say. "You let me know if you need anything."

I fetch my bag and leftover can of Royal Crown from the back room and head for the front door before Amada has a chance to stop me and sit me down for story hour. We're not supposed to come and go through the front, but when the owners aren't here we bend the rules a bit. Parking in the back lot is a bitch—not to mention parking is ten bucks a day, which adds up.

"Enjoy the rest of your day," I stop short of the doorway to bid Odessa adieu before I leave.

She glances up, oblivious for a second, and then her gaze focuses on me. "Oh? I didn't realize you were leaving."

I offer an apologetic wince. "Tuesdays are my half days. If there's anything else you need, Amada will be happy to assist you."

Her gaze travels to my colleague, who despite being polished and presentable, still retains the crazy eyes of someone in the midst of having a mental lover's quarrel.

"I should probably be on my way, as well," she says, sliding a pair of emerald and resin clip-ons from her lobes and placing them gently on the tray. Checking the radiant timepiece on her lithe wrist, she says nothing, adjusts the strap of her bag over her shoulder, and follows me out.

The midday sun beats down from a cloudless sky and a blanket of Palm Shores humidity wraps around us as we pound the exclusive Arcadia Avenue pavement, Odessa with her long-legged stride and click-clacking heels and me in my noiseless secondhand Demi Kitterman ballet flats that have seen better days.

"I can't stop thinking about that dress," she says with a slight chuckle, tucking a strand of hair behind one ear.

"I'm happy to hold it in the back for a few days, if you want more time to think about it?"

We stop half a block from the shop, where my fifteen-year-old Accord looks out of place amongst the shiny black, white, and silver luxury imports that line the street. They say Palm Shores is the Range Rover capital of the world, but I'm beginning to think Bentleys are on the cusp of dethroning them.

"No, I shouldn't," she says with a wave. Odessa shifts on her feet, facing me, lingering like she isn't ready to go.

I'd be lying if I said it didn't weird me out.

I'd also be lying if I said it didn't flatter me.

I've been a ghost for thirty-five years. Not in the literal sense, of course, but in the sense that people can feel my presence but they never see me. They only ever look through me. I can't count how many times doors aren't held open for me, how many times people cut me in line or block the ancient grains aisle at Great Earth Food Market with their overstuffed shopping carts and pretend not to hear me clear my throat or notice that I smiled politely and said, "Excuse me" like a decent human being.

And at work, it isn't much different.

Most of the time, people only see me when they need my help. And even then, they treat me like I'm only halfway human, a rung or two beneath them. There are copious amounts of Annette Townsends out there and while it's a shame, it's also par for the course.

It doesn't bother me half as much as it used to though. I learned quickly and early on not to give miserable people an ounce of my energy, and somewhere around age thirty I stopped wallowing in my own pity every time I felt left out or extraordinarily friendless.

I have my crazy mother and my crazy-loyal boyfriend, a job that I love, and a place of my own.

I don't need to be seen to be happy anymore.

I don't need a robust social life and a million fake friends who only text when they want something.

"I'm sorry for intervening earlier with your customer," she says. "I hope I didn't make you uncomfortable. It's just that it's difficult for me to stand by and let someone treat someone else like—"

"Oh my goodness. Do *not* apologize. I'm over it. Honestly."

Over the years, I've become good at compartmentalizing, at taking unpleasant experiences and shoving them out of my mind, almost to the point where it's as if they didn't happen.

An advertisement-wrapped tourist bus carrying a bunch of retirees whooshes passed us, leaving a plume of diesel stench in its wake. I hold my breath until the air clears.

"Can I take you to lunch?" she asks.

I'm certain I've misheard her. "I'm sorry?"

Odessa offers an unhurried, gracious smile, hands clasped in front of her chest as if she's begging. "I'd like to take you to lunch. That is, if you're free. I just feel awful about earlier."

There's a glimmer in her brilliant gaze, as if she's half kidding about the guilt, half not.

"Oh." I lift my brows, glancing around. Normally Tuesdays are when I catch up on laundry, visit my mother for a bit, and run miscellaneous errands before binge-watching some shitty TV show and taking a two-hour, candlelit bubble bath with my ear pods in.

My routine is sacred.

Not even Sean has been able to charm his way into one of my priceless Tuesday afternoons.

"If you're busy, I understand. We could always do it another time."

"I just ..." I bite my lower lip. I don't want to offend Odessa. I also don't want to risk pissing off my employers should they catch wind of me fraternizing with clients. "I sort of ... I already had plans ..."

She smiles though her eyes turn glassy. "No worries, Cate. Totally understand. Another time?"

"Of course," I lie, burying my guilt into a tiny compartment until I no longer feel it.

While I appreciate Odessa's kind offer, I'm getting the impression she wants to be friends—and I don't do the friend thing. Not anymore. I haven't for some time and I've found my life has been better for it.

Or that's what I've managed to convince myself anyway.

"Wonderful." She digs into her bag and retrieves a key fob, pointing at the jet-black Maserati sedan behind her. "Why don't I give you my number? And you can just get a hold of me whenever you're free?"

We exchange numbers and go our separate ways, the ball firmly, regrettably in my court.

I leave Palm Shores and head over the bridge to the land of less glitz and glamour, all the while wondering ... *what if?*

Maybe one lunch with Odessa DuVernay wouldn't be so bad.

She seems perfectly harmless.

What's the worst that could happen?

4

"ARE you going to tell my mother?" Aviana worries the inside of her lip as I crumple a cellophane snack cake wrapper in my hand, one I found wedged between the wall and the back of her bed when I was turning down her bedsheets for the night.

She's bingeing again.

I imagine if I were to scour her room, I'd find boxes of chocolate cupcakes shoved in the back of her closet, bags of sour candies and sour cream and onion potato chips stowed beneath sweaters in her dresser drawers, and carefully concealed cans of non-diet root beer in her bathroom vanity.

"Of course not." I wouldn't dream of it.

She rakes her silky, russet-brown hair into a loose top knot and secures it with a hair tie from her wrist before climbing into bed. Her pajamas—a polka-dotted button-down with matching shorts, are almost bursting at the seams.

Aviana is beautiful—a near spitting image of her father right down to the striking gaze that can't decide if it wants to be blue or hazel. But Mrs. DuVernay has her convinced otherwise. If it were up to her, Aviana would be thirty pounds lighter and three years away from her first nose job. Not only that, but she has Aviana convinced her hair is too fine, her feet are too wide, and her eyes are too close together—the sorts of things that can't be fixed by a plastic surgeon.

It kills Mrs. DuVernay that Aviana is nothing like her.

Not even their personalities share a single commonality.

Mrs. DuVernay is harsh, cunning, and calculating.

Aviva is sweet, innocent, and inclusive.

Yin and yang, those two.

"Is something bothering you lately?" I ask because I know she tends to binge more when she's stressed. When something eats away at her, she copes by consuming copious amounts of contraband. I'll make sure to dispose of the evidence in my apartment trash, where Mrs. DuVernay won't see it.

Aviana shrugs, picking at a loose thread in the blanket bunched up in her lap.

I take that as a yes.

"I'm failing pre-chem," she says. "Like ... really failing it." Her lower lip trembles. "If my mom finds out ..."

"Can you talk to your teacher? Get some extra help? Find a tutor?"

"School's out in eight weeks. Even if I got straight A's on everything the rest of the semester, I'd only come out with a D and I'd have to retake the class again next year. With a bunch of freshmen. Which will be humiliating. And I have to have at least a C in order to get into Chadwick."

I take her hands in mine, drawing in a long, deep

breath as I gather my thoughts. "You're only fifteen. You should be enjoying this time in your life, not stressing over the future. You'll get into Chadwick. I know you will. And if you have to retake chemistry, then so be it. You won't be the first person to have to do that and you won't be the last."

Aviana's eyes water.

There's something else.

It's not just pre-chem.

"What? What is it?" I give her soft hands a reassuring squeeze.

"Remember Braden?" she asks, referring to the boy she's been crushing on since seventh grade.

"Of course."

"He's dating Alyssa now." A thick tear slides down her rosy cheek. She swipes it away before I can hand her a tissue from the nightstand. "That traitor whore."

My chest tightens and aches for her. Alyssa and Aviana have been best friends since elementary school, close as sisters. The emotional anguish she's experiencing must be torrential.

I would know.

I'm familiar with what it's like seeing someone you love in the arms of someone who betrayed you in the worst way.

"Aviana," Mrs. DuVernay's unanticipated intrusion steals this moment from us without warning. I turn to her. She stands in the open doorway, hands splayed against the framing. I hadn't heard her come home. "What is it, darling? What's the matter?"

She rushes in, hand over the empty cavity where her heart should be, and perches on the opposite side of the bed, face still covered in the day's makeup. She's been friendless for several months now. What she does and where she goes this late at night, I've yet to figure out, but it seems to be happening more and more these days.

"We're good, Zsofia." The warmth in her tone a moment ago is now gone. "You may show yourself out."

I rise, hands folded in front of me. Head tucked. Submissive and docile. The way she likes me.

"Would you like me to draw you a bath?" I ask.

She turns to her daughter, and I imagine she's contemplating how much time her teenage crisis is going to take. With an exaggerated sigh, she cups a palm over her daughter's still hand. I swear Aviana flinches.

"I'll draw my own tonight," she says. "Why don't you head up to your apartment. We'll see you first thing tomorrow."

"Yes, Mrs. DuVernay." I leave the room, but I linger out of sight around the corner. Aviana won't open up to anyone but me. We have a bond. One that means more to me than she'll ever know.

I love her in ways Mrs. DuVernay doesn't quite know how to love someone.

Without conditions, without expectations.

I love her as she is. Perfectly imperfect. The best parts of her father—thank God.

I was five years old when my mother, Mrs. DuVernay's first personal assistant, walked out one sticky Saturday afternoon and never came back. The DuVernays kept me safe, sheltered and fed, all the while believing she would one day return.

But she never did.

And as the years passed, I suppose the DuVernays— Mrs. DuVernay in particular—grew burdened by my presence. At first, I was a pet project of hers, a little girl she could dress in gowns the color of cake frosting with bows to match. But the years yawned on, ushering the dawn of my pre-teen era. The saccharin sweet, surrogate daughter she had created had turned on her, becoming moody and opinionated and, worse yet, willful.

In the blink of an eye, I was relocated from the ballerina-pink suite, where Aviana now sleeps, to the garage apartment, given daily lists of never-ending chores, and a new set of rules so I'd know exactly where I stood in the hierarchy of the DuVernay household—at the very bottom.

I'll never forget the day I tried to run away at age fourteen, bags packed and tears streaming down my face as I called Mrs. DuVernay every name in the book, silently hoping she would see the error of her ways, understand what she'd done to me, how badly I was hurting.

I just wanted her to love me, like she did before.

But Mrs. DuVernay simply laughed, an evil cackle of a thing, equal parts comical and heartless, and she told me I had nothing, I was nothing ... without her.

And she wasn't wrong.

I had never attended school. I didn't have a penny to my name. No identification of any kind nor any knowledge as to how to get anything. My mother had immigrated to the States illegally when I was a baby. Mrs. DuVernay assured me that should I leave, it would only be a matter of time until I was arrested by ICE and deported to Russia, where I wouldn't know a soul, wouldn't be able to speak a single word of their language.

My entire life—at least that which I can remember—has been spent inside the unapologetic sprawl of the DuVernay estate.

Sometimes the devil you know is the better option than the devil you don't.

"Are you sure, darling?" Mrs. DuVernay asks Aviana.

While her tone is genuine, I know better. She's only kind when she wants something, only gives a part of herself so she can collect a part of you later. Always keeping score, that one. "You know I'm here if you ever need to talk."

"I know," Aviana says with the appeasing obligation of a fifteen-year-old.

"But you were crying," Mrs. DuVernay says. "And you were about to tell Zsofia something … I don't understand why you can't talk to me about this."

It's quiet for a beat, the tension so ripe it wafts toward the hallway, like hands wrapping my neck. I hold my breath. Just like that, the conversation went from heartfelt to accusatory. Mrs. DuVernay has the art of flicking perfectly fine conversations into arguments down to a science.

"It's different with her," Aviana says. Her voice is muffled, and I imagine her chin resting against her polka dot pajama top as she speaks into her lap. Making eye contact with Mrs. DuVernay can be akin to looking into the eyes of Satan himself when she's in one of her moods.

I exhale, shuddering.

Mrs. DuVernay releases a breathy moan. "*I'm* your mother. *Not her*. You are not to discuss personal matters with the help. *Any* of the help. You know that."

Once upon a time, she treated me like her own flesh and blood.

Now I'm *the help*.

"It's just boy drama," Aviana says.

"Regardless, Aviana, she's not your mother and she's not your friend." Impatient exhaustion colors her inflection, each word cut into short little snips. She's ending the conversation, seeing to it she has the last word. It's what she does.

I don't stick around to hear the rest of the lecture. I can only imagine the conniption fit she'll throw if she were to catch me eavesdropping ... a little something I've honed over the years. An outsider would be amazed to learn the secrets that reside in the DuVernay household.

They're everywhere, always. Hiding in plain sight.

You just have to know where to look.

5

CATE

"I GOT ASKED OUT YESTERDAY," I tell Sean as he stands next to my bed and slips a white t-shirt over his chiseled, sun-speckled shoulders on Wednesday night.

"Wait, what?" he squints, examining my face, his expression wild and prepared for a laugh.

"Not like *that* ..." I smirk. "This customer came in Monday. This woman." I wrap the thin gray sheets around my body, leaving only my arms and shoulders exposed. "And then she came in again Tuesday. Super sweet. We were walking out at the same time and she asked me out to lunch."

Sean's angled jaw is loose. "And you went?"

"Of course not."

"Right." He tugs his jeans up before working the fly, his belt buckle clanging when he fastens it. "Why'd she ask you to lunch? She trying to sell you something?"

I roll my eyes. "This crazy lady came in today, wanting

a refund on a non-returnable locket. Threw a fit. Threatened legal action. Snapped her fingers in my face and everything. The other woman came to my defense."

He chuffs. "Like you need anyone to come to your defense."

"I know. But anyway. She did. She put the crazy lady in her place. After that I let her try on this gown she had no intention of buying, and then I showed her a bunch of earrings that aren't on the floor yet."

"Aw." He tilts his head. "You two are besties already."

"Stop." I suppress a smirk.

"So why didn't you go?" Now fully clothed, he takes a seat on the edge of my bed, the full-sized, clearance-priced, mail-order mattress dipping proportionally to his average weight.

"Because it was Tuesday afternoon ..."

He rolls his eyes. "Ah. Of course."

"Plus if Elinor or Margaret ever found out ..."

"What? They'd fire you? Yeah, right. You're their number one. They need you more than you need them."

I let the reality of his words sink in a bit. I outsell Amada and a couple of the part-timers three-to-one, and I've been there the longest. Sean has a point.

"Might not be the worst thing ... making a friend, turning over a new leaf or whatever. Then next thing we know you'll be asking me to move in with you. Spoiler alert: I'm going to say yes."

"Dork." I reach for his shirt and tug him close, leaning in to steal a kiss.

If Sean were a dog, he'd be a golden retriever.

Thick, sunny-gold hair. Big brown eyes. Straight white teeth. Pink tongue.

Playful. Faithful. Loyal. Classic. A safe sort of ordinary.

Hell, the man even plays on an Ultimate Frisbee league with a group of guys from work.

I know what to expect with him. He's always in a good mood. There isn't any amount of overtime or oppressive heat wave that can shake the guy, and I adore him for it.

"What's her name? This friend?" he asks before rising off the bed. He grabs his wallet and keys from my night-stand, cramming them in his worn back pocket.

"Odessa DuVernay." I draw out each syllable and splay my hands wide, as if I'm holding an imaginary banner. I don't know why I just did that—perhaps her name feels so grand on my lips that it needs a little extra fanfare.

"Never heard of her."

Sean is a people person in every sense of the word. I can't take him anywhere without us running into someone he knows. An old high school soccer friend. A former colleague from the summer he spent doing landscaping between his freshmen and sophomore years at college. A cousin's former nanny. A client whose guest house he pre-wired six years ago.

He never forgets a name—or a face.

And don't get me started on his penchant for making fast friends with complete strangers.

I like to tease him, pretend that it annoys me (and at times it does, like when we're in line for movie tickets and he's holding it up with his friendly small talk), but I secretly admire him for it. It's a special skill, being able to talk to anyone, anywhere, about anything.

Sean more than makes up for the things I lack.

My mother always refers to him as my "better half."

She probably isn't wrong.

I try not to think too much about the small handful of things he gets from our relationship. Regular sex, maybe?

Someone to send funny memes to when he's bored on his lunch break? A woman to make him feel loved?

Perhaps for him, those things are enough.

Or at least, enough for now.

And I do love him. In my own way. You don't stay with someone for five years and not love them. It isn't his fault that I keep him at an arm's length. We don't go crazy with the romance. We've never exchanged love letters—or even anniversary cards. We've maybe exchanged Christmas gifts once since we've been together—the first year, I believe, and only because it seemed like the kind of thing you do when you're trying to impress someone in the beginning.

He got me flowers once. I told him they were lovely but that he didn't have to waste his money on things that die. I'd rather that he spend that twenty bucks whisking me off to the Palm Shores art museum or renting bikes at the pier.

Memories last forever. Just like my mother. She re-lives the brief seven years she shared with my father in her dreams on a nightly basis, as evidenced by the various words she cries out in her sleep.

If ever a day arrives when Sean decides he's tired of waiting for me to come around, the breakup would be painful yes, but not messy.

It would be a clean break.

I would detach the Velcro holding my heart to his, collect his things in my apartment into a single box, and place it outside the door for him to retrieve at his earliest convenience. And I would want nothing but the best for him.

Okay, that's a lie.

I'd be devastated—but I don't want to think about that right now.

Lord knows he deserves better than me, and one of

these days he's going to wake up and realize that. Until then, I suppose we're both biding our time.

Ignorance is bliss and all of that.

"We exchanged numbers," I tell him, though I don't know why.

"You going to text her?" Sean asks.

I shrug, tamping down my excitement because I'm still not quite sure. The number of people I like in my life I can count on one hand, and now all of a sudden there's Odessa.

I've never needed a second hand to count my people before. It's weird. And I don't want to get my hopes up. She was probably just being kind. Or throwing dollars at her guilt for intervening. It's a classic John Cabot move— throwing money at things to feel better.

To this day, I have no idea if the quarter million in hush money he threw at my mother after leaving us completely absolved him of his guilt or merely "took the edge off," as Odessa would say.

"Are you sure she wasn't hitting on you?" Sean's hands rest on his narrow hips, his forehead covered in lines.

I laugh. "Yes. She's married. And it wasn't like that at all."

He swipes his shiny black phone off my dresser, checks the screen for two seconds, and slides it into his front pocket. In a few minutes, he'll leave. He'll climb into his truck and drive the ten minutes to his place in the slightly nicer section of town, and I'll smoke a Newport on my apartment balcony. Later, he'll text me goodnight, tell me he loves me, and that'll be that.

Another day in the books.

I still don't know why he stays, but I learned early in life that it's better not to question good things—at least not out loud. Think your thoughts, but for the love of God, keep them to yourself.

Asking questions always leads to uncomfortable truths.

As my mother always says, "When in doubt, leave well enough alone."

So that's exactly what I do.

It has yet to serve me wrong.

6

Zsofia

"WHAT ON EARTH are you doing out here?" Mrs. DuVernay slides the patio door closed behind her before striding toward me in her billowing silk robe, a nearly full wine chalice in her left hand. "I thought you were retiring for the night?"

I bite my tongue. She ordered me to my apartment twenty minutes ago, when she was attempting to comfort Aviana, but it's much too beautiful of an evening to waste it inside the stuffy, sterile confines of that makeshift prison cell.

Above, the stars spread over us like a blanket, the air warm but breathable thanks to the miniature thunderstorm that passed through a short while ago. Crickets and bull-frogs perform an evening symphony. In the distance, boats motor through the Twincoastal and yachts anchor down for the night, bobbing on dark waters. From here, the horizon is infinite and the unknown is a little easier to digest when I think about how small we are in the grand scheme of things.

I was actually enjoying this … until now.

I'm about to rise from my pool lounge chair when the icy sensation of Mrs. DuVernay's slender hand grips my shoulder.

"Stay." She takes the lounger beside me, draping the fabric of her robe over her long legs and placing her wine on the glass side table. "Beautiful evening, isn't it?"

"Yes, Mrs. DuVernay."

My body stiffens from head to toe, an involuntary reaction anytime I'm uncertain of what Mrs. DuVernay has up her sleeve. It's different during our routines, when everything is scheduled, and I'm ticking off the to-do list one by one. At five AM, I rise, grab a quick shower, and dress for the day before making my way to the main house. Once in the kitchen, I brew two cups of espresso. Mr. DuVernay takes his Americano-style while Mrs. DuVernay prefers hers with a splash of steamed whole milk and a packet of Sugar in the Raw—a combination she believes to be sinfully decadent. I place their morning beverages—alongside a bowl of organic oatmeal with raw brown sugar and a toasted cinnamon bagel with Italian cream cheese—on a covered tray outside the master suite before heading to Aviana's room to wake her for school.

While Aviana showers, I make her bed and lay her clothes out, grateful for the fact that she wears a uniform. I can't imagine what it would be like dressing a teenager with free rein of her closet.

Mrs. DuVernay prefers that I blow dry Aviana's hair each morning, using three specific products that are meant to help volumize and add body and shine to her fine locks. She always says it looks better when I do it, and Aviana doesn't seem to mind. She uses the time to scroll through her phone, catching up on all things social media before we head out. Plus it's kind of our time together—we listen to music and chat a bit.

Almost like a couple of friends.

By seven-thirty, I'm driving Aviana to school. On a good day, Mrs. DuVernay will have me run a few errands around the city. Whenever possible, I take my time, always blaming traffic or long lines if ever I'm questioned. On days my errands take me across the bridge to West Palm Shores, I milk every ounce of it, intentionally taking detours and longer routes.

Every second spent outside the gates is a second I cherish.

It's a miracle they agree to let me leave at all, though I suppose by now they're confident in the fact that I have nowhere else to go, not a single friend to call upon for help, and not a penny to spend should I ever try to leave. The car, the driver's license Mr. DuVernay gave me, they give the illusion of freedom some days, but the moment I return through the iron gates of Artemis Cove, that illusion shatters all over again.

"You're quiet tonight," she says, as if it's different from any other night. "Entertain me with your thoughts."

Mrs. DuVernay reaches for her wine glass, lifting it to her full mouth and taking a careful sip.

"Nothing on my mind, really," I lie. "Just enjoying the nice night we're having."

She scoffs, indulging herself in a more generous sip the second time. "Sometimes, Zsofia, I don't think you appreciate how truly fortunate you are."

A lump forms in my throat, my mind teetering on the edge of the unknown. She could be going anywhere with this, and it's been a while since my last chastisement. Not only am I her personal assistant, but I also serve as her personal whipping post when she's had an off day—which is most days, if I'm being honest.

"You haven't a single, solitary problem in the world. Not one," she says, peering out at the glassy, infinity edge pool before us. This time of night it looks dark, deep, and murky. In the morning it's brilliant, crystalline—much like the Twincoastal in the distance.

The thing terrifies me either way, so I always keep my distance. Close but never too close.

I don't know how to swim.

Mrs. DuVernay never took the time to teach me as a child, nor did she think to hire someone to do the job for her as she did with Aviana. Sometimes I wonder if she secretly hoped I would fall into the pool and drown.

A single, unfortunate accident and she'd finally be rid of me.

"I'm grateful for all you've given me," I say, monotone. It's true and yet in so many ways it isn't.

For everything she's given me, she's taken twice as much.

"Do you have any idea how much I would pay for the luxury of an empty mind?" she asks with a huff. Angling toward me, she adds, "Life gets burdensome. And it's filled with disappointment after disappointment. I wish you knew just how easy you have it here. The most stressful part of your day is making sure our coffees are made just right and on time every morning."

She laughs, helping herself to another sip of wine.

"Oh, to be you," she says, her gaze fixed on the still water ahead. "To live in a place like this, surrounded by all this serenity. Not a single pedestrian problem clouding that pretty little head of yours. Do you know how many people are out there struggling to get by, eating twenty-five-cent packs of ramen noodles and working cubicle jobs, barely able to pay their rent, maxing out their credit cards on car repairs and medical bills..." She sighs, though I don't think it's a sympathetic gesture. "And don't even get me started on dating. You're not missing out on anything, I promise you that. From what I hear, the Palm Shores dating scene leaves much to be desired. Just a bunch of retired men acting like virile, twenty-something stallions. That and tourists passing through, trying to get quickies in their corporate-sponsored hotel rooms before flying home to their wives. It's all silly, really. Tragically cliché."

Glancing at my lap, my fists clenched so tight my nails dig into my palms, I let them unfurl. I splay them across the tops of my thighs as I drag in a long, slow breath. A few more minutes of indulging her with my company and I should be able to head inside for the night—for real this time.

Mrs. DuVernay rolls to her side on her chaise, cupping one hand under a perfect cheekbone. "I'm saving you from a lifetime of disappointment and heartbreak. I just wish you could see that."

"I do—"

"—no. You don't," she says. "I can see it in your eyes. Like right now. You're looking in my direction, but you won't make eye contact with me. You resent me. I know you do. I feel it. And quite honestly, I don't understand it. You have everything you could possibly need right here. You've been given this beautiful, stress-free life. A slice of cake without those pesky calories. And you don't even realize it. Do you know how many people would *kill* to be in your shoes? *Do you?*"

Her wine chalice is vacant now, the glass completely transparent, and her words have the softest blur to them. This likely wasn't her first drink of the night.

"Sometimes I look at you and I want to hug you," she says, her bright blue eyes glinting cold in the moonlight. "And other times I look at you and I feel sick about this whole thing. Your mother left us in quite the situation. You know that, right? What were we supposed to do with you? She left and we had this five-year-old child who wasn't even supposed to be in this country. Your mother was working on getting her green card, but she didn't have it yet. She was still here illegally. We shouldn't have hired her, but we did because we were quite fond of her and more importantly, we trusted her. We believed she was going to get her green card and everything would be fine and she was one hell of a housekeeper. Not to mention she was willing to work for a fraction of what everyone else wanted to charge. But I digress.

"I guess what I'm getting at here is that life gave us lemons, you and I. We didn't ask for this situation. And I don't know about you, but I'm doing the best I can. I don't think I could live with myself if I just turned you loose, like you were no longer my problem. I mean, what would you do? Where would you go?

"You don't have any kind of legal identification. You've never attended school a day in your life. You wouldn't be able to get housing or a car of your own. You don't know the first thing about life in the real world. Honestly, you'd be living on the streets and sleeping with dirty and disgusting men for a ridiculously sad amount of money, and the whole thing just breaks my heart to even think about."

Mrs. DuVernay reaches for her glass, frowning the instant she discovers it empty.

I don't know why she feels the need to remind me of the things I already know—realities I know like the back of my hand because she's mentioned them to me time and time again over the years.

Next month I'll be thirty-one.

A year ago, I'd have told myself that if I haven't left yet, I probably never will.

Lately, I've been thinking about it though. Seriously thinking about it. Thinking about it more than I should. Daydreaming of walking out all the time and never looking back. But my daydream always ends the second I set foot outside the iron gates of the Cove.

I never quite know what happens after that.

"Well this is unfortunate." She examines her hollow wine goblet with an unfocused stare. "Run in and pour me another glass, won't you? And while you're at it, check on my husband. Tell him to join me out here. It's much too lovely a night to let it go to waste. We could use some one-on-one time actually. The man's been working like a maniac trying to land the Rothwell contract. I hardly see him at all these days."

I don't tell her that she's absent more than he is most nights, nor do I tell her that he doesn't seem particularly bothered by that fact.

Instead, I climb out of the lounger, reach for her glass, and head inside.

My body aches from all the tensing, but I make my way toward the wet bar off the dining area, inhaling and exhaling deep breaths until the pain becomes tolerable.

"Zsofia." Mr. DuVernay emerges from the darkness of the west hallway, joining me at the bar. His hair is slicked back, damp from an evening shower, and a thick robe the color of Brandywine censors his athletic body. Whether or not he's wearing a shred of clothing beneath it remains a mystery. And also, none of my business. Though it doesn't stop my mind from wandering curiously, innocently in that direction. "Fixing the missus her nightly special?"

I nod. "She's by the pool. And she'd like you to join her."

He reaches for a cut-glass bottle of his favorite decanted bourbon, pouring two fingers' worth into a spotless crystal tumbler he plucks from an open shelf along the wall behind the sink.

"Would she now?" Mr. DuVernay swirls the amber liquid before taking a sniff, and then he laughs a breathy sort of laugh, as if his wife is being cute by wanting to spend time together for once. "So kind of her to remember I still exist."

All these years I've spent observing their marriage, and I've yet to understand why he tolerates her, why he stands by her faithfully and loyally. She gives him every good reason to leave—and then some—and yet he stays.

It certainly can't be love.

I can only assume it has to do with Aviana.

Aviana and money.

Though sometimes ... secretly ... I can't help but hope that part of it has to do with me, too.

7

CATE

HAUL DAYS ARE MY FAVORITE.

Margaret and Elinor arrive at the shop shortly after nine Thursday—a full day later than intended. They park in the back, because the ten dollar per day charge is toll booth change to them, and unload their newest haul from the trunk of Margaret's glistening black *suburbitank*—Elinor's word, not mine.

This time the ladies are fresh off a long weekend in Manhattan, where they go once a season to find the best "treasures" as they call them. They have a driver, a local retired long-haul trucker, who takes them up and down the coast in Margaret's beast of an SUV, and they almost always come back with a ridiculous amount of stuff—all of it Tetris-packed, utilizing every available square inch of the interior.

"What'd we get this time?" I ask, sliding my hands in the back pockets of my navy pencil pants that stop just above my ankles. I'm going for a Jackie O look today, complete with a paper-white blouse and a Fernanda Puccelli neck scarf in tasteful, psychedelic colors.

"Oh, Cate, you're just going to die when you see what we found," Elinor says, flourishing her hand at me. Her nails are painted baby blue today, an unexpected departure from the classic red she's gone with for the past two years. "Three words: are you ready?"

"I'm ready."

She spreads her fingers, pawing at the air with wild, wide eyes pointed at me. "Hawthorne. Makeup. Compacts."

"No way," I say. "I always thought those were a myth."

And the only reason I thought that was because Margaret and Elinor have been on the hunt for these unicorn makeup mirrors for as long as I've known them. Supposedly there were only twenty-eight ever made—each of them solid gold with Piedmondt diamonds embedded in the floral logo on the top of the compact. Finding them was hard enough, finding them in good condition, even harder. And finding them for less than ten grand a pop? Impossible.

Collectors know the value of these, and they also know better than to undersell. Each year that goes by makes these compacts shoot up in value ten, sometimes thirteen percent.

They're like an index fund, only prettier.

"I'm afraid to ask what you're going to charge for these …" I wince as Margaret digs into a box and removes a small, bubble-wrapped, tissue-paper-covered compact.

She pulls the packaging away as if she's peeling the delicate petals of a rose, and then she turns it toward me.

It's stunning.

This thing must be at least one hundred and fifty years old, but it looks as if it just left Hawthorne's infamous studio in Old Cotswold and time traveled to Palm Shores, Florida.

I reach for it, but she pulls it away, tsk-ing me.

"Gloves," she says, her tone gentle yet firm.

"Of course. Was getting ahead of myself, wasn't I?" I reach beneath the counter and retrieve a pair of white lint-free gloves, the kind archivists and museum curators wear, and she hands me the exquisite piece. Her stare rests on my hands, and she's probably checking for nicotine stains.

"You'll never believe where we found these," she says, carrying on.

"*These*? How many are there?" I ask, softly unclasping the mirror.

"Elinor saw this flyer for some random estate sale on the Upper East Side. We weren't planning to go but at the last minute we decided to check it out." Margaret tilts her head as she speaks, her sparkling gaze never leaving the makeup mirror for one second. "Anyway, we walk in and there was a table of vanity items ... boar bristle brushes and handheld mirrors and perfume trays and the like ... and then three of these just sitting there. Three!"

"That's ... wow ... I'm speechless."

"I know. I still can't believe it. I swear we pinched ourselves about a dozen times the whole way home. Elinor insisted they ride in her lap the entire time. She didn't want to risk them knocking against something and getting a scratch. Never mind the fact that they were bubble-wrapped so tight you could probably drop them off the Empire State Building and they'd bounce right back." Elinor rolls her eyes, chuckling at her best friend. As much of a handful as these two can be at times, I wish our customers could see how much passion goes into stocking the store. These women do their research. They scour the ends of the earth in search of their "lovelies" as they call them. I suppose, in a way, they price accordingly.

I re-clasp the mirror and hand it to Margaret, opting to visually inspect the other two. The less these are handled, the better, even if they are in pristine condition.

"Oh. While I have you ... a customer stopped in the other day, wanting to return a locket she'd purchased."

Margaret rolls her eyes. "Let me guess, it was the Longcheau."

"Yep."

"I told 'Nor that one wasn't suitable for sale, but she just wouldn't listen. Did she sign a purchase agreement?"

I nod. "She did. She was aware that it was a non-returnable item, but it sounds like she's going to challenge that."

Margaret peers over her skinny glasses, the seed-pearl chain dripping to her shoulders. "Well good luck to her. A contract is a contract ..."

"I wrote her name and number down. It's on your desk. By the phone," I say.

"Perfect. I'll be sure to pass that along to 'Nor since she had the wise idea to put that locket on the floor in the first place." Margaret collects the compacts, cradling them in her arms like fragile baby birds, and steps lightly to the office. The ladies carry in a few more boxes from the back of the SUV, stacking them neatly in their office over the course of the next hour. When they're finished, Margaret declares that she's "absolutely famished." Elinor reminds her they "just had breakfast three hours ago at the Sailcloth Club with Gaynelle and Birdie."

Nevertheless, the women bicker for a few more minutes before locking the office door and waving goodbye on their way out.

It's been a painfully slow morning, so the moment they're gone, I retrieve my phone with the sole intention of killing some time—only I'm met with zero emails, zero messages, not a single soul requesting an ounce of my time.

If I were twenty-five, I'd be bothered by that.

At thirty-five, the only thing that bothers me is that we're having a slow day, and it's only getting started.

Outside, two women pass by, bathed in sunshine, one of them laughing so hard she has to hold on to the other one to keep from toppling over in her designer stilettos. I imagine they're sharing an inside joke, something only the two of them would get.

It's been a long time since I've shared a laugh like that with someone.

My mind wanders to Odessa. The warmth of her smile. The soft, sweet scent of her floral perfume—not too imposing, not too commercial. Her effortless, laidback demeanor. How easy it is to like her ...

But when I try to imagine the two of us as friends, everything grows murky. The image of the two of us dining at a restaurant makes me physically cringe because any restaurant Odessa frequents likely has food on the menu with names I couldn't possibly begin to pronounce. Shopping with her would be another slap in the face as my budget isn't Palm Shores friendly and someone like her wouldn't dare venture to the non-prestigious *Outlets of West Palm*. I try to picture what it might be like visiting her palatial home on the coast. It has to be immaculate, and I'm sure she has full-time help to keep it that way. My place is five-hundred-sixty square feet of curry-and-cat-piss (thanks to the previous tenant), furnished with the kinds of things you buy online with free shipping then assemble yourself five to seven business days later when it arrives in a ripped, dented box.

The idea of the two of us becoming friends is more

comical than anything. Seriously. This is the unimaginative crap cancelled sitcoms are made of, and I'll be damned if I'll live the kind of life some desperate newbie TV writer in LA can pitch to a boardroom full of showrunners for a quick buck.

I'm a Cabot, damn it.

If my life were turned into a TV show, it would feature my deadbeat father lying on his deathbed (surrounded by Scrooge McDuck piles of money, because this is TV, and we need ratings) as my four siblings and their mother battle over their inheritance—and then in walks the kid sister none of them knew existed.

Dun, dun, *dunnnnn* ...

I lock the shop door, flip the sign, and head to the back for a Newport and a swig of Royal Crown.

8

ZSOFIA

MRS. DUVERNAY'S closet floor is a mess—a mess I'll have to clean up when she's gone.

"How is it I have all of these beautiful pieces and yet I've nothing to wear?" Her fingers tangle in her silky hair, resting just above her ears before turning into fists. Across the room, the dressing room mirror produces three of her. A sickly jolt travels down my spine at the thought of there being any more of this woman.

"Did you check the weather forecast like I asked?" She turns to me, lips bunched and brows raised as far as her Botox-filled forehead will allow.

"Rainy and sixties."

"Ugh. Springtime in the *sticks* ..." She kicks a periwinkle cashmere sweater with a bare foot and struts to another corner of her dressing room, returning with an armful of designer denim. She squeezes past me a second later. "Please don't stand in the way. You know I *abhor* when you do that."

I step aside to the threshold between the closet and the bedroom as she tosses the pile of jeans on the bed beside her first suitcase. She's simply visiting her mother in upstate New York, but the way she's packing, you'd think she was visiting some European dignitary and staying for a month.

"Remind me when the reunion is?" Hands on her hips, she stares at the flayed-open, half-filled suitcase.

"Saturday. Four to seven PM at the Goldworth Town and Country Club."

"Four to seven? So is it afternoon casual or cocktail attire?"

"The invite didn't say."

"Of course it didn't. You sent the RSVP, didn't you?" she asks, ever the micromanager.

"Yes. For one."

"I'm going to have to apologize in person for showing up alone." She rolls her eyes, sniffing. "God forbid Charles takes time away from his company. The man acts like the whole place is going to fall apart if he isn't there to personally wipe everyone's rear ends."

She doesn't mention Aviana. I suppose in her mind, Aviana has a valid excuse—she's still in school. But I doubt it bothers Mrs. DuVernay to leave her behind. She's always left her behind to gallivant around the world, taking extravagant, opulent vacations whenever her mood called for them. This isn't any different, even if her destination is a little less than glamorous.

Mrs. DuVernay throws her hands in the air and storms into her dressing room, plucking sweaters and dresses from wooden hangers.

In all my years living with the DuVernays, I've never

seen her make such a fuss over a visit back home, nor have I seen her spend more than a few days at a time in the presence of her mother. Their relationship is complicated and contentious on the best of days, toxic and venomous on the worst. The only times they're not spitting down one another's throats and flinging backhanded verbal jabs is when they have drinks in their hands, and even then I've seen things get dangerous.

It's funny how you can love someone and hate them at the same time.

I used to feel that way about Mrs. DuVernay.

I used to love her, used to see her as a mother figure.

But when things became complicated, I added a layer of resentment to that love.

That love has been gone for a long time.

Years. Years that blur into one another. Years that feel like one, big, long, endless stint in hell.

Now all that remains is what I can only describe as hate.

"Your flight leaves in four hours," I remind her, standing in the doorway of the dressing room with my hands clasped in front of my hips.

She shoots me a look. "I know that."

"Why don't I finish packing for you?" I offer, but only because it will allow me a break from her. "No need to get worked up before you travel. I can make you a drink if you'd like?"

Mrs. DuVernay hates to fly, which I don't think is a fear of flying so much as it's a control thing for her. She requires at least one Xanax pre-boarding, which means no alcohol for the duration of the flight. In the hours leading up to her departure, she's incapable of being anything other than wicked and short-fused, more so than usual.

Dumping the clothes at her feet and lifting her empty palms in the air, she exhales. "Fine. I'll be in the *en suite*."

"Should I pack seven outfits or ten?" I ask before she disappears.

"Ten ... plus two extras," she says. "Going to play it by ear. If my mother decides to take liberties with my sanity again, I'll be on the next flight home."

Mrs. DuVernay disappears into her bathroom, swinging the door closed halfway. A moment later the sound of drawers sliding open and slamming shut mixes with the distinct snap of metal makeup compacts and gold-handled cosmetic brushes slapping marble counters follows.

I return to her dressing room and select outfits. I start with her basic go-to pieces: black leather leggings, silk blouses, skinny jeans, cashmere sweaters. And then I move on to accessories: patterned headbands, oversized earrings, Lucite cuffs, and silk scarves. I choose her shoes last, ballet flats, pointy-toed kitten heels, nude wedges, and designer sneakers fresh from their boxes.

I imagine there are women out there who would die for Mrs. DuVernay's closet, everything curated to perfection, tailored, labored over, imported from the finest couture houses. Some women see something they like and buy it without a second thought, but Mrs. DuVernay takes her time. She thinks about her purchases with careful precision, sometimes for weeks at a time, buying only the items she truly loves.

It's an impressive amount of self-control.

I carry an armful of her clothing to her bed, laying them flat beside her open suitcase. Peering toward the bathroom, I catch a glimpse of her mirrored reflection as she fusses over her toiletries, lining up her infinite collection of oils and creams and serums, nauseatingly expensive beauty counter purchases and night potions that promise to stop aging in its tracks.

Mrs. DuVernay is obsessed with preserving her youth, convinced growing old is a tragedy, each wrinkle a battle scar for those less fortunate, the ones on the front lines of the war on aging. Around Palm Shores, agelessness is the hottest thing and no price is too high if the results are guaranteed.

I couldn't disagree with her more.

I think growing old is an honor. Special in its own way since not everyone has that privilege.

My mind wanders to my mother, wherever she is. She's in her fifties now and I can't help but imagine what she looks like. Would I recognize her if I saw her? Unless she met some rich, handsome stranger who swept her away and affords her with all the comforts of life, I imagine she's showing her age.

She probably looks similar to Eunice, the DuVernays' housekeeper. They would be about the same age. In some ways, Eunice has filled that gaping motherless hole over the years. Despite the fact that she only comes three days a week, from nine to three, she taught me how to cook and bake, how to do laundry, and on top of that, she found the time to teach me how to read. Somehow I was able to convince Mrs. DuVernay that I taught myself. As savvy of a woman as she is, her fatal flaw is always believing what she wants to believe.

I imagine it's easy to believe anything you want when you're convinced you're never wrong about anything.

Another mental image of my mother fills my head, this one taking shape like a photograph that doesn't exist. The two of us, matching saffron hair, wide eyes, and even wider smiles—ones so massively jubilant they make our faces hurt.

A tightness in my chest steals the wind from my lungs, as it does whenever I think of my mother, so I force my thoughts away, focusing on the task at hand.

I roll and fold Mrs. DuVernay's outfits, and then I stack them neatly in the left half of her suitcase before tugging the zipper closed on that compartment. On the right, I'll place her underthings, her French lace panties and brassieres made of the finest Italian silk.

"Are you about finished out there?" Mrs. DuVernay calls from the bathroom.

"Almost," I say, unzipping the right side of her suitcase.

It's then that I see the lingerie.

Hand clapped over my mouth, I suck in a startled breath and take a step back.

"I'm checking in for my flight now," she says from the next room. "I'll have you drop me off at the airport in about an hour. Is your car gassed up?"

My throat is too dry to swallow, and I try to utter a response but my voice is rendered to a creak. If Mrs. DuVernay is simply visiting her mother in New York, why would she need all these negligees? I've been around long enough to know she doesn't prance around the house in silk robes, teddies, and see-through underthings.

Pulling myself together, I finish stocking her suitcase with bras, panties, and socks, and I zip the right side closed. A moment later, Mrs. DuVernay struts out of her *en suite*, two oversized cosmetic totes in hand. I take them from her, praying she doesn't see the tremble in my hands, and find a place for them in her luggage.

Checking her watch, she exhales. "Aviana's still not home. I was hoping to see her before I left."

"She's at art club," I remind her.

"Yes, Zsofia. Thank you for that. I'm well aware of my

daughter's schedule. I was simply remarking that I'd love to see her before I go, not asking where she was." She scoffs, pawing a hand at me. "I just can't with you today."

Mrs. DuVernay yanks her sealed luggage off the bed and wheels it to the door. She doesn't have to say another word to let me know that I'm expected to carry the seventy-pound behemoth down the polished wood stairs to the foyer.

I dim the lights, close the door, and follow her out, pulling the bag behind me, the wheels whirring steadily against the wood floor. Her dainty hand curls around the shiny banister as she makes her way downstairs, each step housing a sort of seductive sway—though that's always been the way she moves, with intention and purpose.

The lingerie comes to mind again.

My teeth clench.

Gripping the handle of the suitcase as hard as I can, I hoist it up and carry it carefully down the narrow, winding stairs, ensuring it doesn't bump against a single railing, step, or balustrade on the way down.

I'm slightly winded when I reach the bottom, though I'm willing to assign that blame to the maelstrom of thoughts swirling in my head, visions of Mrs. DuVernay and some exotic mystery man tangled in hotel sheets, laughing and making a fool of her loving, loyal husband.

In spite of everything this woman has put Mr. DuVernay through, he loves her beyond reason, beyond logic. He's never sought so much as an ounce of attention from another woman, opting to hole himself up in his study or motor around the waterway in his boat instead of meeting his friends for drinks at the Sailcloth.

He is fiercely, inexplicably, infuriatingly loyal to her.

I always knew Mrs. DuVernay was self-serving, but this is ... beyond.

This is intolerable.

Unacceptable.

She must be stopped.

9

CATE

"OH, Cate, you should smell this one. I just got it last week." My mother is seated on the rickety bench of her assemble-yourself vanity in the corner of her twelve-by-twelve bedroom.

"Top notes of lily and iris with ambergris base notes. Dries down to a light yet sultry scent." She presents me a bottle of cheap perfume, champagne-colored liquid enveloped in thin glass carved to resemble some celebrity's face.

I imagine she bought it at the outlet mall for a steal due to its questionable authenticity. Ambergris is rare and pricey, controversial, and harvested from whales. I doubt this bottle contains a milligram of the real stuff.

It's Friday evening, and her petite frame is wrapped in a faux silk kimono covered in screen-printed lilies. Her gaze finds mine in her mirror, and I rise off the foot of her bed to indulge her.

"It's pretty," I lie, ignoring the tickle in my throat and the sting in my nostrils that tends to happen to me when I inhale the cheap stuff. "It suits you."

Three sprays later, she places the glass bottle on the corner of her vanity, nestled between four others she keeps on a regular rotation—all of them bargain-basement finds marketed to make women like her feel like old-world glamour is within their reach despite their less-than-glamourous budget.

"So what movie are you two seeing tonight?" She reaches for a jar of drugstore cold cream manufactured by a company that spends more money on ads than research. She unscrews the cap with patience and places it aside as though it were the most delicate thing on the counter.

"Some superhero blockbuster monstrosity." I let him pick because that's the kind of girlfriend I am. That and I've never been big into movies. I find the special effects too distracting, and even when I try not to, I'm always finding continuity errors or plot holes. Sean says it's because I think too much and I'm always looking for flaws in things. He's probably right, but it's not something I can turn off. Believe me, I've tried.

Mom wipes the cold cream from her face with a wet white washcloth. Or at least it used to be white. These days it's taking on more of a gray tinge. Reaching for a small glass vial of gold-hued oil, she disperses four drops into her palms, and then slicks them together, warming the fluid between her fingers before tapping it around her eyes and pressing it into her flushed cheeks and forehead. Upon closer inspection, the oil is also a drugstore brand, and I imagine it promises the same results its hundred-dollar counterpart promises.

My mother has never been able to afford the nicer

versions of things, but it's never stopped her from pretending.

Pretending is kind of what she does.

I can't count how many times I've watched her get dolled up on a Friday night with her bubble bath, hair, and makeup routine ... just to stay in and binge-watch game shows. It started after Dad left us for his other family. I assumed it was a phase at first, but phases are temporary and we're going on thirty years now.

If I think about it too much, it dampens my mood, so I try to consider it like a vice.

I smoke, and she dates her television.

She doesn't judge me. I don't judge her.

"It's just what I do," she'd say when I'd bring it up as a kid and later as a mouthy teenager. The older I got, the more I understood people generally do the strange and unconventional things they do because it makes them feel safe.

Perhaps my mother, despite her authentic, working-class beauty, felt undesirable and rejected after my father's betrayal, and so putting on a little makeup and getting date-night ready made it so she could look at herself in the mirror without dying a little on the inside, without having to fear the sting of rejection all over again.

At least that's my theory.

I bet even my mother has no idea why she does the things she does.

That's what happens when you're emotionally stunted. I'm convinced her emotional age came to a screeching halt at seventeen, when her family was evicted, and she and her two older sisters were forced to do what they had to do to survive. To this day, she won't say much about those years on the street, but I can only imagine.

All I know is she was twenty-nine when she met my father, thirty-one when she had me, and thirty-six when she found out he'd been living a double life—complete with a wife and four kids in Rhode Island.

All that time he'd been traveling to Newport "for work," it turned out he'd been going home. His *real* home.

It was his wife who cracked his bullshit lie one day, and she felt the need to deliver the bombshell in person—at our house. We lived in Orlando at the time, in a little two-bedroom bungalow in an unassuming but safe neighborhood with good schools. I'd just started kindergarten, and my teacher was Mrs. Lamb. I don't remember much else about that time in my life, but I remember that particular day as if it happened yesterday. I'm sure Mom does too.

She was making dinner—shepherd's pie—and it was burning because she'd forgotten to set the timer. The kitchen was filled with smoke, and, once she silenced the smoke alarm, she went around opening windows and fanning dish towels to clear the air. After that, Dad ordered pizza and carried me on his shoulder to the living room so we could watch the evening news while we waited for the delivery guy. During commercials, he filled my head with promises of a trip to Disney World for my sixth birthday and let me take sips from his can of Royal Crown.

The doorbell rang, and I sprang up to answer it. I could practically taste the cheese on my tongue as I grabbed the check and the two dollar tip off the table by the door and prepared to greet the delivery driver.

But it was a woman.

A beautiful, sad woman with angled features, skin like milky glass, and hair the color of burnt umber. Eyes so clear you could almost see through them. Despite her quivering lip and glassy gaze, she was one of the prettiest things I'd ever seen. Like a rare doll you place on a shelf, forbidden to touch. Fragile and beautiful. Prettier than a theme park princess.

Life as Mom and I knew it came to a screeching halt from that moment on.

We've never discussed that day in any kind of great detail. She has her memories of what happened, and I have mine. Everything else I've puzzled together over the years, savoring what bits and pieces of information she's let slip here or there.

Some days I can't help but wonder how different our lives would have turned out had my father not been a liar and a con. He cheated on his wife, he cheated on my mother, yes. But he also cheated me out of any semblance of a normal childhood, any chance at ever knowing a normal, less fractured version of my mother.

For that, I hate the man.

My mom finishes her nightly skincare routine, rises from her vanity bench, and adjusts the belt to her kimono. There's an understated peacefulness on her face, though her eyes are filled with the same melancholy that colored them on that fateful day.

I don't think it's ever left.

"You look radiant, Mom," I tell her because she needs to hear it from someone. I'll say about anything to see a spark of light in her eyes.

"Thank you, Catie girl." She reaches for my face and cup my chin. Her gaze remains dimmed. "So sweet of you to say that."

I follow her down the short and narrow hallway, past the hall bath and the second bedroom that houses her outdated, virus-filled desktop computer. We stop when we reach the humble living room with her overstuffed pleather recliner and the brown microfiber sofa she bought off Craigslist for twenty-five bucks two years ago. A knitted blanket covers the back of it, obscuring stains and tears and little bits of fluffy cat hair from the elderly Himalayan she adopted from a moving neighbor three years ago.

"The funniest thing happened at work this week," I say as she lowers herself into her favorite chair and reaches for the TV remote.

She stops, glancing up at me mid-grab. "Oh yeah?"

I tell her about the crazy locket lady and Odessa yelling at her.

Mom frowns, turning her dead-eyed stare to the TV. She doesn't find the amusement I was hoping.

"Rich people." She tuts and mutters something under her breath.

That's the other thing about Mom ...

When Dad left, she had her private investigator friend dig up as much dirt on my father as she could. It was then that she found out Dad was loaded. Disgustingly wealthy. His home in Rhode Island was massive, his children all attended the best private schools in the area, and his eight-car garage was filled with rare and exotic cars. After more digging, it was discovered that his great-grandfather invested in the railroad back in America's Golden Age. My father's family weren't exactly the Rockefellers, but they were close enough, which came in handy when I had to do a family tree project in the fourth grade. All I had to do was Google the "Golden Age Cabots of Rhode Island" and voila.

I imagine leaving his first wife would've been expensive for him. Whether or not he truly loved my mother, we'll never know. Nor does it probably matter. All we do know is he chose money over her and because of that, my mother has waged an all-out internal war on anyone who has it.

"Wasn't that nice of Odessa though?" I ask, choosing to redirect the conversation for her sake.

Mom rolls her eyes. "I guess?"

It's always been us versus them. I don't know why I expected that to change.

I nod. "You'd like her, Mom. She's actually super nice. She asked me to get lunch with her—"

I don't have a chance to finish, to tell her I declined the invitation, before Mom launches into her signature diatribe.

Batting a hand at me, her chipped manicure the color of fruit punch, she says, "I'm sorry, Catie girl, but why would some Palm Shores rich bitch want to be friends with you? People like that, they like to network. They like to make connections. In the end, their relationships come down to what you can do for them and nothing else. No offense, Catie, but what could she possibly want with you?"

I'm silent and she laughs, maybe trying to soften the landing of her harsh, heavy words, but it's too late.

Mom extends the footrest of her recliner, glaring at a lifeless TV on the other side of the room. "I'm just saying, it's not like you have the kind of money to be able to keep up with all the things she probably likes to do."

"You didn't let me finish ... I told her no." I make my way to the recliner, bending to kiss the top of her head, which smells of discounted floral shampoo. "Have a good night, Mama."

"You too. Tell that man of yours I said hi. Where is he anyway?"

"He had to work late," I say. "We're meeting at the theater."

Warmth colors Mom's expression, but within seconds I realize it's only because the TV screen is glowing to life.

"He's a good man," she says.

"I know."

"A keeper." She changes the channel to her game show.

Here we go again ...

Mom shoots me a look. "You might want to think about locking him down before he finds someone else to lock down ..."

I head for the door, stepping into my tennis shoes. The longer I linger, the more she'll feel the need to get in one last lecture before I go.

"Right. I know," I say. "You tell me this every time. If he ever decides to leave me for someone hotter, nicer, not terrified of long-term commitments, then that's his prerogative."

I kiss the top of her head one more time before giving her shoulder a gentle squeeze.

She means well and she's doing her best.

The pre-rain scent of nitrogen saturates the humid air when I leave Mom's apartment. I climb into my car, heading for the movie theater, passing the bridges that connect West Palm Shores with its showy, glow-y sister. The lights across the Twincoastal twinkle this time of night, reflecting off the sky and into the bay. What it would be like living in one of those houses on the water, the ocean so close you could almost dive off your rooftop into the salty currents below?

It's a little cooler there too, being right there at the Atlantic. In the summer, West Palm Shores becomes damned near unbearable sometimes, like slogging around in a sauna, the air so wet and thick that it sticks to the insides of your lungs.

On a nice day, Palm Shores is a literal breath of fresh air.

I come to a stop at a red light, one known for being notoriously slow from this direction. A lipstick-red Ferrari idles beside me, the engine growling like an Italian beast as the driver gives it a few revs. I steal a glance. A silver-haired fox sits behind the steering wheel with a giggling blonde beside him, breasts to her chin. The guy doesn't look funny. He looks like someone who takes himself too seriously; permanent scowl, sprouted hair-plugs, and a golfer's tan.

The light turns green, and they're off, long gone before I so much as press my foot on the gas pedal.

For no other reason besides bored curiosity, I try to envision what a typical Friday night is like for Odessa. I bet her husband whisks her off to some exclusive, reservations-only hotspot before finishing off with drinks at one of the sailing clubs around here. Seems like anyone who's anyone is a member of one of those, even if they don't sail.

Driving on, I continue my pointless reverie, imagining Odessa in a little black dress, teal-bottomed stilettos with crystals on the heels, and distractingly red lips that compliment her icy blonde locks. I try to picture her husband. I don't want to believe she's shallow, so I imagine him to be equally attractive, similar in age and interests. I tell myself they were high school sweethearts, hopelessly in love for all time, with a robust, yet realistic, sex life.

It's funny how mismatched our lives are— Odessa in her thousand-dollar dresses, and me two seconds from checking my bank account balance to make sure I can swing twelve bucks for a movie ticket and five bucks for popcorn.

Up ahead, the theater sign flickers and, as if on cue, my phone vibrates in the passenger seat, probably a text from Sean asking where I am. Another stoplight later, I turn into the parking lot and find a narrow spot in the back, between an overparked minivan and a grass-green electric sedan.

Climbing out, I lock my car and trot inside, shocked that Sean has his nose buried in his phone and not chatting up some strangers about God knows what.

"Hey," I say. "Sorry. Stopped at Mom's and lost track of time."

He glances up, his mouth forming a forgiving, lopsided grin as he slips his arm around me. It doesn't bother him that we've missed the previews and the first seven minutes of the movie, and honestly, I almost wish it would.

We head to the ticket counter, each buying our own tickets, because I've always been a go-Dutch kind of girlfriend. Then we head to theater number eight, managing to snag the last two seats together in the front row.

While Sean gets comfortable, I lean over and whisper that I'm going to grab us some snacks. It's the least I can do since it's my fault he's missed the beginning of the movie. Before he can protest, like the gentleman he is, I'm out of there, stepping over crushed popcorn and spilled Mike and Ike's.

The concession line is eight people deep, so I slide my phone out of my pocket to kill time while I wait. I read two quick news articles and check the ten-day forecast for the hell of it—even if it's notoriously unreliable in these parts.

It's an hour later, as we're nose-to-screen with Sean's movie and I'm daydreaming about random things ... a funny exchange I had with one of my favorite customers last week, the basket of laundry that still needs sorted, the refill on my birth control that I forgot to pick up yesterday ... when I'm blindsided by a different kind of thought.

I'm becoming my mother.

We each have our vices, our unflinching routines, our reasons for everything.

We live in constant fear that the rug is about to get

swept out from under our feet at any moment, that everyone around us is a liar.

For decades, we've both built fortresses around ourselves to feel safe, and by doing so we've made ourselves prisoners.

Prisoners of fear.

Livewire energy jolts through me—a literal Eureka moment or something, I don't know. I reach for Sean's hand, though it happens when some superhero bad guy leaps onto the screen and Sean turns to me with a giddy grin, thinking it was the scene jump that scared me.

He slips his arm over my shoulders, pulling me tight.

My neck cramps a little from the odd angle he's put me in, but he's smiling and totally into this and deserves to be happy, so I go with it.

I don't want to be a prisoner of fear anymore.

I don't want to be sixty-six years old, reliving the same horrible night over and over, dating my television set …

"I'll be right back," I tell Sean a minute later. Hunched, I tiptoe over sneakers and sandals until I reach the end of the aisle.

When I make it to the hallway, I dig my phone from my bag and pull up Odessa's contact information. My heart hammers, working its way from my chest to the back of my throat before settling in my ears. With pulsating fingers, I tap out a text message to Odessa, asking if she's free for lunch next week, and then I head outside for a smoke while I wait for her reply.

10

ZSOFIA

I'VE DECIDED I'm leaving.

I don't know how, but I am. I *will.*

This time, I mean it.

"You're making me uneasy with all that pacing," Mr. DuVernay says. "Why don't you join me for a drink? Something to take the edge off whatever's bothering you. Besides, a man shouldn't drink alone on a Saturday night."

Mrs. DuVernay has been gone a full twenty-four hours, the house awash in unspoken ease with a hint of peacefulness despite Aviana and her noisy group of girlfriends upstairs, blaring music mixed with giggles and text message chimes.

I take a seat on the end of Mrs. DuVernay's chesterfield as he fixes himself another finger of bourbon. Soft jazz plays through speakers in the ceiling, and the curtains are pulled, displaying a cloudless night sky and well-lit yachts bobbling on the waterway.

I swear he walks lighter when she's gone, his shoulders slightly less rigid and his eyes that much softer.

We are prisoners, and the warden is away.

"This is a good one." Mr. DuVernay adjusts the volume on his music, bumping it up a couple of notches, though it still isn't loud enough to drown out my thoughts.

The suitcase crammed with lingerie won't leave my mind.

Whenever I close my eyes, it's there.

For hours—all night—I laid awake, trying create a scenario where I told Mr. DuVernay, trying to convince myself he deserves to know. He deserves to know right away.

In the good scenarios, he explodes, declares he's going to leave his wife immediately, and begs me to go with him.

In the bad ones? He accuses me of lying, of making the whole thing up and scheming to wreck his marriage.

I haven't the slightest idea how he would act, given the fact that he's rarely ever upset about anything. All these years of living here and I've yet to learn Mr. DuVernay's hot button topics. The most stressed I've ever seen him is after a long day at work, and he tends to keep to himself during those times, choosing to self-medicate with a Cuban cigar, a glass of bourbon, or an afternoon on the water, weather permitting.

Mr. DuVernay takes a seat in the chair next to me, leaning back and crossing his legs wide. He's in navy slacks and a white button down, cuffed just below his elbows. His eyes are fixed on me.

"Is something bothering you?" he asks. "Is your back hurting again? You're sitting there all stiff and hunched."

I straighten and offer him a smile. "I didn't realize."

Mrs. DuVernay's black lace teddy fills my head again,

and I have to look away. It's half-past nine on Saturday night—her family reunion ended at seven. I'm sure she's likely holed up in a hotel room with this mystery man, expensive liquor flowing through her veins, long legs parted, lips swollen.

The threat of bile rises in the back of my throat. I swallow again and again, until the liquid leaves—but the burn remains.

Mr. DuVernay watches me.

What I wouldn't give to know what he's thinking ...

Suddenly his gaze leaves mine, traveling to my mouth before stopping at my cleavage, where I left my shirt unbuttoned *just enough*. The entire thing lasts no more than two seconds, but it happened, of that much I'm certain.

He clears his throat, re-crosses his legs, and glances out the window.

A trumpet wails in the background, screaming as loud as my thoughts.

I've spent hours upon hours figuring out a way to get out of here, most of them requiring ungodly sums of money or a safe place to hide—both of which I don't have. But there's one route that necessitates neither of those things ... an option that would require seducing Mr. DuVernay.

Up until yesterday, I was adamantly against this strategy. I'm not a homewrecker. I'm not a husband stealer. I'm not the kind of person who can hurt someone and not lose an ounce of sleep over it.

But I'm also a woman with dwindling options, a woman desperate to do whatever it takes to break free.

The lingerie in the suitcase changed everything.

Why should Mrs. DuVernay get to have her fun and take a match to her wedding vows, while her husband sits here at home on a Saturday night, loyal and clueless?

Mr. DuVernay is my only ticket out of here. He's the only way I could ever truly be free from his wife.

I tug down on my shirt with modest subtlety so as not to make it obvious, and then I readjust my posture, focusing on the closed cigar box on the table in front of me. From my periphery, the gentle weight of Mr. DuVernay's gaze lingers.

He fixed me a drink earlier, and I've yet to touch it, though mostly out of habit. Mrs. DuVernay doesn't allow me to drink.

I reach for the wine glass and take a sip, smiling internally.

Mrs. DuVernay isn't here now, is she?

"How is it?" he asks, watching me swallow. I lick an imaginary drop from my mouth. His fingers rap on the overstuffed arm of his chair as he studies me. The red wine lingers on my tongue and I catch a trail of his intoxicating Italian cologne. I picture him in the boardroom at his office, leading his team of highly-educated, giant ego'd sharks with his signature effortless confidence, charm, and wit.

He's a made man, that much I know.

Mrs. DuVernay brought family money to the marriage, but from what I've been able to gather, she never shared it with him. After his parents died, he used his inheritance to buy a fledgling drop ship company in West Palm Shores, and over the years he turned it into a multi-million-dollar corporation with international stations in London, Moscow, and Beijing.

"Lovely." I take another sip.

"Take your time, Zsofia." He chuckles, raking his fingers beneath his dimpled chin. "The night is young."

My stomach somersaults.

If I'm reading between the lines, he's asking me to stick around *all night*.

There'll be another drink after this, I suppose. And possibly another.

Conversations.

Flirting?

My stomach somersaults, my fingers tingle with uncertain electricity.

This is wrong.

And this is also necessary.

Elbow leaning against the arm of the sofa, I rest my chin against my hand and gaze at the man beside me, and for the following hour, he entertains me with stories about his childhood holidays in Naples and Paris and Rome, his boarding school antics in West Chester, and his wild summers in the Hamptons as a ne'er do well teenager, looking for trouble any place he could find it.

His mouth is curled into an amused, wistful smile and when he's done, he empties the last of his bourbon into his mouth and says, "I shudder to think of how I might have turned out had Mrs. DuVernay not walked into my life when she did. I'd probably be back east, commuting ninety minutes each way and running a fledgling car dealership."

"That's oddly specific," I say.

"My girlfriend at the time, Cassandra, her father owned a bunch of dealerships along the coast," he says. "She always told me if I married her, he'd probably give us one to run. You know, so his daughter would always be provided for. And it sounded like a good deal at the time. I just had to finish school, marry the girl, and I'd have a career waiting for me."

"But you didn't want that."

His eyes hold steady on mine, and he has the strangest

expression, like a man thirsty to talk about himself, his younger days specifically, and that thirst is finally being quenched.

"I thought I did at the time." He glances down at his empty drink, tilting it from all angles. "And then I met her."

Mr. DuVernay rises from his chair, making his way to his mini bar to refill his crystal tumbler. The silence between us—save for the piano and saxophone duet playing —is palpable.

He still loves her...his wife.

But there's a distance. Emotionally. Physically. You'd have to be blind not to see it, heartless not to feel it. I live it every single day.

My fingernails dig into the leather beneath me, and I try to relax, but a blood-boiling undercurrent remains. Mrs. DuVernay has betrayed her beloved in the worst way, and here he sits on a Saturday night, waxing poetic about his wife and giving her praise for saving him from a life of running car dealerships.

Mr. DuVernay returns to his chair, fresh drink in hand, and sinks into the cushy seat. He offers me a pensive sort of half smile, and my insides tear at the thought of him missing his wife in this moment.

He'll never leave her on his own, not without the most compelling of reasons.

He's miserable and he hasn't the slightest idea.

He needs someone to show him the light, prove to him that a world of possibility exists beyond the stucco walls of this Mediterranean eyesore.

Drawing a cleansing breath, I finish the rest of my red wine and set the glass aside.

"I've always wanted to learn to play the guitar." I turn to his massive collection in the corner of the room. Mrs.

DuVernay doesn't show interest in his passions. She finds his "guitar plucking" to be juvenile, a midlife crisis he took too far.

Mr. DuVernay leans forward, eyes wide, engaged. "Really? You've never mentioned that before."

I shrug. "I didn't want to bother you."

"Don't be ridiculous." He stands, making his way to the corner and plucking a shiny acoustic from its stand before shutting off the music. When he returns, he takes the seat beside me. Placing the guitar in my lap, he slips his left arm around my shoulders, his hand taking mine, curling them together until our fingers are placed on the neck of the instrument.

The room spins and my gaze grows unfocused, nerves or wine, I'm not sure which, but before I know what's happening, he takes my other hand in his, strumming my fingers gently against the metal strings. The vibrations travel through me, settling in the deepest part of my middle.

With every chord, Mr. DuVernay comes alive, his voice laced with boyish excitement as he explains what we're doing in great detail.

"I tried to get Aviana into this, but you'd have thought I was torturing the girl," he says when he removes his arms from around me after a few minutes.

My body relaxes, and I exhale. I'd been so tense in his pseudo-embrace.

I suppose you could say that I've always had an innocent, tamped-down crush on Mr. DuVernay—and perhaps there have been instances of dubious flirting here or there over the years depending on one's own interpretation of flirting...but never once have we been this close physically.

Not ever.

My head spins, and my body reels with a cocktail of want and disgust.

Gently, as if handling a Fabergé egg, I hand him his guitar.

"Can I ask you something?"

"Anything." He gives me his full attention, reaching for his tumbler of bourbon and pulling a modest sip between his lips, tender as a kiss.

"Am I a burden?"

His blue-hazel eyes widen and without hesitation he says, "Good God, of course not. I'm happy you're here with us. In fact, I can't imagine my life—our life—without you."

Mr. DuVernay's hand finds mine, his soft palms a distracting contrast against his calloused, guitar-playing fingertips.

"I just want to thank you...for everything you've done over the years. You and Mrs. DuVernay," I add because I can't sell her out yet. "I don't know where I'd be right now if it weren't for the two of you opening your home to me."

He studies me for a moment. "Zsofia, what prompted this? What's this really about?"

I hesitate, so he thinks this isn't easy for me ...

"The other night, Mrs. DuVernay made a comment. She said she felt I was resentful and unappreciative." I bevel a hand over my beating heart. "I'm not. And I guess I just wanted to make sure you knew that as well."

His striking face tilts to one side as he pores over me with a soulful expression. Lifting a hand to my cheek, he says, "You're special to us, Zsofia. To Aviana. To me, in particular. You've been a bright light in a sometimes very dark place. Sometimes I look at you and it can turn my entire day around. There's a simplicity, an innocence in you that makes me believe there are still good people in this world."

My heart beats wild, free.

His words are unexpected.

And they give me hope.

"I still think about ..." his voice trails off, his hand leaves my cheek, and he takes another swill of bourbon.

I open my mouth to protest, but he lifts a finger to silence me. This topic is strictly forbidden—but the woman who forbade us is a thousand miles away...

"I should have protected you from Malcolm." His eyes are pained, remorse colors his voice. "I had no idea ..."

I resist the urge to tell him "it's okay," because he seems like he wants to vent, to get something out that he's been forced to hold in for ages, and I'm not about to keep him from that.

Sixteen years ago, Mr. DuVernay's twenty-one-year-old half-brother stayed with us for a summer. I was fifteen and completely enamored with the tawny-haired, sun-kissed Ivy League graduate who swam laps in our crystalline pool every morning in his white swim trunks, snuck me my first glass of wine, and gave me my first toe-curling kiss in the butler's pantry with everyone having dinner just around the corner. Malcolm was the spitting image of his brother, same almond-shaped eyes that couldn't decide if they wanted to be blue or hazel, same boyish grin and presence that captivated any audience within earshot.

We were in love—or so I thought.

The pregnancy came as a shock to us both, but Malcolm shouldered the blame. From the other side of the DuVernays' master bedroom door that night, I listened as they discussed my situation until the sun came up the next day, their pacing footsteps against the wood and hushed whispers forever ingrained in my memory.

The following day they forced him to leave and told him never to set foot in Palm Shores again. I begged him to take me with him, throwing myself at his feet as he wheeled his bags to the door, but he didn't say a word, not even a "goodbye," and then he was gone.

Mrs. DuVernay told me to clean myself up and meet them in the living room.

It was then that the fate of my unborn child was explained to me.

I would birth the baby in the home with the help of a private midwife. They would adopt the child and raise it as their own. Mrs. DuVernay cried tears—happy tears—as she explained what a blessing in disguise our situation was. Early in their marriage, they had tried to conceive, but after a string of devastating miscarriages that wreaked physical and emotional havoc on a younger Mrs. DuVernay, they decided not to have children.

But this was her chance, she said. The baby would have DuVernay blood, it was family, it was meant to be. She promised the child would have the most beautiful life and would never want for anything. I wasn't in a position to say no to that, seeing how I lived in a tiny studio apartment above the garage, not a dollar to my name.

As the months went on, my pregnancy ignited something primal in Mrs. DuVernay. She became hyper-focused on the baby. I was hardly showing when she had the nursery painted a soothing shade of yellow. From the moment the plan was set into place, I had to listen to Mrs. DuVernay talk about *her* baby and all the things they were going to do together.

It was as if I were growing her new best friend, someone

to craft and shape into whatever she wanted it to be. It didn't matter if it was a boy or girl—it was going to be hers.

Aviana came two weeks early and in the middle of a tropical storm. Labor moved quickly and with main roads closed and traffic backed up for miles, it was a miracle the midwife made it in time to catch her.

Mrs. DuVernay held her first, wrapping her in a blanket and carrying her off into the next room the instant the midwife was finished giving her a perfect APGAR score.

Within a week, the nannies arrived—one for daytime, one for nighttime—so Mrs. DuVernay could sleep.

For the first five years of Aviana's tulle-and-crinoline life, I wasn't allowed to watch her, hold her, or so much as look at her, as Mrs. DuVernay was terrified I might get attached or do something crazy.

I see Malcolm every time I look into her eyes, whenever she smiles.

She's a dead ringer for her biological father, which means the same could be said for her adoptive father too.

Sheer luck.

"Not a day goes by that I don't wish I would have protected you from him," Mr. DuVernay says. "And now that Aviana's fifteen...I look at her and I think about how young she is, how innocent. And then I think about you at that age..."

He rises from his club chair, pacing for a moment before refilling his drink. He's downing them faster than usual tonight. Making his way to his sound system, he puts a crackly Louis Armstrong record on.

"It's in the past," I say over a jazzy spray of trumpets. "And we got Aviana out of it so...something that perfect could never be a mistake."

He carries his half-filled glass back, pointing a finger at

me. "I admire your spirit, your optimism. I suppose we took a dark situation and turned it into something wonderful, didn't we?"

He takes a seat beside me, settling in, arm wrapped around the back cushions, legs spread just enough that his thigh rests against mine.

My throat is dry, tight, and my palms prickle, damp on the tops of my thighs. At the same time, the room tilts. I lick my lips, silently willing him to make the first move.

It has to be him.

I would if I could, but one wrong interpretation of this situation could be fatal for me. If I'm misreading the signs, I would make a complete fool of myself and this plan of mine would be dead in the water.

Not to mention, I'd never be able to look the man in the eyes again—an uncomfortable fate if I'm to be stuck here the rest of my life.

Swallowing the lump in my throat, I think about Mrs. DuVernay in the arms of another man tonight, and I reassure myself that I'm doing the right thing. She has no idea how good she has it. She'll only know once I take it all away.

The husband, the picture-perfect life ... the daughter.

Aviana deserves to know the truth—and she deserves to have a real mother, one who loves her more than life itself.

And, besides, I could never walk away from my daughter and leave her to be raised by a monster the way my mother did to me.

"Well. I suppose it's getting late." Out of nowhere, Mr. DuVernay rises from beside me, leaving a surge of cool air in his place. Tossing back the remains of his bourbon, he heads over to the record player, the music finishing with a soft scratch before we're engulfed in silence. "Goodnight, Zsofia."

11

CATE

I GET ready for my *date* with Odessa in the back room of the shop the following Friday afternoon, using the mirror that hangs on a chain behind the door. Red lipstick. Pearl studs in my ears. Hair pulled back into a low chignon. One of those trendy, oversized headbands with a knot on the top. My outfit is neutral—black linen shorts, a breezy white tank, and strappy sandals.

We're meeting at the Archipelago Café two miles from here, starting with coffee and conversation, and then we'll progress to shopping, I suppose. It's been years since I hung out with another woman outside of work by choice, and despite the fact that I could throw up at any given moment, I'm actually excited. Low-level excited, but excited none-theless, especially after spending the weekend obsessing over my sudden revelation—that I was turning into my mother.

I give myself another once over in the small mirror,

smooth a stray piece of hair, stick an emergency nicotine patch on my stomach, and head to the front of the store, waving to Amada on my way out. Last Friday, when I texted Odessa and asked if she was free, she told me she was out of town until Thursday and that Friday afternoon would be "lovely."

For the second time ever, I had to ask Amada to cover half of my shift (the first time was three years ago when Sean's aunt died and I accompanied him to the funeral in Tallahassee). Naturally Amada was concerned, texting me randomly all weekend asking if everything was okay…

Ten, maybe fifteen minutes later, I'm strolling into the air-conditioned Archipelago Café, greeted by a twenty-something hostess with shiny white teeth and even shinier fuchsia lips.

My heart skitters in my chest, and my armpits prickle. Oh my. I have no recollection of driving here—time must be in a vacuum or something.

"Right this way, Ms. Cabot," the hostess leads me to a window-side table in the next room.

"Cate!" Odessa rises and wraps me in a warm embrace. She smells like a million dollars with a hint of expensive shampoo. "I've been looking forward to this all week!"

We sit across from one another, and she's grinning ear to ear.

I don't think anyone's been this excited to see me…ever.

A server whose nametag reads CAMILLE deposits a tray of petit scones and pastries (complimentary, she says), and then takes our orders—a London fog for me and a double espresso with steamed 2% milk and one Stevia for Odessa.

"How have you been?" she asks, unfolding a white linen napkin and laying it across her lap. "What's new with you?"

There are few things I loathe in this life (besides fake people and those tiny lizards I always find in my apartment bathroom), and one of those things is small talk. But I came prepared. Prepared to tell the truth. I don't want to be someone I'm not—especially if we're on the verge of forming some kind of friendship.

"Odessa ..." I begin to say, reaching for the ice water in front of my place setting.

"Yes?"

Silverware tinkles around us, piano music plays softly in the background, and the blaring afternoon sun filters through windows, dappling off the crystal chandeliers that hang above us.

"I want to be completely upfront with you about something."

She straightens her spine, unblinking, exuberant demeanor fading by the second.

"I don't ... I don't really do the whole friend thing," I say.

I wait for a response, a micro-expression to clue me in on how she's taking this news, but I get nothing.

"I haven't had many close friendships," I continue, wiping my dampening palms against the tops of my bare thighs. "Not ones that have meant anything or lasted more than a year or two at a time. I don't like a lot of people or maybe I push them away or maybe I rub them the wrong way and they get tired of me, but I'm trying to change that. I'm trying to put myself out there more, I guess. And you're nice. You're so nice. Over the top nice." I laugh, feeling the real-time flush of my cheeks as I awkwardly stumble through this monologue I've practiced in my head a dozen times. "And I want to get to know you, but I want to be myself. I don't want to pretend to be the kind of person I think you want me to be."

She shifts, subtly, eyes narrowing.

"I don't live in Palm Shores," I say, reaching for my water. "I have a shitty apartment just outside of West Palm. I have a long-term boyfriend whom I adore but I won't let him move in with me because I have this whole thing about personal space. I have a mother who can't deal with the real world on her best of days. I smoke a pack a day, and I have a mean soda addiction— the cheap, sugary stuff—not the naturally-flavored carbonated water everyone's obsessed with these days. Also, while I work at Smith + Rose, I can hardly afford to shop there. All the nice things I own, I buy secondhand. Oh, and on top of all of that, I don't do small talk. So … if you're okay with all of this, then great. If you don't think we're on the same page or you're inter- ested in something more superficial or transactional then—"

"—Cate." Odessa's hand shoots across the table, covering mine, which I now realize is shaking. Her full, pink-painted lips spread into a smile. "My husband doesn't look at me the way he used to. I have a teenage daughter whom I'm convinced speaks a completely different language. I practically have to bribe her with shopping sprees to spend an ounce of time with her. I had this circle of friends, close friends, for years. And now I'm … now I'm on the outside of that circle. I don't care that you live in an apartment outside of West Palm. I'm not a fan of smoking personally, but as long as you're not blowing it in my face, it shouldn't be a deal breaker."

She pauses to wink as our drinks arrive in gorgeous china tea cups with matching saucers. Little tufts of steam rise from the tops, dissipating into nothing.

"Anyway," Odessa stirs her latte, clinking her tiny spoon

against the rim of the cup. Taking a sip, she peers across the table at me, eyes glimmering as she leans closer. "Why don't we skip any and all talk of the weather or the past week, and you tell me about the boyfriend thing. I'm intrigued."

I love a woman who skips small talk and goes straight for the good stuff.

Sucking in a breath, I exhale the tension from my shoulders and dive in. She listens with intention, nodding and never once scrunching her nose or asking questions laced in judgement. Seamlessly, the conversation navigates through the unconventional waters of my five-year-relationship to my mother's penchant for dating her television before setting sail for my formative years. I tell her about growing up in Orlando the first five years of my life.

And I tell her about my father too—something I've rarely shared with anyone. When I'm finished, I sip my tea and reach for a blueberry scone—anything to shut myself up. I'm not normally this chatty (or open for that matter), but Odessa has this calming presence about her. Once I started yammering on, I couldn't stop.

I'm two seconds from turning the conversation to her when her phone rings from inside of her bag.

"Oh my goodness. I'm so sorry." She dips a lithe hand inside to retrieve it, pressing the red button to silence the ringer. "*Oh*."

"What is it?"

"I ... I'm so sorry. Something came up at home." She retrieves her wallet next, counting out a few bills and placing them in the center of the table. "Forgive me, Cate. I'm afraid I have to cut our afternoon short."

"Is everything okay?"

"Yes, yes. It's nothing serious. I just need to handle something at home." She slips her bag over her shoulder, scanning the area to ensure she has everything. "I'll text you later … we'll figure out another time to get together. I'll make this up to you, I promise. Again, I'm so terribly sorry about this."

"Odessa, it's fine."

I've never seen anyone exit so quickly, but before I have a chance to process what just happened, she's gone.

Camille comes by, asking if I'd like the check. I nod before glancing at the forty dollars Odessa placed on the table, which is more than enough to cover our drinks.

That strange high I'd been riding for the past half hour has morphed into something different. Vulnerability? Exposure? I poured my heart and soul out to a stranger, and she left without explanation. An old familiar line of thought takes my ear, convincing me Odessa had become bored with me, disenchanted with my brave honesty, and that she decided to pretend her phone call was an emergency.

The chilled air sends a spray of gooseflesh down my arms and across my thighs. Peering out the window, I spy Odessa climbing into her Range Rover and peeling out of the parking lot, nearly hitting an oncoming BMW in the process.

Maybe it *was* an emergency?

I spent all weekend convincing myself it was time to change my old ways, to not automatically assume the worst with people. It seemed so easy in theory. In practice? Not so much.

I hand the twenties to the waitress, collect my things, and show myself out. When I get to my car, I peel the nicotine patch from my stomach and light up a Newport. Driving home, I decide to give Odessa the benefit of the doubt.

But just this once.

12

Zsofia

I'M HANGING up the last of Mrs. DuVernay's dry cleaning in her closet when her presence darken the dressing room doorway. Her stare is weighty but I don't dare meet it. She's been back from New York since yesterday and she's yet to say more than a handful of words to me.

I've been giving a lot of thought lately to my escape plan; the logistics of it mostly, but also the repercussions.

Turning to leave, I stop short. She's blocking me in.

"How long have those been sitting at the cleaners?" she asks. "I swear I haven't seen that sweater in weeks."

"I must have forgotten. I'm so sorry," I say, head tucked. "Did you have a nice trip?"

Her gaze is pinched in my direction, sliding down her straight nose as she scrutinizes me. "And why would you care about a thing like that?"

"Just trying to make conversation."

"Ah. Right. To prove you don't resent me." She laughs.

I don't.

"What's the matter? That pretty little head of yours still empty?"

If she only knew the thoughts inside my head ...

If she only knew the drinks I shared with her husband, the kindness and attention he showered on me, the way our bodies brushed against one another in casual, pseudo-flirtations that can only be the beginning of the inevitable.

I fully appreciate the hypocrisy in all of this, but I'm a woman forced into survival mode. Besides, you can't destroy something that's already shattered. Her marriage was ruined the day she found love in the arms of another man behind her husband's back.

"I should check on the laundry." I glance past her shoulder toward the exit of her master suite.

"Yes. We'd hate for you to ruin yet another load of towels." She turns to the side so I can pass through. I'm almost to the door when she calls out, "I'm going to take a nap. Please be sure Aviana keeps the noise down when she gets home."

I close her door behind me and check the time. Once I switch the laundry, I'll have to head out to pick Aviana up from school with a quick stop at the grocer to grab a few items for tonight's supper.

I hate to cook.

It's my least favorite duty.

But Mrs. DuVernay is always on some exotic diet or claiming some new trendy food allergy and she likes to "save her calories" for the weekend, when she and Mr. DuVernay go out for dinner and drinks at the latest Palm Shores hotspot.

The only perk is that occasionally Aviana will wander out of her room, following her nose to the kitchen where she perches on a counter stool and volunteers to peel potatoes or chop parsley. It's a tiny sliver of time together, but it's our silver of time together—something I'll no longer have when I'm gone.

I finish with the laundry five minutes later and head to the kitchen to grab my keys off the counter, bumping into Mr. DuVernay filling his Nalgene bottle with triple-filtered refrigerator water. He's shirtless, body slicked in sheen, hair damp with sweat, towel draped around his muscled shoulders. He must have taken the afternoon off of work and gone for a run.

"Oh, hi," he says when our eyes meet. "Heading out?"

I nod, swallowing the bulge in the back of my throat. "Picking up Avi then going to the grocery store."

He takes a sip of water, his blue-hazel eyes capturing mine before slowly scanning the length of my body. He doesn't even try to hide it. He may not have acted on his inhibition-less intentions last weekend, but I imagine he's been giving it plenty of thought all week. And now that I think about it, I've hardly seen him the last seven days. When he hasn't been holed up at work, he's been hiding out in his study, door locked.

I think he wants me ...

"See you in an hour." I give him a tiny wave and an ingenue's smile.

On the other side of all of this—is freedom.

13

Cate

I HAVEN'T SEEN nor heard from Odessa for a week when she walks into Smith + Rose one afternoon, a gift bag hanging from her arm and two paper coffee cups in hand with the Archipelago Café's logo on the sides.

Shit.

Elinor and Margaret are in their office in the back.

"Hi!" She places her things on the glass counter. "So I come bearing gifts ..."

She's in a mood—a bright, bubbly, sunny Palm Shores kind of mood. But I've been having a day—a shitty, stuck-in-traffic-on-the-way-to-work, so-busy-I-haven't-had-time-for-a-smoke-break kind of day. Not to mention we had a flood of customers this morning who made a mess of the store and not one of them purchased a single thing.

I shouldn't take it out on Odessa—and I won't. I just wish she would've given me a heads' up that she was coming in today.

"You really shouldn't have ..." I say as she slides a cup toward me.

"London Fog, right?" she asks before reaching for the gift bag. It's pale pink with gold-flecked tissue paper. "Open it."

"Odessa ... I can't accept this."

She bats a hand at me, eyes rolling. "Don't be ridiculous. I felt so awful for leaving you like that last week. I wanted to make it up to you."

This friendship is still new, and there's still a lot we need to learn about one another. Maybe, in my rambling stupor last week, I should've mentioned I don't do gifts. I don't accept them. I don't give them.

"Come on," she nudges the bag. "I can't wait to see your face when you open it."

She bounces on her toes, slicking her hands together. I steal a glance toward the back, noting that the office door is still shut. They had a conference call a little while ago, but I haven't the slightest clue how long it's going to last. It always depends on whether or not Margaret is in a chatty mood, or Elinor is suddenly starving and wants to wrap things up.

"You really didn't have to do this," I say again. Dipping my hand into the tissue paper folds, my fingertips graze buttery soft leather. A moment later, I have a creamy blue Tournesol minaudière with a silver tulip clasp in my hands. "Odessa ... this is too much."

"Do you love it?" She does the tiniest squeal, clapping her hands together. "I saw it and immediately thought of you. I just had to get it."

I pause for a second.

The way she worded that made me assume she was shopping at Tournesol on Worth and happened upon this clutch, but I know for a fact this bag is from two spring collections ago. I'd had my eye on it for the better part of a year, obsessively watching the high-end re-sale websites, but even the worst of the used ones were still hundreds of dollars more than what I could afford so I eventually accepted the fact that I would never own one.

Regardless, even if it had been sitting in her closet, the original packaging collecting dust, I still love it and it's a kind gesture.

"It's beautiful," I say, clutching it against my chest and sighing. "Thank you."

She reaches over the glass counter, wrapping me in one of her perfume-scented, long-armed hugs just as the back office door swings open.

Clearing my throat, I pull away, hiding the gift bag under the counter and praying the ladies didn't see that.

"Hello," Elinor offers a generic greeting to Odessa as she wanders up front, and then she turns to me. "Cate, when you have a second, we have a few boxes in the back room that are ready for the floor. Finally putting out those Hawthornes ..."

"I'll take care of that this afternoon," I say, silently curious to see the markup. The ladies took their time pricing them out, getting appraisals and liability insurance just in case someone were to drop them or worse—steal one.

"Marg and I are running out to grab a bite," she says, hand over her stomach. "We'll be back in a bit."

The instant they're gone out the back door, I apologize to Odessa.

"I'm actually not supposed to be overly friendly with customers," I tell her, wincing, shoulders up to my ears. "I should've mentioned that before ..."

Her lips are shaped into an 'o' and she places a hand

over her heart. "I had no idea. I hope I didn't get you in trouble?"

"I don't think they saw anything."

"That's a ridiculous rule, by the way," she says. "We're grown, adult women. Who are they to say we can't be friends?"

"It's not that I don't agree with you, but they sign my paycheck, so ..." I slip my hands in my back pockets, brows lifted, gaze averting.

Odessa waves. "Well, I suppose I should get out of your hair. I don't want to get you into any more trouble. Seems I'm good at that, no?"

"Before you go, you want to see something?"

"Of course."

Slipping on a pair of white gloves, I head to the back office to grab one of the makeup compacts. Odessa has an affinity for beautiful things and the first day we met, she said she loved things that came with histories and meaning. I might not be able to gift her the equivalent of a Tournesol bag, but I can at least impart her with a story.

"So this is a Hawthorne makeup compact," I say when I return. "In the mid-nineteenth century there was this man, this jeweler, Simeon Hawthorne, who lived in the Cotswolds. He mostly made rings and little trinkets for local customers, but eventually he started making these palm-sized mirrors, intricate, inlaid diamonds, truly breathtaking works of art. So Simeon Hawthorne had three daughters and a wife, all of whom were his world, and he was always telling them how beautiful they were and thought they should each have a little mirror to carry around with them wherever they went, and he told them every time they looked in their mirror, they would see them the way he did —beautiful. One night, there was a terrible storm in his village and a lantern in his bedroom was knocked over in the middle of the night. Simeon, his wife, his three daughters, and his workshop burned to ash—all that was left were twenty-eight compacts that were stored in a box with a stone lid beneath a floor board in the kitchen. As of last year, there are only twelve accounted for in the world, which makes these pieces incredibly rare. If more people knew about them, I imagine they'd be priceless. Here."

I hand Odessa a pair of gloves and the compact.

"You're not going to believe this," she says after a moment of examining the piece with careful fingertips. "I think I have one of these at home."

"No kidding?"

She flips it over, tracing a finger along Simeon's signature rose emblem on the underside, which if you look closely, is drawn using the initials of his wife and daughters.

"Yes." Her eyes light up. "It's exactly like this, only it has a yellow diamond daffodil on the front. Yes ... I remember that logo on the bottom. It belonged to a distant family member, I believe. Honestly, I don't recall how it landed in my hands, but it's been stuffed away in a drawer for years. Do you think your owners would like to see it?"

Without hesitation, I nod. "It took them decades to find this. Yes, yes, yes. Bring it in—that is, if you're willing to part with it. They'll probably make you an offer you can't refuse."

"How much do these go for anyway?" she asks as she examines the tiny price tag hanging from the underside. A second later, she gasps. "Oh, my word ..."

Odessa hands it back, and I take a look myself.

Fourteen thousand seven hundred dollars.

Holy shit.

I'm not sure who would pay that much for an antique

compact, but I know the ladies wouldn't have procured these if there wasn't a market for them, and with their connections, I'm sure it won't be long before we have buyers making special trips to the shop just to see these beauties in person.

"Like I said ... there are only twelve of these accounted for in the world," I say.

Odessa stares at the piece, speechless, hand pressed at the base of her throat.

"You okay?" I chuckle once.

She exhales. "I just can't believe all this time I've had one of these and had no idea how special it was."

Now that she knows the story (and the value), I doubt she'll want to sell it to the shop. Not to mention, I doubt she needs the money. But whatever. It's her decision.

"So is everything okay?" I ask, changing gears. My tongue tingles in anticipation of my next smoke break. "From the other day?"

She chuffs, laughing off my question. "Yes. Teenage daughter drama. No need to bore you with the details."

Odessa peruses the other little trinkets and novelties on the glass countertop, and I study her for a second. I gave her every last detail of my and Sean's relationship the other day and she can't even tell me what happened with her daughter? The thing that was so important she had to blast out of the café like a SpaceX rocket?

I force the annoyance down, to the deepest part of me, where I can no longer feel it.

"How's everything with Sean?" she asks, lashes batting, full attention on me. It occurs to me that I don't yet know her husband's name. We were so busy talking about me the other day that we didn't have a chance to get into any of her things.

"Believe it or not, I'm kind of, sort of thinking of maybe letting him move in." The words make me nauseous, but it feels good to get them out. I still can't believe I'm considering this. Sean can't either. He thought I was joking when I brought it up. We're still working out logistics with our leases and I haven't committed to anything yet, but it's a start.

"Good for you." Her eyes gleam, as if she's genuinely happy for me. "I know you said you were working on opening up a bit more. Seems like you're already making big strides."

"Well, it's not a done deal, but yeah."

Checking her timepiece, she sucks in a breath. "I hate to dash so soon, but ..."

"No worries." I shrug and try not to think about the freedom afforded to women like her—the bottomless bank accounts, the ability to do whatever your little heart desires with each and every hour of your day. I don't hold it against her—we're all dealt the hands we're dealt—but I'd be lying if I said it didn't make a portion of my human ego envious.

But good for her.

"I'll text you soon," she says at the door. "Last Friday deserves a complete do-over. My treat."

When she's gone, I lock the front door, flip the sign, and take my break, calling Sean to chat for a second.

"I'm sorry, but who the hell just gives someone they've only met a handful of times a thousand-dollar handbag?" he asks after I fill him in.

"I know." I take a drag. "I'm all for a genuine friendship, but I don't want to feel like I'm being bought, you know? And I don't want to feel like I owe her anything. I can hardly afford a Hallmark thank you card, let alone a thousand-dollar bag. What the hell do I do?"

"There's got to be a catch. She wants something from you."

"Like what? I told her I live in a shitty apartment in West Palm. She's seen my car. She knows I lack connections or money. I literally have nothing to offer her ..."

"Maybe she's trying to lock you into some pyramid scheme or something, selling protein shakes or makeup or those really ugly earrings my mom is always buying from those catalogs."

I exhale a plume of smoke as an afternoon thunderstorm rumbles in the distance. "She doesn't seem sales-y though. All she ever wants is to talk about me ..."

"Maybe she wants to be you?" He snorts into his receiver. He's kidding, I think.

Fat rain drops begin to fall from the sky, plunking against the cars parked in the back lot.

"Maybe she's obsessed with you," he adds, "like in those Lifetime movies my sisters always watch."

"Babe. She drives a car that costs more than what I make in two years and she looks like a cross between an angel and a supermodel. I promise you she does not want to be me." I stub out my half-smoked Newport and toss it in the nearby trashcan before heading inside. "Break's over. Call you tonight?"

"Love you," he says.

Ever since I brought up the possibility of moving in, he's been showering me with "I love yous" every chance he gets. I don't tell him it makes me twitchy to hear that fifty times a day, that it feels non-genuine and a tad creepy when spoken in excess.

Nobody loves anybody that much. If they do, there's usually a catch.

I take a swig from my RC cola can in the break room, buying a couple of seconds. "Love you too."

One of these days, maybe the twitching will stop, maybe I'll learn that there isn't a finite number of "I love yous" a man can give you before they run out, and maybe I'll even stop second guessing everyone's motives—especially people who drop thousand-dollar bags in your lap like candy at a parade.

There has to be a catch.

14

Zsofia

"WHERE'S MRS. DUVERNAY?" I ask Mr. DuVernay in his study Friday evening.

"Painting the town, I suppose. Doing what she does." He silences his record player. "Why don't you come in for a second? Close the door behind you."

Heat creeps along my neck, settling in my ears. I shut the door and make my way across the room, hardly feeling the ground beneath my feet.

"I wanted to ask you about something," he says, perched on the edge of his desk.

"Of course." I nod. "Anything."

"Do you think Aviana is doing okay?"

Not what I was expecting.

At all.

"It's just—She won't talk to me anymore. And I know she doesn't talk to her mother. She tells us everything is fine, but she seems distant lately, pulling away. Maybe she'd said something to you? Have any insight?" He points to the sofa. "Take a seat if you'd like."

I sink into the middle cushion, hands in my lap, clearing my throat. "Well, she's a teenager, sir. I think we both remember what it was like to be fifteen. All the emotions ... the confusion, trying to figure out where you fit in this world."

"Do you think maybe you could talk to her? Try to get her to open up?"

And betray her trust? Never.

"Um." I search for the right words, something diplomatic. "Last time I did that, Mrs. DuVernay wasn't very happy about it."

He rises from the edge of his desk, taking the spot beside me, glass of bourbon in hand, the permanent prop that it is. "So we'll just have to do this when Mrs. DuVernay isn't home."

Is this double speak?

Did he lure me in here under the guise of talking about Aviana so he could get me alone?

The room is stuffy, hotter than before—or maybe it's the intensity of his gaze that makes me feel I'm on fire from the inside out.

The idea of stealing Mr. DuVernay away, of showing him how much better things could be, of using him to get out of here holds all the appeal in the world to me. But the thought of actually kissing him—of going through with this, terrifies me to my core.

I haven't been kissed, even touched, since his brother— and that was close to sixteen years ago.

In the dim light of his study, he could almost pass for his brother. An older version, of course.

Malcolm would be in his late thirties now.

I assume he's married. A couple of children perhaps, beautiful like him ... like our Aviana.

I can't help but wonder if he thinks of me, of *us*, as much as I think of him.

"So what do you say?" Bourbon trails from his breath, strong and abundant with a hint of spearmint mouthwash and his citrus vetiver aftershave. "This could be our little secret."

A vision of his wife bursting through the door fills my mind turns my blood to ice water. It paralyzes my intentions, but only for a moment. He doesn't even know where she is tonight and even if she were here, she wouldn't set foot in his cigar and cedar scented mancave, because it gives her an instant headache.

"You remind me so much of my wife in her younger days," he says. His fingers spider across the top of my knee, and he gives me a boyish smile, though perhaps it's the alcohol. "But you're softer, kinder. She's a tiger. You're a kitten."

I don't know what to say to that, so I marinate in this awkward silence, attempting to regulate my runaway heartbeat.

"You're a very beautiful woman, Zsofia." He pulls in a sip of his drink. His palm is still and warm, resting on the top of my knee. Our eyes catch and, for a second, he looks at me with more depth than ever before.

Is he thinking about what would have become of me had I not been given to them all those years ago? The woman I'd be now? So much more than this biddable servant they've molded me into?

His empty hand lifts to my face, cupping my jaw, and his thumb traces my lower lip, leaving a path of effervescent tingles.

"I have an incredible amount of self-restraint, Zsofia,"

he says. "But lately you're making it impossible for me to use an ounce of it."

My stomach twists, knotted and nauseous.

No. This is what I've wanted.

This is part of my plan.

I swallow the vigilant lump in my throat and force the words out. "Then don't."

His eyes drop to my mouth for a moment. "Are you sure this is what you want?"

"More than anything." And it's the truth. This is my ticket out of here.

I close my eyes until the heat of his mouth finds mine and accept a kiss from a sex-starved man who tastes like freedom.

15

CATE

ODESSA PICKS me up from work Tuesday afternoon.

That's right.

I've deviated from my sacred Tuesday post-work ritual in favor of hanging out with a woman whose intentions are still murky. It isn't like me to continually give anyone the benefit of the doubt, but at this point, curiosity might be steering the ship.

Whatever her end game is, I'll find out.

If she is trying to rope me into some pyramid scheme, I'll have no problem politely declining, and she'll be the one walking away with her tail tucked after having wasted all this time and money. When it comes to my time and my wallet, I've zero problem saying no to anyone about anything.

But that's neither here nor there.

I climb into the passenger side of her Range Rover, the black leather soft and cool beneath my thighs as I buckle up.

I reach into the Tournesol clutch she gave me two weeks ago and retrieve a check for five grand.

"I know it's a little less than you were probably expecting," I say after remembering her kaleidoscope eyes when she saw the sticker price on the first compact. "But they said that's the wholesale price. And it's more than they paid for the ones they got in New York."

Last Wednesday she stopped in so Margaret and Elinor could check out her diamond daffodil Hawthorne, and the ladies asked for a few days to put together an offer.

"No, this is great," she says, taking the check and folding it before slipping it into the front pocket of her Balworth bag. "The thing was just sitting there in a drawer, not being used. I'd rather it go to someone who'll appreciate it."

Odessa steers toward the main road before hanging a left at the light. She's taking me to some French restaurant for lunch, and then we're catching a matinee of some film festival flick I've never heard of. I didn't tell her I'm not into indie movies because it seemed like she put so much thought into planning this afternoon for us and she'd already purchased the tickets.

"Do you mind if I jet home for two seconds?" she says. "I've been running around like mad all morning and I forgot to drop something off for my assistant. It won't take long."

"Not at all."

"You're the sweetest." We head away from the shopping and entertainment district and drive toward the ocean, the houses growing more gargantuan with each passing block. Ten minutes later, we're turning into a gated neighborhood. An ornate sign nuzzled in a tropical landscape reads ARTEMIS COVE, and the security bar automatically lifts once her car approaches.

Coasting through lush, winding streets with paradisiacal names and the kind of jaw-dropping mansions I've ever only seen in magazines, I struggle to keep my cool and to keep my gawking to a minimum.

We turn onto Laguna Terrace, and, once we reach the top of the hill, she accelerates into a circle driveway, coming to a stop outside a stucco garage with an unapologetic five stalls.

I note the house number—422—and it makes my heart smile a bit.

Sean's birthday is April twenty-second.

"Two secs." She flashes a smile before reaching into the backseat and grabbing a medium-sized shopping bag. Climbing out, she trots to the garage, presses in a code, and disappears inside. She isn't gone more than a minute before she returns.

It's only when Odessa steers around the second half of the circle drive that the bubbling limestone fountain with a multitude of spitting fishes along the perimeter and a marble mermaid in the center comes into view. If those are the kinds of luxe frivolities the DuVernays spend their money on, what treasures and oddities inhabit the inside of their *humble* seaside abode?

"I swear, I'd forget my head if it wasn't attached some days," she says as we pull onto the main road. "We should still make our reservation, so we're good."

"No worries," I say, ogling another slice of real estate heaven to my right. This one is pink and, while it isn't exactly my taste, I could easily put that aside if it meant waking up to the sound of the ocean crashing in the distance every morning.

"Oh my God." Odessa's hands grip the steering wheel until her knuckles whiten and she peers into the rearview mirror. From the passenger side mirror, I catch the flashing lights of a traffic cop behind us. "I think I might've been speeding ..."

"It's fine," I say. "Stay calm. They're just doing their job. I'm sure he'll let you off with a warning, and we'll be on our way."

She digs into her purse with shaky hands as the cop approaches us and produces an ID, rolling down the window.

It's a scorcher today with that unrelenting sun and not a puffy white cloud in the sky. A bead of sweat trickles from his hairline, catching in his eyebrow. "Do you know why I stopped you, ma'am?"

"I'm so sorry, Officer." She hands him her ID. "I guess I'm not sure."

"You were going eight over in a construction zone," he says.

I don't mean to, but I make a face. I spotted a few random orange cones back there, next to a sewer gate, but there weren't any workers or signs. If there were, I missed them.

Odessa gasps, as if she's done the most horrible thing in the world. "I had no idea. I can't believe that. I'm so sorry."

He inspects her license before studying her face. "I just need to check your registration, make sure everything's current, and then I'll let you get on your way."

"Of course." She points to the glove compartment, and I retrieve a half-folded slip of white paper and an insurance card.

"I'll be right back," the officer takes the items and returns to his car.

Odessa's chest rises and falls in quick succession, and her hands have a chokehold on the steering wheel.

"You okay?"

"This is just ... a little embarrassing, that's all," she says, almost breathless.

"I've been pulled over half a dozen times," I say. "It's no big deal, really. These guys just want to keep the road safe for everyone. Sounds like he's going to let you off with a warning."

Her gaze lifts to the rearview for a moment, her cheeks flushed. "This has never happened before."

I place my hand over hers. "Seriously. Don't be embarrassed. It's not a big deal."

The officer returns a few minutes later, handing Odessa her things and, as promised, letting her off with a warning.

It isn't until she's on her second cocktail at Franco, an hour later, that she appears to be over it. She's smiling now, her back less rigid, her cheeks still flushed, but this time from the alcohol, not from the public humiliation of being pulled over for speeding.

"Tell me about your husband," I blurt when we finish our second course. Fortunately, the menu here is prix-fixe, so I didn't have to worry about mispronouncing anything.

"What about him?" she asks, fingers delicate around the stem of her martini glass before she takes a sip.

I'm not drinking. I don't drink. It's a control thing. I prefer to keep my inhibitions in a vise-like grip at all times.

I shrug. "I don't know ... what's his name, for starters? What's he like?"

She bites her lower lip before breaking out into a girlish grin. "He's handsome."

"Duh," I snicker.

"He's intelligent ... driven ... independent ..." her gaze rests on her glass for a second. "He can be detached sometimes. In his own world. Sometimes it feels like we're drifting in two entirely different directions and other times it feels like we're in the passionate throes of those early years, you know? Marriage is funny like that."

I wouldn't know ...

"How did you meet?" I ask, taking a sip of my sparkling water. I fight off the sour wince that threatens to own my expression when the sugarless, tasteless disappointment assails my tongue.

I'll have a Royal Crown later.

"College." Her mouth flickers into a wistful curl that's gone before it has a chance to fully form.

"So how long have you been together then?"

Peering through a fringe of dark lashes, she points a playful finger across the table. "Is this a roundabout way of asking how old I am, Cate Cabot?"

"Of course not," I lie as I do a quick mental calculation. If she met her husband when she was in college and their daughter is a teenager, that places her roughly somewhere in her mid-thirties? Add a bit of Botox and filler and her ageless face makes sense.

"I'm teasing you," she says. "The longer you're with someone, the more the years tend to blur together. I can tell you we've been together so long, I hardly remember what life was like before him."

"That's romantic."

"Maybe," she says, twisting the stem of her glass and appearing to be lost in thought for a moment.

"You must still love him though," I say, "if you're sticking it out through all the ups and downs."

Her angular face tilts to the side. "Sometimes I see myself growing old with him. Other times I fantasize about running off with some dashing stranger, starting a new life. But I could never do that to my daughter."

If I'm reading between the lines correctly, it sounds like

her daughter is the glue holding their marriage together ... at least for now. I resist the urge to offer her advice seeing as how I have zero experience—and I don't want to overstep my boundaries here. Our friendship is still budding, not yet in bloom, and unless she asks for my two cents, I'm keeping those pennies in my pocket.

Before she has a chance to add anything more, our third course arrives.

I haven't the slightest clue what it is, only that it looks pretty and smells ... interesting.

"*Bon Appetit,*" she says, selecting the appropriate fork.

I wait until we're finished with our dessert course and Odessa swipes the check away before I have a chance to protest—not that I could afford to—and then I speak the one thing that's been on my mind ever since she gave me that gorgeous bag two weeks back.

"Odessa?" I ask.

"Yes?" She takes a bite.

"I don't know what kind of friends you had before me ... but I want you to know, you don't have to buy me gifts and treat me to fancy meals to get me to hang out with you."

She chews, swallows, and reaches for a glass of water, eyes averted.

"You've been so generous," I say. "And I don't ... I can't reciprocate these kinds of things."

"And I don't expect you to," she says, dabbing her mouth with a lace napkin, intense blue gaze meeting mine. "Cate, I enjoy this. Truly. I enjoy your company. You're unlike anyone I've ever met, and I find your honesty absolutely refreshing. I hate the idea of you feeling indebted ... now I feel awful."

I reach across the table, my hand over hers. "Please. Don't. Don't feel bad. I just don't want you to think you have to try to impress me. That bag? It's the nicest thing anyone's ever gotten me. And this French food? I have no idea what I'm eating and I sure as heck can't pronounce most of it, but this is easily the best meal I've eaten in my life. So thank you. Really. But I hope you're not worried about trying to win me over because that's completely unnecessary. At the risk of sounding like a total weirdo ... I'm really enjoying getting to know you."

And it's true.

She's an enigma, a giant question mark, and kind-hearted to boot.

I couldn't dislike her if I tried.

"You're sweet to say that." Odessa glances at the napkin in her lap before digging into her bag and producing several large bills, which she slips into the check folio. "Movie starts in forty minutes. Shall we?"

We leave Franco and head to the nice theater across town, the one with the heated leather recliners and the wait staff that personally deliver your soda and popcorn, and we spend the afternoon watching some fancy film with uniquely attractive actors I've never heard of.

When it's finished, I sneak away for a quick smoke before spritzing myself with perfume, popping a mint, and climbing back into the air-conditioned buttery leather seats of her SUV.

Within twenty minutes, she's dropping me back at my faithful Honda. With its dull paint job and saggy suspension, I remind myself it's what's inside that counts. I can't remember the last time it broke down or the last time it needed anything other than an oil change and fresh brake pads. I can't imagine what Odessa shells out for maintenance on this thing. It's probably more than what I make in a week.

"We should do this again soon." She hugs me across the console and her perfume sticks to me when we're done. "Maybe I'll come your way next time? I'd love to meet Sean too. He sounds lovely."

"He is. And we should—we will." I chuckle. "I mean, yes to all of that."

I don't recognize myself right now, making plans with a new friend—smiley, giddy, and agreeing to introduce her to my boyfriend, inviting her to my neck of the woods. It's almost like speaking a new language—foreign and exotic with a dash of newness to make it fun.

This new leaf I'm turning over is emerald green and as refreshing as an early spring after a gray-brown Florida winter.

I climb out of her car and get into mine, instantly craving the leathery aroma of her Range Rover. I inhale her perfume off my shirt. These things, too, are foreign and exotic with a dash of newness to make them fun.

I have a feeling we're going to be great friends.

16

Zsofia

MRS. DUVERNAY CLAIMS she's meeting "a friend" again for lunch today. Third time this week. Given the fact that she has no friends, I can only assume this "friend" is her secret lover, and for that reason, I'm camped outside the café shortly past one in the afternoon, waiting for her to arrive for the 1:30 reservations I made on her behalf. I'm supposed to be dropping off dry cleaning. Fortunately the dry cleaner's is on the way. If she spots me—and she won't— I'll simply explain that I stopped to grab a mango bubble tea from the café on the corner.

It's been three weeks since Mr. DuVernay kissed me in his study.

And that's all it was—a kiss.

There was a bit of heavy petting too, but none of it lasted more than thirty seconds before he peeled himself off of me, slicked his hands through his hair, gasped for air, and wore an expression unlike any I've ever seen on him—sheer panic and a tinge of self-directed disgust.

He paced his study for a minute, mumbling about how wrong it was, how he crossed a boundary that he swore he'd never cross, and then he swore me to secrecy before ordering me to my apartment above the garage.

For four straight days, he avoided me like the plague.

On the fifth day, he cornered me in the laundry room and kissed me again, this time slipping his hand under my shirt. The next day he found me in the kitchen while Mrs. DuVernay was out and about, and I imagine things would've progressed further had there not been a delivery at the front door that required a signature. Two days later, he called me into his study and told me to shut the door, but Eunice barged in with her Oreck and feather duster, not realizing he was working from home that day.

It would seem the universe is conspiring against us.

Some days I'm okay with that. Kissing him doesn't empower me as much as it leaves a feeling akin to dirt beneath my nails. When it's over, I wash my mouth with antiseptic mouthwash until I can no longer taste him on my tongue.

Regardless of my moral qualms, this is nothing more than a necessary evil—and I remind myself of that every time he comes on to me.

Most of the time, I close my eyes and pretend he's Malcolm, but, of course, I would never tell him that. In his eyes, I was victimized. I never told anyone that Mal gave me more time, love, attention, and affection than anyone ever had, and I relished every moment we shared. Those sweltering summer months were the most blissful ones I'd ever known, until it all came crashing down with a missed period and morning sickness so severe I couldn't hide it.

Slumping in the driver's seat of my car, I slip on a pair of black, oversized sunglasses I stole from her closet this morning and tuck my hair into my shirt. At 1:32, Mrs. DuVernay is seated at a table for two in the outdoor patio section of the restaurant.

Bold.

It isn't but two minutes before a man strolls up in a gray linen suit, white button-down with the top several buttons undone. His hair is slick and dark, oiled and finger-combed back, lush with a hint of wave, and his skin is a sun-warmed, youthful, exuberant shade of bronze.

Even from the opposite side of the street, across several lanes of Palm Shores traffic, I can tell he's gorgeous enough to make Mr. DuVernay the equivalent of a shriveled prune —no easy task.

The two of them are locked in an embrace.

He caresses her face a second later, and then kisses her, shameless and unhurried.

When their PDA show is finished, they take their seats, hands locked from across the table as their server delivers a bottle of wine and two glasses. My stomach churns as she laughs and bats her manicured hand and gives her lover a kinder, sweeter, more playful version of herself than she gives the rest of us.

If he only knew.

I roll down my window and snap a few pictures, my phone's camera zoomed in so close the two of them take on a fuzzy form. It's better than nothing.

I stay a few more minutes, stewing and steeling my resolve because, sooner or later, Mr. DuVernay is going to want to go all the way with me, and I need to be mentally prepared for that. Then I pull out of my parking spot, shielded by an out of place eighteen-wheeler.

Exhaling, I check the rearview, assuring myself there was no way she could have noticed me. Then again, why would she? I'm meaningless to her, a sub-human assistant born solely to do her bidding. A harmless object in the background.

But she's about to learn that the last person she should have underestimated ... was me.

17

CATE

ODESSA WANDERS into the shop late Wednesday afternoon, a shoebox-sized container in her arms and a smile on her red lips. Her icy hair is pulled back tight, secured in a classic French twist. An ivory jumper and diamond studs finish the look.

"Hey, stranger," I say, hands slipped in my back pockets. "I had no idea you were coming in today."

She strides across the marble floor, heels click-clacking, and leans over the glass counter to air kiss my cheeks. A second later, she places the container down and peels back the lid.

"You said your bosses were here on Wednesdays, right?" she asks.

"They're in the back right now. Why? What's up?" I glance at the contents, spotting a vintage Winthrop watch with a sapphire bezel, a set of aquamarine-and-diamond teardrop earrings, a black and white gingham Oppenlander scarf, and a snake-shaped brooch with emerald eyes ... amongst other things.

"I was cleaning out my closet the other day. I was going to donate a few of these things, but I wasn't sure if maybe they were worth something? I had this horrible vision of these beautiful things sitting in the bottom of a clearance bin ..."

I inspect the watch, which is easily older than I am. It's flawless. Not a single scratch. It's as if no one's ever worn it.

"These are incredible," I say. "Let me run this to the back super quick."

Odessa smiles, hands clasped in front of her narrow hips. "Actually, I can't stay. I've got a million things to do today. Why don't you text me whenever they're done looking everything over, and we'll go from there?"

"You sure?" I ask, box in hand.

"Of course." A second later, she gifts me with a wave, disappearing out the door as fast as she sashayed in a minute ago.

I'm halfway to the back office when I pass the display case that houses our costume ring collection.

"No way," I whisper. Sitting the container aside, I stoop to take a closer look at the opal ring with the glistening diamond halo—the very same one Odessa purchased the day we met.

For a second, I contemplate the notion that maybe we got a lookalike in recently? It's not like that was the only opal costume ring in existence. But I'm the one who handles new inventory displays and I know for a fact I wouldn't have missed something like this.

Why would she have returned it? And when? This would explain why I've yet to see it on her ...

I think about the compact ... and the box of small valuables before me. And then I think about the casual lines she'd dropped about her marriage, how her husband doesn't look at her the way he used to, about how sometimes she dreams of running off and starting a new life.

Perhaps she's decided to leave and she needs money, and this is the only way to stash away a good chunk of it without her husband noticing. I doubt he's aware of half of the things in this woman's closet. Most husbands are blissfully ignorant in that department.

Carrying her things to the ladies, my mind spins with a million questions—all of which I'm dying to ask her, none of which are any of my business. The smallest piece of me is hurt that I've opened up so much to her, left no topic off the table, and yet there's so much I still don't know about this woman.

———

SEAN RUNS his palm along his bristled jaw Wednesday afternoon, leaning back in one of the breakroom chairs, belly pooched with the takeout Thai he surprised me with after he finished a job in the area. I've filled him in on the latest chapter in the Odessa saga and apparently rendered him speechless.

"I don't know," he says after a never-ending moment of contemplation. "The whole thing is just strange to me. I mean, I'm loving this new side to you, don't get me wrong. But I've got a bad feeling about this woman and whatever the hell she's roping you into."

Sean never has a bad feeling about anyone. If anything, he's incapable of seeing anything other than the best in even the worst of individuals—something that's driven me crazy more times than not over the years.

"There's more," I tell him, sliding my phone across the table. "Look at that. You type her name into a search engine and it's like she doesn't even exist."

His arms fold across his chest and he shrugs. "It's not unheard of for people to pay to have search results cleaned up. Some people don't like to be discoverable—especially people like that. They don't like other people digging into their business, trying to figure out how much money they have or whatever."

"True." I grab the phone again. "But I did a search for her husband. Got a hit."

A second later, I show him a website for some drop ship company headquartered in Jupiter. It lists Charles DuVernay as the CEO alongside a headshot of a handsome older man in a classic black suit and red tie combo, temples flecked with gray and deep worry lines between his dark brows.

"How old do you think he is?" I ask.

Sean squints, leaning in to get a closer look. "I don't know. Fifty? Fifty-five? Somewhere in there?"

"She told me they met in college and their daughter is fifteen," I say. "There's no way she's more than thirty, thirty-five unless she's had a facelift and even then, it's too natural-looking."

"Welcome to Palm Shores ... Who knows, maybe she was a student and he was her professor?"

"You don't think any of this is strange?"

His brows lift and his smile fades. "Oh, no. I think all of it is weird as hell and I think you need to start distancing yourself from this chick before she makes a lamp shade out of you or steals your identity or some shit."

"Oh my God," I say.

"What?"

"What if that's what she's doing? What if she's trying to leave her husband and wants to steal my identity?"

"I was kidding ..."

"I know, but remember the other week when we were trying to figure out what she could possibly want from me?"

"Pretty sure that woman can afford to buy a new identity on the black market without having to go through all the effort of stealing one from some random person."

A random person with average credit and a mere four hundred dollars to her name at any given time ...

He has a point.

"Honestly, this woman's more trouble than she's worth. You need to just slowly back away from this whole thing and maybe forget it ever happened," he says. "I wasn't going to say anything, but the whole friendship kind of seems too good to be true. I don't want you getting hurt ... like before."

I don't know if he's referring to my last friendship with a chatty hairstylist whose talkative demeanor I mistook to mean more than it apparently did ... or the one before that, the Texas girl who moved into the apartment next door and asked to borrow my Wi-Fi password until hers was set up. For a month she kissed my ass, even inviting me over for a "girls' night" of mud masks and Outlander. But as soon as her Wi-Fi was up and running, she started brushing me off and making excuses. Five months later, she moved away without so much as a goodbye.

I didn't even like the last one that much anyway, but the rejection stung the same.

"You're right."

Sean checks the time on his phone. Our lunch break is over. Reaching for my hand, he gives me that sweet-natured, lopsided grin that always puts me in a better mood, and pulls me in for a hug. His breath is warm on the top of my head, and I inhale his average Joe cologne, the same drugstore scent he's been wearing since the day we met.

A minute later, I walk him out and unlock the front door.

Margaret and Elinor aren't back yet. I'm guessing they're having one of their three martini lunches at the Silver Anchor down the street, so I use the opportunity to grab my phone.

Sean's right—I need to step back from Odessa, end this on my own terms before I find myself disappointed by yet another friendship gone sour.

But I have to know about the ring ...

If I don't ask now, every time I see an opal I'm going to think of that damned ring and the fact that she returned it when someone else was working and never once mentioned any of it to me.

Did she think I wouldn't notice?

Did she think I wouldn't happen upon it in the display case?

I decide to call her rather than text. Texts are too easily misinterpreted

"Hi, it's me ... leave a message," her familiar voice plays from her voicemail greeting after five rings.

"Odessa, hey." I remind myself to keep it light, casual. "Question for you ... I saw your opal ring back in the case a little bit ago. I was just wondering if everything was okay with that or ...?" I pause, beginning to wish I'd have thought about exactly what I was going to say before I dialed her number. "No big deal or anything. I was just wondering. Hope all is well! Talk to you soon ..."

I don't want her thinking I'm upset about it. I'm not. At all. I'm simply curious.

Curious and disappointed.

Maybe Sean's right.

Maybe this whole "friendship" was too good to be true.

18

Zsofia

I COUNT out forty-five hundred dollars in cash—what's left of the five grand I got from selling my mother's daffodil compact to Smith + Rose minus the ten percent fee the check cashing place charged.

My escape plan is three-pronged: win Mr. DuVernay's favor, find an ally on the outside, someone I can trust and reach out to if I need a place to lay low, and put together enough money to buy me time to figure out the rest once I'm gone.

I tried returning that opal ring the other day when Cate was off, but I'd lost the receipt and the girl working the register refused to give me cash, saying she'd have to process the return manually and the owners would cut me a check. I've been doing that lately—buying things with the debit card the DuVernays gave me for menial errands and then returning them for cash. I started out at smaller places, mainstream chain stores mostly, and I kept my purchases to less than a hundred dollars so as not to make it obvious, but it wasn't adding up fast enough, so that's when I wandered into Smith + Rose. I needed to start aiming for bigger ticket items.

Four thousand five hundred dollars, plus the eight hundred I'd collected running my exchange-for-cash system might last me a couple of months out there, three at most, so I had the wild idea today to grab a few things from Mrs. DuVernay's closet and take them to Smith + Rose. It took a bit of work, but I ended up with a small slew of expensive-looking vintage items I never recalled seeing her wear in all my years of knowing her—things she won't notice are missing.

I shove the cash into a white sock and tuck it into the bottom of my last dresser drawer.

The makeup mirror I sold once belonged to my mother, one of the only things she left behind that day. For years, I've kept it hidden away in the back of my closet, not quite wanting to part with it but not exactly feeling a nostalgic attachment to the one thing that represented the fact that my mother left me here to be raised by that monster.

Lately, I've been wondering if I, too, am becoming a monster.

The stealing ...

The lying ...

The pretending ...

The using ...

It's a miracle I manage to get any sleep at night with all the guilt demons haunting my thoughts.

Heading to my bed, I lie down and tuck my hands behind my neck, gazing up at the motionless ceiling fan above. My thoughts wander to Cate, the kind and unsuspecting shop girl at Smith + Rose. I've grown quite fond of her over the past couple of months and I pray that when I eventually tell her the truth, she doesn't slam the door in my face.

If she'll give me a chance, I'll explain everything.

If she doesn't give me a chance, it'll be my own fault. One of the first things she stressed to me was that she loathed superficial friendship, that she was an honest person with nothing to hide. How will she feel when I tell her my name isn't Odessa DuVernay? That the only Odessa DuVernay that exists is the one on the fake ID they make me use so I can run their errands …

I was so concerned with winning her over, getting her to like me and trust me … that I didn't think about how any of this might hurt her.

My eyelids grow heavy, fatigue and exhaustion settling into my bones despite the fact that it's only four o'clock in the afternoon. I haven't started dinner yet, but the thought of laboring over the coq au vin Mrs. DuVernay requested for tonight's menu makes me want to rip my hair out in fistfuls.

I've always loathed cooking chicken, with its humanoid pink flesh and sticky white strips of fat that cling to the kitchen shears with every snip.

I promise myself a short nap, fifteen minutes tops, and then I'll head downstairs—only I've barely closed my eyes when there's a knock at the door.

Just like that, I'm awake again.

No one comes up here.

Ever.

With my heart lurching up the back of my throat, I push myself up and make my way to the door, stopping in front of the dresser mirror for a quick once-over in case it's Mr.

DuVernay. He's yet to take things this far, but something tells me that's all about to change ...

Cheeks flushed and fingertips on fire, I clear my throat, tuck a strand of hair behind my ears, and ready a smile as I get the door.

Only it isn't Mr. DuVernay.

It's his wife.

"Zsofia," she says, monotone, arms crossed. "I'd like a word with you."

Oh, God.

"Of course." I step aside, lips trembling as I speak.

She slams the door behind her, gaze darting to every corner of my plain and simple spread. The twin bed with the white blanket. The walnut dresser with the missing knobs on two of the drawers. The mismatched lamp on the wicker nightstand. This place could easily pass for someone's storage attic. You can hardly tell anyone lives here, but I kind of think that's the point.

"Is everything okay?" I ask, the silence killing me. She could be here for any reason, any reason at all, and the sooner we get on with this, the sooner I won't feel the need to expel the contents of my stomach all over her thousand-dollar heels.

She turns to me, gaze laser-focused. "Obviously not. Mind telling me how this magically teleported to a shop on the other side of town?"

Producing a silver watch with a sapphire bezel, she dangles it in front of my face.

Shit.

It takes everything I have to maintain a poker face, despite the fact that I've clearly been caught ... I just don't understand *how*.

"What else have you pawned?" she asks. "What else have you stolen out from under me?"

Mr. DuVernay ...

"God, you're pathetic," she spits her words at me. "Anyone with half a brain cell knows Winthrop timepieces have registered serial numbers. These are twenty-thousand dollars for Christ's sake. I'm just grateful that nice woman at the shop called me today to ask if I was aware someone had come in today and tried to sell my watch."

If I could see myself right now, I imagine my face is the color of that lipstick she always wears in the fall, the matte red that's nearly as dark as blood.

"And apparently, several other items as well," she continues. "A scarf, earrings ..."

She prattles off the list of all the items I stole from her closet this morning.

Arms folded, she squares her shoulders with mine. "Tell me, Zsofia, what were you planning to do with your proceeds? Don't tell me you were planning a little vacation, a little getaway."

Mrs. DuVernay snickers, her face shadowed and menacing in the dim light of my garage apartment.

"Apparently you sold them my great-grandmother's makeup mirror as well," she says. "And they paid you five thousand dollars for it, is that correct?"

I try to answer, but my throat is so dry and constricted the only thing that comes out is a rasp of air.

"*Answer me,*" her voice booms through the small space that separates us, sending a barb of shock through my chest. "Where's the money, Zsofia? Where's my five grand?"

Again, I can't speak and within seconds, Mrs. DuVernay is tearing my room apart, dumping out drawers and shoving my mattress off its frame, tearing through my closet. The hot sting of tears blinds my vision, and by the time I wipe them away, my space is barely recognizable.

"Do yourself a favor and hand it over now," she says through clenched teeth. Her stormy eyes flash with an unspoken threat, a silent dare to call her bluff.

Lumbering across the room, I bring myself to my knees and sort through the spilled pile of socks and undergarments next to my dresser until I locate the hidden cash.

"Here," I say, handing it to her a moment later.

She yanks it from my hands. I don't tell her that's only ninety percent of it. There's no getting back that other ten percent, nor do I mention where the additional eight hundred came from. There's no undoing what I've done.

"I'm also going to need your car keys, your debit card, and your cell phone," she says. "Clearly you are not to be trusted."

19

CATE

"I'M GOING TO GET YOU!" Sean's teasing threat is followed by a cacophony of kid-sized giggles.

I've taken up residence in a lounge chair next to his parents' pool Saturday. Several yards ahead, Sean swim-chases his nieces and nephews around in the water, pretending to be a shark. They scream and laugh and doggy paddle away as fast as their little arms and legs allow until he catches one of them, and then they start all over again.

His brother-in-law mans the grill next to the patio, shooting the breeze with Sean's dad. Inside, his mother and sisters are probably putting candles on his niece's seventh birthday cake and gossiping about my withdrawn state today.

Normally I try to put my small-talk-hating ways aside when it comes to his family. They're good people (save for the one narcissistic sister that everybody tolerates and her braggadocios attorney husband) and they're his earth, moon, and stars. Visiting them can sometimes feel like a social chore for me, and oftentimes I leave with cheeks sore from smiling so much, mentally exhausted from all the conversating.

But today I haven't the energy to so much as attempt to fake it.

"You doing okay over there?" Sean asks, bobbing up and down as one of his nephews climbs over his back.

I nod, force my lips to curl at the sides until they show some semblance of a convincing smile, but he must not buy it, and soon he's swimming to the ladder. Within seconds, he climbs out, wraps himself in a sunbaked beach towel covered in faded flamingos, and takes a seat at the foot of my lounger.

"You have to let it go," he says.

"I'm trying."

This past Wednesday Odessa dropped off a box of items she wanted to sell, one of which was a Winthrop timepiece worth tens of thousands of dollars. Later that afternoon, Elinor happened to be going through it all and thought it was odd that she'd have so casually tossed it in with a few "lesser" items, not so much as a velvet pouch to keep it from getting scratched. Deciding to check its authenticity, she pulled up the Winthrop database and typed in the serial number on the back. When it showed as registered to a local woman by the name of Aviva DuVernay, she decided to give her a call.

I wasn't overly concerned at first, wanting desperately to give her the benefit of the doubt. Crossing my fingers in hopes that Aviva DuVernay was an aunt or grandmother or sister, a family member who gifted her the watch. But the woman on the phone confirmed she was indeed the owner of the watch—and subsequently the other items Odessa had carried in with her that morning. None of them were to be sold, she said. She promised to be there within an hour to retrieve her items, but my shift was over and Amada arrived early of all things, so I wasn't able to stick around. But I did linger in my car, waiting and watching for the other Mrs. DuVernay to arrive.

Elinor never asked her relation to Odessa, but later that night, I was able to confirm that Aviva—not Odessa—is married to Charles.

I don't even know who that woman was—*Odessa*.

Or why she lied.

And she never returned my phone call about the opal ring.

Indignant, I tried calling her yesterday, mostly for the hell of it, but it went straight to voicemail. Didn't ring once. Clearly she has no desire to speak to me.

"You want to get in the water with us?" Sean nods toward his sibling's splashing progeny.

"I'll just watch." I reach for the can of RC cola I brought with me. His parents are hardcore Coke drinkers, complete with a Coca-Cola themed half bath off their rec room. I tried to convert them once, but it was an epic waste of time. And his father told me that when I visit, I have to BYORC—bring my own RC. So I do.

"I hate that you're not having fun." He steals a glance at his brother-in-law and father as they watch us. Rivulets of chlorinated pool water drip down his forehead, and the mid-day sun makes him squint. "She's already taken weeks of your life that you'll never get back. Don't let her take this day from you too." His hand finds the top of my knee, and he gives it a squeeze. "You think she's sitting around in her big ol' house thinking about you right now?"

"It's not that. I just want to understand."

"And you never will because that chick is psycho, and psychos don't feel remorse and they have zero self-awareness. She's not going to call you up and apologize and 'fess up to all the lies. She's probably moving on to the next victim. You dodged a bullet. Be grateful."

As per usual, Sean's right.

"Going to get back in the water. Hate for you to miss out on all this madness. Sure you don't want in?" He winks as he lets the damp flamingo towel fall off his shoulders.

Cupping a hand over my eyes to shield the sun, I entertain his invitation.

He's a good man, my boyfriend.

I should probably get serious about the whole locking him down thing.

There are a million Odessas in this world.

But there's only one Sean.

Rising from my chair, I peel off my swimsuit cover up and plunge into the deep end of the pool.

Screw Odessa.

In my mind, that lying con artist is dead.

20

Zsofia

"YOU HAVE TO DO SOMETHING." I hunch over Mr. DuVernay's desk in a low-cut top, eyes brimming with tears. I smell like gardenia and desperation, and he's my last hope —my only hope.

It's been a week since Mrs. DuVernay confiscated my car, my phone, and my money, rendering my escape plan worthless, all that parading around like a better version of her for naught. I hated wearing her clothes and her shoes. Some days I'd scrub my skin raw trying to get her scent and all that makeup off, and ensuring I placed everything right back where I found it was always stressful. Once, I'd painted my nails ballet slipper pink and I'd forgotten to remove the polish before dinner. I thought for sure she'd notice ... but of course she didn't—she was too concerned with herself as per usual.

"I'll try to reason with her," Mr. DuVernay says, voice low. His hand covers mine and his eyes have yet to veer lower than my neckline. "She's still quite— upset—and I have to say that I don't blame her. What you did—stealing from us—it's unacceptable. You're going to have to build back her trust. *Our* trust."

His hand leaves mine, and he leans back in his chair. There's a pressure on my chest, as if I can feel him pushing away from me even if he isn't touching me.

She has him snowed, convinced I can't be trusted. And he's a smart man. I'm sure he's putting all of this together.

"Mr. DuVernay, there's something you should know."

He lifts a brow. "And what might that be?"

"Your wife has been seeing another man."

He doesn't flinch, doesn't blink, doesn't show an ounce of emotion.

"She packed *lingerie* for the New York trip." My voice is just above a whisper. "And the other week, I was out running errands and I saw her having lunch with this dark-haired man. They were kissing, holding hands, and drinking wine."

"Now is not the time for your antics. This revelation of yours has curious timing, wouldn't you say?" He rises from his chair, checking his phone before sliding it into the side pocket of his charcoal suit slacks. "Anyway, I'm leaving in the morning for Chicago. I'll be gone a week. Aviva's birthday is next weekend, so I'd like for you to arrange a small gathering. Order her favorite cake—the lavender champagne cake from La Mie. And get her mother and her cousin, Deborah, on a flight out here. No more than a two-night stay, please. I'll leave an emergency credit card in the drawer next to the refrigerator for you. I trust you won't do anything to get yourself into trouble again."

"Mr. DuVernay ..." I can't believe he's brushing over the bombshell I dropped a moment ago. "I don't think you understand. I have pictures. On my phone. The phone she took from me. If you get it, I can show you."

His lips press into a flat line as he draws in a hard breath, eyes closed. "Please. I can't with all of this. I've got to pack my bag for tomorrow. Plane leaves early. I suggest you make yourself scarce for the rest of the evening. My wife and I are having a night in together, and I don't need anything to set her off."

"But if you—"

"—Zsofia," he skewers my name, hand slicing through the air until it becomes a balled fist.

I flinch.

"Don't make this situation any worse than it already is. For you. For me. For everyone involved." Making his way around the desk, he places a firm palm on the small of my back and ushers me to the door. "Now, run along."

For the first time in months, my situation is unquestionably hopeless.

21

Cate

"THINK I'm going to visit my father." I take a long, slow drag from my cigarette, staring at the ceiling fan above my bed Saturday night, covers tugged tight beneath my bare arms as Sean lies next to me.

"Wait ... what?"

I exhale. "I want to meet the bastard."

"Yeah. I heard what you said ..." He rolls to his side, propping himself up on his elbow as he stares at me in the dim lamplight. "... it's just ... you've never mentioned this before, and you're so casual about it. I figured you'd written him off."

"Oh, I have."

"Then what's this about? What exactly are you wanting from this? You really think this is a good idea? After what he did to you and your mom? I mean, what kind of expectations do you have here?"

I take another drag, letting the smoke burn my lungs.

"None. None whatsoever. I mostly want him to see me in the flesh, you know. Like a human reminder that he has a daughter he walked away from thirty years ago, not some problem he can sweep under his quarter million-dollar Cabot rug. That, and I want to see what he looks like. I can't remember, and I hate not knowing. It keeps me up at night sometimes."

"You've never mentioned that before."

I sit up, stubbing out my cigarette in the ashtray on my dresser, and then I lie back, gaze fixed to the wobbling fan above.

"It's never been worth bringing up."

I don't remember much about my father. The things I do remember are more like fragments of memories. Shards of remembrances, some of them hazy, others crystal clear. A pack of cigarettes. A can of cola. His Francesco Chiara cologne. Every once in a while, a customer's husband will wander into the shop smelling like my father, and I always find myself making my way around the store the second they're gone, inhaling what's left of that undeniable pong of oakmoss and vetiver, hoping it'll help me remember something new, but it never does.

"Why now?"

"He's got to be, like, seventy or something." I leave out the fact that I've done extensive research on my father's side of the family, and the average Cabot man seems to croak around age seventy-two.

"Okay, but what prompted this? Is it the whole Odessa thing?"

I turn to him, unfazed. "Does it matter?"

He lies back, chest rising and falling as he contemplates an answer, only a moment of silence passes and all he does is slip his arm around me and pull me close.

"When were you thinking of going?" His question arrives after a noticeable delay.

I inhale his chlorine water skin and press my cheek against his warm chest. "I'm off next weekend, and there's a direct flight from Miami to Newport."

"Damn."

"It was one hundred and fifty round trip, last I checked, so it's not that bad."

"No, I meant damn as in ... you're going that soon."

"Kind of feeling like getting out of here anyway. Need a change of scenery." Plus a part of me is curious to visit the Cabot homeland. There's an entire suburb south of Newport that my great-great grandfather helped found. There are streets and bridges and libraries named after him. Even if my biological father is a philandering asshole, I can still appreciate the accomplishments of my ancestors.

"I'm going with you."

"Sean—"

"—you're not doing this alone." He pauses for a beat, his heart drumming harder in my ear. "You're making all of these changes, and I'm happy for you. I just don't want you to take on too much at once. If you go there, and he's the giant jackass I think he's going to be, I don't want you to have to deal with it by yourself."

Early in my relationship with Sean, there were moments I would find myself jealous of him, secretly resenting the fact that he grew up in one of those *perfect* families. The parents with the unshakable, decades-old marriage. Eleventy-million siblings and cousins. Both sets of grandparents a short drive away. Sunday suppers with extended family and enough food to feed an army. Game nights and Christmas traditions and those cheesy "live, love, laugh" signs on every wall and shelf in the house.

I used to think he could never begin to understand the depths of my jaded outlook on life.

Now I realize he doesn't need to.

His compassion is enough.

"How do you think your mom will take this?" he asks.

"I'm not telling her."

"Seriously?"

"She wouldn't understand. This is about me. And I don't want to hurt her."

Sean kisses the top of my head. "You're a good daughter."

"I know."

"Your dad really missed out."

"Duh." I snicker. He snickers. Sitting up, I reach for my lamp and turn out the light before returning to his arms, the ones that feel like home more than I allow myself to admit. "You're staying over tonight."

"Figured ... you shutting off the light and curling up with me and all." He squeezes me tight. "A guy could get used to this."

And he should.

I'm renewing my lease next month and I plan on asking him to move in.

The brief residence Odessa DuVernay took up in my life may have been a confusing waste of my time, but I can honestly say I'm in a better place now than I was before that fateful day when she walked into Smith + Rose and bought that opal ring. I don't claim to know how it all works or why she, of all people, was the one who emboldened me to change my ways. But she did. And I'd changed. And for the first time in my life, I'm looking forward to the future.

I'm grateful we met, if only for that reason.

And if I'm lucky, we'll never meet again.

ZSOFIA

I'M CHANGING the bed linens in the first guest suite Friday afternoon when I notice a spot of blood on one of the sheets.

My blood.

My cuticles are raw, cracked, dried out from all the washing and cleaning Mrs. DuVernay has been punishing me with this past week. I've polished silver and china, hand washed curtains, dining linens, and pillow coverings. My knees are bruised from waxing floors and washing baseboards by hand, and there are times I'm barely able to support my weight by the end of each day. My body aches with each step, each lift of an arm and fluff of a pillow.

The last three nights, I've cried myself to sleep—partially from sheer exhaustion but mostly out of physical pain.

She's essentially sentenced me to hard labor, twelve, sometimes fourteen hours a day.

Shuffling into the guest bath, I wash the blood from my fingernails and massage a bit of lotion into my dry skin. It's thick and scent-free, some *au naturale* French brand Mrs. DuVernay's mother insists on using when she visits, but it stings when it works its way into my fissured flesh.

Mrs. DuVernay's mother and cousin are coming into town later today, visiting for her birthday weekend. I've had a monster of an anticipatory headache all day. Her mother is the worst—worse than Mrs. DuVernay, if that's possible.

When she's here, she waltzes around the house like she owns the place (and I suppose she does, it was her family's money that made its purchase possible). And she's always nitpicking and criticizing, finding little tasks for me to do, millions of ways for me to "make myself useful" as if I wasn't already juggling a trillion other tasks. And she has this bell—this tiny, sterling silver bell that she rings when she needs me. Mrs. DuVernay says it's the way she beckons her staff back in New York, and she's not about to change her ways on my behalf. Yelling is unbecoming and uncouth, she says.

The bleeding on my hands finally stops, and I return to the bedroom, stripping off the stained sheet before making my way to the linen closet to grab a replacement.

I pass Mrs. DuVernay's bedroom on the way, the door ajar enough for me to sneak a glance inside, where I hear the tell-tale beeps of the hidden wall safe in her closet. She mostly keeps valuables in there ... emergency cash, her diamond engagement ring (not the fake one she wears when she travels to exotic touristy islands).

If I had to guess, that's where she's keeping my car keys, cell phone, and wallet. The safe only opens with a six-digit code, one not even her husband knows.

I must have some texts or missed calls from Cate. She's likely wondering what happened, why I stopped coming around. By now she's seen that the opal ring is back in the case and she's probably scratching her head, dying to know why I returned it. Either way, I miss her, but thinking about her too often is painful. Any foundation of the friendship I worked so hard to kindle has probably died to ash.

Padding down the hallway, I grab the fresh sheet and return to the guest suite. Our visitors will be arriving sometime this afternoon, and I still need to set out those iris-scented candles her mother likes—the ones in the milky glass jars—and place chocolate mints on their pillows before waiting for the fresh flowers to arrive. Normally I'd run out to the grocer and grab a couple of hydrangea bouquets but seeing as how I'm no longer allowed to drive or leave the house, I had to call the florist and place an order, asking them to put it on Mrs. DuVernay's tab.

I finish Mrs. DuVernay's mother's room and make my way to the second guest suite where her cousin will stay. This one is half the size and lacks the sweeping ocean views, but it's in a quieter location of the house, and I quite prefer the décor of this one to the other. The other is over the top, ornate. Dark wood. Floral everything. This one is crisp and clean, white and bright.

I'm making the bed a few moments later when I spot a blue and orange BELGROVE SECURITY truck pulling into the driveway. The other day I overheard Mrs. DuVernay on the phone with the security company, requesting someone to come out and install more cameras.

By the time this man leaves today, there won't be a single space in this entire house without coverage.

This can't be the rest of my life.

I won't allow it.
For now I'm bent, broken.
It's only a matter of time until I snap.

23

Cate

"THEY'RE BOARDING OUR ZONE NOW," Sean says Friday afternoon, nudging his elbow against my arm.

I've been planted in the waiting area outside our gate since the second we made it through security, nose buried in my phone, Googling anything and everything Odessa DuVernay in vain while he hit up the snack bar and magazine stand. "You having second thoughts? You haven't said a word since we got here."

He keeps his tone light, but his wringing hands tells me he's annoyed.

"No. No second thoughts." I exhale, darken my screen, and rest my phone in my lap. "Sorry. I just can't stop worrying about ... *her*."

Sean pinches the bridge of his nose. "Seriously, Cate?"

I rise, securing my bag over my shoulder and scanning my space for my carry on.

"You've got to let this go," he says.

"I want to. Believe me, I want to. But it's like this riddle I need to crack," I say. "I literally lie in bed awake all night trying to piece it together, and none of it fits. And then I Google her, it's like she doesn't even exist, and that only makes me want to look harder."

"Clearly she's going through something and wants her privacy. I'm sure she'll reach out to you if she needs anything."

"What if she's sick, Sean?" I ask. "What if something's happened to her? She told me she doesn't have any friends."

His brows lift and he pushes a breath between his lips. "Maybe there's a reason for that ... anyway, she's a wealthy woman. I'm sure if she needs any kind of help, medical or otherwise, she has the resources for that."

The final boarding call for our flight blasts through the speakers.

We exchange wordless glances before wheeling our way to the jet bridge, tickets in hand. Within twenty minutes we're mid-air, bound for Rhode Island, and he hasn't said a word to me. In fact, not only is he not speaking, his nose is buried in a thick paperback—and Sean is hardly a reader.

It isn't like him to be annoyed. I've seen him smile and shrug away the most irritating of situations, but this is different. A scowl adorns his normally agreeable expression and his arms are ridged, fingers gripping his book until his knuckles turn white.

Perhaps I've been a bit distant lately, a little preoccupied. And I can count a handful of times when he's asked me if anything was wrong and I clammed up, not wanting to bother him with my private fixation on this mystery woman. But I don't think any of that warrants the silent treatment.

I spend the next hour quietly stewing, mentally berating him for overreacting. I can practically feel the fight we're about to have the second we check into the hotel, the words bubbling up the back of my throat, simmering beneath the surface.

But when the pilot announces our descent the ridiculousness of it all swoops in on me, how pointless it is for me to obsess over a woman I barely knew, and how important Sean is to me. Despite what I've always told myself, I wouldn't fare so well if he ever decided to break this off.

He's the only good thing I've got in this world, the only thing that makes me smile and keeps me sane. I can declare that life would go on without him until I'm blue in the face —but I'd only be fooling myself.

Reaching for his hand, I practically have to pry it off his book. A quick scan shows me he's on page eleven, as if he'd been reading and re-reading the same few pages over and over this entire flight, his mind unable to focus.

Sean isn't a man who overthinks, who worries. At least I didn't think so. Perhaps I don't know him as well as I thought I did.

I interlace our fingers and squeeze his hand, and it feels like forever until he squeezes it back, but when he does, I know he's accepting my nonverbal apology, my quiet promise to do better, to be the girlfriend he deserves.

From this moment on, I vow to stop ruminating over the whereabouts of Odessa DuVernay.

24

ZSOFIA

I COLLAPSE in a chair by the pool Friday night, joints stiff and bones aching through to the marrow. Mrs. DuVernay's birthday party was this evening, and while it was just Mr. and Mrs. DuVernay plus her mother and cousin, I was run ragged for hours on end, serving course after course, fetching cake and candles, uncorking bottles and re-filling wine glasses.

Not only that, but all the effort I'd put into preparing the guest quarters this week had been for nothing, as our visitors opted to stay at a hotel at the last minute without explanation.

It's not quite midnight but the inside of the house is dark, everyone having retired for the evening, thank goodness. The sickly-sweet scent of buttercream icing and dessert wine lingers, mixing with the sea salt air and the chlorine wafting off the top of the heated pool.

I'd throw up if I could, but I can hardly motivate myself to move another inch.

I just need to sit here a while, in the stillness, dragging fresh air into my lungs until I can revive my spirits enough to move to my apartment. In six hours, I'll be expected in the kitchen, tiptoeing around the marble tiles preparing coffee and breakfast while making as little noise as humanly possible.

Hot tears cloud my vision, stinging for a moment before rolling down my cheeks.

I can't live like this.

My mind travels to my mother for a moment. Perhaps this is the very thing she endured, the very thing that caused her to flee without a second thought. Maybe she was exhausted, browbeaten, and at the end of her rope, and Mrs. DuVernay made her an offer she couldn't refuse.

"Zsofia, what are you doing out here?" A puffed Mrs. DuVernay trots across the patio in heels. "You scared me half to death. I thought you'd gone home for the night."

Home.

As if I lived somewhere outside this hellish compound.

That's a joke.

I drag in a breath of salty air and let it linger while I muster some semblance of composure. "I was just taking a moment for myself."

"And why would *you* need a moment?" She takes a seat in the lounge chair beside me, gathering the hem of her satin robe and covering her bare legs. A glass of wine rests in her opposite hand, nearly filled to its glassy lip.

I don't answer her. It's best that I remove myself from this situation.

It saps all of my physical strength to push myself back into a standing position, and I have to stop and brace myself on the back of the chair when my knees threaten to give out. This was the first chance I'd had all day to sit down.

"What's going on with you lately?" Her words are clipped. "You've been acting strange all night. Everyone noticed. It was quite embarrassing for Charles and me, having to excuse your behavior."

My jaw tenses and my hands grip the chair back until my knuckles throb. Half of me wants to give her a piece of my mind, the other half knows better.

I imagine I haven't seen the worst of her punishment yet.

If there are seven levels of Mrs. DuVernay's hell, there's a chance I haven't seen beyond the first quite yet.

"Just a little tired, that's all," I decide to take the middle road, politely giving her the satisfaction of knowing her punishment is effective while also being honest. "It's been a long week."

She takes another sip, chuffing. "You act like you have it so bad."

My lips flatten and my nostrils flare with each breath. Try as I might to bite my tongue, I feel the sharpness of the words rising from the back of my throat, burning like fire every silent second that passes.

"How much longer are you going to punish me?" My heartbeat whooshes in my ears, drowning out the ocean in the distance.

"Until you learn your place in this household." It's dark near the pool, but Mrs. DuVernay's eyes flash in the moonlight as her glare possesses me. Her fingers curl around her goblet as she studies me. "By the way, what were you planning to do with all that money? You realize five grand will hardly buy you a thing in this town, yes? You might be able to stretch it out a month, maybe two, three if you're resourceful ... but then you'll be out on the street, providing sexual services to junkies and dirty strangers."

She turns her attention toward the end of the property, where waves curl and crash into the shore.

"I suppose it doesn't matter, does it? It's not like you're going anywhere. Have a seat, Zsofia. There's something else I've been wanting to say to you," Mrs. DuVernay pats the seat beside her, the one I occupied in peace and silence until the elegant lush half-sashayed, half-ambled outside. Resigned, I sit. "I know you're in love with my husband."

"That's not true—"

Mrs. DuVernay lifts a finger to silence me. "He told me everything. About the late night talks, the flirting, the perfume, the suddenly-pretending-to-be-interested-in-guitars. Apparently you told him about my affair."

Her casual, confident tone is a slap in the face.

"Fortunately with all of your ... questionable seduction techniques ... he brushed it off as a desperate attempt to win his favor." She swirls her red wine, which in the dark appears to be the blackest of black. Turning to me, she tilts her head and sighs. "Mr. DuVernay will never leave me. Ever. You should know that."

The wind brushes her pale hair across her face and she lets it stay, apparently lost in thought.

"Did I ever tell you how we met?" she asks, though I don't say a word. I don't care to know. "He was dating my best friend in college, but they were all wrong for each other. Whenever we'd be together, in a group of what have you, he was always looking at me, always finding excuses to sit near me or make conversation with me. But he and my friend were practically engaged at that point. I believe her Daddy Dearest had already offered him a job running one of his car dealerships back in New Jersey or somewhere like that. Anyway, Charles asked me to help him pick out an engagement ring for her one weekend. I answered by giving him a big fat no, and then I kissed him. Let me tell you something, Zsofia, you have to be ruthless in this life if you're ever going to get anywhere. The things you want, you have to be willing to take risks. Terrifying risks. That kiss could've gone very badly for me. And I lost all of my friends after that. But I got Charles. And he was the only thing I wanted."

I bite my lip, dying to know why she would run around on a man she risked everything to be with and knowing the answer doesn't matter.

"You aren't ruthless enough." She winces in my direction. "My husband likes a challenge. He needs to be impressed—and you're ... well, you're pathetic." Mrs. DuVernay's mouth titters into a smirk and she shakes her head. "The thought of you throwing yourself at him, so desperate, honestly makes me want to throw up in my mouth a little."

This woman can work my fingers to the bone all she wants, but I'm not going to stand here and take her verbal abuse. I gather my strength and rise from the chair.

She takes another sip from her chalice before setting it aside and joining me. Squaring her shoulders to mine, she folds her arms across her chest and peers down her straight nose. She can barely strand straight without leaning, and each exhalation is bathed in the pungent, sweet stench of expensive wine.

I imagine this could be the drunkest I've ever seen this woman, and that's saying a lot.

"I have to be honest with you about something," she says, voice slipping and slurring. "Sometimes I look at you, and I wish I could shove you into the ocean like I did your pathetic mother."

My eyes lock on hers and my breath holds in my chest as I question what I just heard.

Did she just confess to murdering my mother?

"You said she left ..." My lower lip quivers, but then it goes numb. Everything goes numb. The birds in the night sky and the crash of the water goes silent, and the warmth of the evening air across my skin disappears.

Mrs. DuVernay rolls her eyes. "Don't be so dense, Zsofia."

"What did you do to her?" The voice that comes out of my mouth is a scream.

Mrs. DuVernay responds with a slap across my face. "Keep your voice down."

I lift my palm, soothing the cherry-hot sting where her hand met my flesh.

"Your mother was a homewrecker," she says, keeping her voice low. "She came into my house and tried to seduce my husband. There are many things in this world I can tolerate, Zsofia, but I draw the line at stealing—husbands, jewelry, or otherwise. In the end, your mother was disrespectful and defiant and she tried to take something that belonged to me, something very near and dear to my heart—so I had no choice but to return the favor."

My thoughts loop and intertwine as I try to make sense of what she's saying.

"You murdered my mother ... and took me as a prize?"

"Don't flatter yourself. I'd hardly call you a prize, though I will say that it's worked out quite nicely over the years, having you here. At least until recently. I suppose the apple doesn't fall far from the tree. I can only hope our Aviana favors the DuVernay side when it comes to temperament in her adult years. Anyway, rest assured I'm not a murderer—I didn't know your mother couldn't swim."

She shrugs, eyes wide as she feigns innocence.

"It was so sad ... by the time help arrived, it was simply too late." She places a bony hand on my shoulder, and I shove it off.

"Don't touch me. You're a monster. You're an evil, wicked woman and you're—"

Mrs. DuVernay rolls her eyes. "What are you going to do? Call the authorities? Sweetheart, your mother's body is probably lying in the bottom of the Atlantic right now—if it wasn't eaten by a shark on the way down. And given the fact that she was here illegally, there's no proof that she ever existed. Not to mention ... you're not exactly a legal citizen yourself. If the police were to find out about you, we'd get a slap on the wrist, but you ... you'd be on the next flight to Russia. Can you imagine? Landing in a country where you don't know a soul? Don't have a ruble to your name? Don't speak the language?" Reaching for my face, she cups my chin in her hand, pinching my flesh between her fingers. "I want you to remember that things could always, *always* be worse for you."

My eyes are locked on hers, but I don't see her.

I see my mother whose life was stolen from her.

I see my daughter who will never know how much I truly love her.

And then I see myself—a desperate, angry woman with everything and nothing to lose at the same time.

Without giving it a single thought, I shove Mrs. DuVernay.

I need her out of my space, I need her to get her hands off me, to stop exhaling her wine-fused breath in my face, to stop spewing her cruel words in my direction.

Her arms flail as she stumbles backwards, reaching out for something to catch her but grasping nothing but the thick night air. Within seconds her fox-fur house slippers catch on the hem of her billowy robe and she spills backwards.

The sick thud of Mrs. DuVernay's head against the concrete ledge of the sparkling pool comes next, followed by silence.

I run toward the water as the reality of what's just happened smacks me in the face.

I'm not a murderer.

I didn't mean for her to get hurt.

I just wanted her to leave me alone.

"Mrs. DuVernay ..." I call her name, but she's face down in the water, body splayed like a sea star, her saturated white robe glowing from the moonlight as it clings to her body.

A spot of red blood lingers on the pool ledge, the same red that matches the liquid oozing from the back of her skull and dripping into the crystalline water that surrounds the lifeless monster.

"Mrs. DuVernay!" I crouch, reaching toward her, but she's too far out—in the deep end no less.

If only she'd hired a swimming instructor for me as she did for Aviana ...

That irony isn't lost on me in this moment.

Sprinting to the pool house to retrieve a buoy or pool skimmer, anything I can use to fish her out, I'm met with a locked door.

If I had my phone, perhaps I could call 9-1-1, but seeing as how that was one of the privileges I lost ...

Making a mad dash inside, I call for Mr. DuVernay throughout the dark house. His study is unlit, void of life much like the rest of the house, so I sprint to the second level, taking two stairs at a time.

Aviana's bedroom door is open, but the room is pitch black. She's at a sleepover tonight, but even if she were home, I can't imagine traumatizing her with any of this.

Racing down the hall, stomach knotted and heart whooshing in my ears, I find the master bedroom door ajar, and a quick peek inside reveals no sleeping Mr. DuVernay, only a closed bathroom door with the outline of light shining around its perimeter.

I'm halfway across the room, prepared to knock on that door, when a certain something catches my eye from the dressing room—the safe, the one Mrs. DuVernay has been keeping my phone and keys and wallet in ... it's wide open.

The flush of the toilet on the other side of the bathroom door serves as a starting pistol of sorts, and with my heart in my teeth and mere seconds to spare, I retrieve my things from Mrs. DuVernay's safe. I'm shoving cash, my phone, and my car keys into every pocket on my body, tugging and pulling my clothes into position to obscure the bulges. The faucet turns on next, as if Mr. DuVernay is washing his hands. It won't be long until he's out of there.

In the endless seconds that pass, an entire scenario plays out in my mind ...

I imagine telling Charles about his wife, lying face down in the pool. I imagine him asking what happened, asking how long she's been unconscious. I imagine him screaming in agony as he pulls her lifeless body from the water, blaming all of this on me.

The last thing I imagine are the police showing up and hauling me away.

Everything they'll need to convict me will be on the

DuVernay's security cameras—I know of at least three that cover the back yard from every angle.

The cash is heavy in my pockets and I feel for my keys and phone, ensuring none of this is a cruel hallucination.

Taking a deep breath, I tip-toe out of the master suite in a hurry, heading down the hall and gliding down the stairs without making a sound—a skill I've perfected over the years. I keep my head low when I pass the wall of windows that showcase the moonlight back yard paradise where Mrs. DuVernay took her final and fatal breath.

Seconds later, I'm in the garage, damp palms gripping my steering wheel as I shift into reverse, foot hovering over the brake pedal, gaze darting from mirror to mirror to ensure I'm in the clear as I leave the DuVernay estate for the last time.

Maybe this makes me a bad person.

But I didn't come this far to trade one prison for another.

25

Cate

"WE CAN KEEP DRIVING if you want?" Sean offers as
our rental car crawls to a stop outside my father's home
Saturday morning.

After a quick continental breakfast at our hotel this
morning, we hit the road, embarking on an unofficial Cabot
Family Tour. For hours we zig-zagged around Newport
and her sister cities, journeying from the George R. Cabot
Library to the Elizabeth Granger-Cabot Memorial Bridge
to the Cabot Liberty Amphitheatre in a quaint park near
downtown Newport. We also passed the birth place of
George R. Cabot, a fully restored Victorian house-turned-
museum which regretfully only offered tours Monday
through Friday from one to four PM. And while we
haven't seen the half of the Cabot legacy, we're now idling
outside 1155 Cherry Glen Drive—a white-painted-brick
colonial fit for a former Commander-in-Chief, with its
prominent American flag out front and its perfectly

trimmed boxwood hedges and red, white, and blue perennials.

A Mercedes SUV is parked in the driveway alongside a Lexus sedan.

I don't know if these are the cars they drive or if there's company.

Perhaps I should have called first. Jumping on a plane and flying here without giving it a second thought was a little rash in retrospect, but I was having a moment. I was feeling emboldened and incensed and my mind was made up ... and now here we are.

"It's okay." I unfasten my seatbelt. "Just park. I'm going up there."

Sean lines our rented Nissan up with the curb and shifts into park. "You want me to go with you?"

"No. I should do this alone."

A second later, I'm trudging up the pristine white sidewalk, barely sensing the hard ground beneath my steps, no recollection of climbing out of the car mere seconds ago. Each breath I take is shallower than the last, and my ears are so hot they're probably glowing.

Clearing my throat, I press the doorbell and take a step back.

There's a little painted rock by my feet next to a small potted plant. Some words are spelled out in child's handwriting. *I love you, Grandpa*, or something like that.

My father is a grandpa.

I wonder if they call him Granddad or Papa or Opa or PawPaw or Poppy or something cute and off-the-beaten path. I wonder if he gives them sips of his RC cola or if he's taken them to meet their favorite theme park princesses yet.

Standing outside this All-American home, warmth and tradition and comfort ooze from every double-hung window, every colonial-style flower ledge, from the Newport-style white-washed Adirondacks to the waving flag saluting from a pole by the garage.

Voices sound from the other side of the door—young and old, followed by footsteps—fast and slow.

An ache stabs through my middle and my throat constricts.

That's my family. A family I will never truly be a part of, blood or not.

A moment later, the door swings open and a tow-headed boy of six or seven stands before me, blinking up with striking round eyes the color of cornflowers.

"Who are you?" he asks, scratching at his freckled nose from the other side of a screen door. The scent of breakfast wafts from behind him—eggs and bacon and pancakes.

I'm definitely interrupting a family affair, which is either beautifully ironic or the worst timing imaginable.

"Hi." I force a smile through trembling lips, my voice shaking in tandem. "I'm looking for John Cabot."

"Uh, I think that's my Grandpa ..." He looks over his shoulder before turning back to me. "Hang on."

The little boy shuts the door in my face, and his footsteps stomp along as he tromps off. I glance at Sean who's watching from the rental car, and I give him a reassuring nod. Moments pass, and I spot the curtains next to the door shift, though I can't see who's on the other side.

Another minute passes, or maybe it just feels that way, when the door opens, and a woman with dark hair like mine but stronger, more Germanic features greets me from the other side of the threshold.

My thoughts jumble for a moment. All this time, I'd rehearsed each and every word I was going to say to my father, but not once did I think about what I'd say to one of my four half-siblings.

"Hi, I'm sorry," she says through the screen. "Ollie said there was someone at the door and then he ran off. Is there something I can help you with?"

She stares back at me with the same cornflower blue eyes as the little boy, and I force myself to snap out of it before she takes me for a solicitor and I get the door slammed in my face.

"Yes, hi. My name is Cate ..." I catch myself before saying my last name. "I'm here to see John Cabot. I'm so sorry for stopping by unannounced, but I happened to be in town and he's an old friend of my family's. I was wondering if I could have a quick word with him?"

The woman—my sister—eyes me up and down, though I don't get the sense that she's the kind to tell strangers off. A glistening diamond ring adorns her left ring finger and for a second, I picture my father walking her down the aisle on her wedding day. All the tears. All the smiles. All the family photos. And while I can imagine everything so clearly, the one thing I can't picture is his face.

All these years, whenever I've tried to imagine him, it's as if I can only see him from the neck down. I suppose when you're a five-year-old you see most of the world that way, so it only makes sense. He had dark hair and blue eyes—that much I remember. Everything else is a blur, but I can only assume there will be some strong resemblance because I look nothing like my mother from the neck up aside from my eyes. From the neck down, we're practically twins right down to the shape of our toenails.

My sister exhales and offers me a gracious if not hesitant nod. "Just a moment. Let me see if I can find him for you."

She shuts the door halfway, just enough so the kaleido-scope of brunch scents linger on the front steps a little longer, mixing with voices on the other side, a TV blaring in the background, a crying baby, female laughter, the tinkle of a toddler toy.

Tears cloud my vision, but I force them away.

I'm used to being on the outside of things.

I'm not used to the intense emotional puncture of wanting to belong, a desire so heavy it weighs my heart to my shoes.

"Can I help you?" A man's voice captures my attention.

I glance up and find a tall silhouette on the other side of the storm door. He reaches for the handle to step outside, and I move back. A moment later, I'm face to face with my father—only he isn't how I imagined him, not at all. I remind myself that my memories are those of a child's and they're decades old.

"Are you John?" I ask, just to be sure.

His hands rest at his narrow hips. He's taller than I expected, skinnier. He no longer has those strong, beefy arms that used to hoist me on his shoulders. And I can't help but notice his eyes aren't brilliant blue, but more of a dull steel. His hair is mostly silver, though his eyebrows retain a few slivers of dark, so at least there's that.

"I am," he says. "And you would be ...?"

"Cate," I say. "Cate Cabot."

Funny. I must have rehearsed this moment a thousand times, but now I can barely mutter my own name.

His eyes narrow, as if he's trying to place me, and just like that, the bittersweetness of this moment evaporates and I regain my mental footing.

"You don't recognize me, do you?" I ask.

"I'm so sorry. I sure don't." He scratches at his thinning

temple, his left wrist sporting what I immediately recognize as a Truesdale Aviator watch—an heirloom piece.

"It's been a while," I say, unable to remove the curtness from my tone. "About thirty years or so …"

He hasn't placed me, but the sorry asshole appears to be trying.

My father chuckles. "I'm sorry. I guess I'm going to need a little more help."

"My mother is Darcy Hicks." I wait for a light to come on in his dull eyes. "We live in Palm Shores, Florida."

His gaze averts, fixating on the idling car over my shoulder, and just when I expect him to carry on with this clueless charade, the man exhales and tucks his chin against his chest.

"You remember me now?" I ask, almost wanting to scream it in his face.

His wrinkled hands lift and he takes a step closer, shushing me with quiet desperation. "You need to keep it down."

"Thirty years is a hell of a long time to keep quiet, don't you think, *Dad*?"

John's expression turns ashen, his head tilts to one side, and then he loops his hand into the crook of my elbow, escorting me away from the front door like the dirty little secret I am. It's a heartless move that would break most people, but I'm not most people, so it only fuels my thirty-year rage.

"Please don't call me that," he says when we're out of earshot of the front door. He releases his hold on me and keeps his voice whisper soft. "I'm not your father."

"Bullshit," I cough, arms crossed.

"Your mother … Darcy … she was pregnant when I met her. Four months along, I believe."

"Convenient."

"I'm telling the truth, Cate. I'm sorry your mother couldn't be bothered to do the same ... have you really believed that I was your father all these years?"

"This is rich." I can't look at the bastard anymore.

"No, no. You need to listen to what I'm saying." His voice is pleading and desperate. "I would hate for you to walk away from this thinking that I'm your father and that I'm denying you. I've made some mistakes in my day, but I'd *never* ..."

"You'd never father a child with your mistress, and then pay her a quarter of a million dollars to shut her up when you get busted by your wife?" I put the words in his mouth, seeing as though he's having a difficult time doing it himself.

John pinches the bridge of his nose, glances at his pristine New England McMansion, and gathers his thoughts. "I don't know what your mother has told you, but back in the eighties, I was doing business down in Palm Shores once a month. I ... sought out her services one night ... and then it became a regular thing. She was already pregnant the first time we met. I ended up getting reassigned for a few years, didn't set foot back in Florida until my territory changed again. Called up your mother one weekend ... against my better judgement ... and we met up. She was managing some department at a hotel, you were just three, maybe four. For the next year or so, any time I was in town, I'd stay at her place. She said she didn't want to confuse you since you were so young, so she had you calling me 'Dad,' and I guess I wasn't thinking about any long-term effects of that. Anyway, my wife ended up finding out. Showed up. Put an end to everything."

"I remember that day. I thought she was the pizza guy."

John winces. "I'm so sorry, Cate. I really am. I'm sorry

you remember that. I'm sorry you remember me. But mostly I'm sorry that you were never given the truth."

"Why is my last name Cabot?"

He hesitates, at a loss for words perhaps. "That'd be a great question for your mother. I imagine it was wishful thinking on her part. From what I remember, she didn't know who your father was ... just that it was more than likely some John she saw one time and never again."

I'm going to be sick.

"Why did you pay her off?" I ask one more question because I'm not quite willing to part with the only version of my past I've ever known.

He scoffs. "Cate, I didn't pay her off. I felt bad for her. She was a good woman. She worked hard. All she ever wanted to do was make me happy. Never asked for anything. I gave her that money because she was a single mom working long hours and I thought maybe she could buy you guys a house with it, save a little for college. Finally get herself a real job. Something respectable."

I don't tell him she gambled almost all of it away after buying a used car and dropping several thousand on home shopping channel junk. But in retrospect, at least she stopped hooking.

"Look at us." He points from my face to his. "We look nothing alike. Nothing."

I study his features, his close-set eyes, his bulbous nose, his widow's peak and dimpled chin. No amount of squinting or wishful thinking could make any of those things match mine.

"I'll take one of those tests ... those DNA tests." His voice is low and his hands rest at his hips. "Obviously you came a long way thinking you were going to meet your biological father. Maybe at least you can leave knowing you're one step closer to the truth? I only ask for your discretion—out of respect for my family."

My family ...

His words sting, even if they have no right to.

"You used to smoke," I say.

He frowns. "It was the eighties. Everyone smoked back then. Haven't touched a cigarette in probably twenty-five years."

"You loved RC cola," I add, though I don't know why. Perhaps I'm searching for validation, perhaps I'm clinging to something akin to a feather in the wind. Proof that my recollections were real.

John cracks a smile. "I did, didn't I? Man, haven't had one of those in forever. You've really got a memory on you, Cate, but like I said ... I'm afraid I'm not your father."

"Dad?" The dark-haired woman steps out from inside, peeking her head around the open screen door. "Everything okay?"

She shields her hand over her eyes as she gazes in our direction.

My nose begins to run. I don't have to look at John to feel him studying me. A moment later, he places his hand on my shoulder, I suppose the way a father would do, and gives it a light clasp.

"I'm glad you came out here today," he says. "You let me know if you need anything else from me. More than happy to help."

John follows his daughter inside.

I can't get back to the car fast enough.

"So ... how'd it go?" Sean dials down the radio volume after I slam the door.

"Drive. Go." I point at the road ahead. I don't want to be on this street. I don't want to be in this city. I don't want to pass another Cabot monument or bridge or library or park.

"What the hell happened?" Sean keeps his left hand on the wheel as we forge ahead, his right hand covering mine. "Jesus, you're shaking. He seemed nice from what I could tell ... I don't understand? What'd he say to you?"

"I'm not a Cabot." I speak four words I never dreamed I'd speak. "Apparently my entire life has been a lie."

"What are you talking about?"

I tell him everything, and by the time I'm done, we're pulling into the parking lot of our three-star hotel.

Sean shifts into park, staring straight ahead. "So, you believe him then?"

"He offered to do a DNA test. Like, he offered multiple times. Doesn't seem like something someone would do if they had anything to hide."

He lifts his hands to his face, blowing a breath through steepled fingers. "I don't even know what to say right now. I'm so sorry, babe."

"This is going to sound ridiculous, but I have to say it." I pick at my cuticles before wringing my hands, thinking of all the family tree projects I did, all the thick biographies I'd read on the Golden Age Cabots and the Cabots who came after them, I think about all the times I Googled John, the hours and hours I spent scouring social media accounts, desperate for a glimpse of what life as a true Cabot might entail. All of it was for nothing. "If I'm not a Cabot ... what am I?"

"Cate ..." Sean doesn't hesitate to take my hands in his, angling toward me as the radio plays an obnoxious pop song on low volume in the background, a song that clashes with this tender moment. "It doesn't matter what you are. You're still you. Nothing changes that."

For a second, I expect him to make some corny joke about taking his last name ... but he doesn't. And I almost wish he would. My thoughts briefly touch on the plane ride here yesterday, his silence, the way he read and re-read the same eleven pages.

"You going to do one of those DNA tests?" he asks.

I nod. I hadn't thought much about it, seeing how everything happened so quickly, but I will. Eventually. When the dust settles.

"How do I bring this up to my mom? It'll destroy her ... or maybe I'll destroy her. I've never felt so betrayed."

Sean squeezes my hands. "One thing at a time, okay? You need to process this first, then you can deal with Darcy. She had to have known this day would come. And hey, if you want me there with you, say the word. You don't have to go through any of this alone."

I lean across the console, resting my head on Sean's shoulders, breathing in his familiar scent until I can no longer decipher it from the plastic new car scent that surrounds us. He wraps an arm around me, and I'm not sure how much time passes as we linger like this, not saying a word.

He doesn't ask me what I'm thinking—which is one of the things I've always loved about this man. He's always there, but he isn't intrusive. Some days it seems as though our entire relationship is too good to be true, and while I seem to be a magnet for assholes, liars, and users, I don't know how I was able to snag this one.

If he's been gaslighting me all this time, I don't know what I'll do.

"Want to head in, raid the vending machine? Check out the hot tub?" he asks, his tone bordering on playful. My faithful Sean, trying to cheer me up.

"Yeah," I say, sitting up. The sooner this weekend is over, the better.

Five minutes later, I'm perched on the edge of our hotel bed searching for a good Pay-Per-View movie we can watch while he's down the hall raiding the vending machine. I land on a slapstick comedy—I could use some laughs and it's exactly the kind of movie Sean would dig, and I press the button on the remote to order it.

When I'm finished, I reach for my phone and delete my search history, which is ninety-percent Cabots and DuVernays.

From this day forward, I want nothing to do with either family.

I've never been a Cabot. I'll never be a DuVernay.

The only thing I am in this moment is never looking back.

My resolve lasts all of two hours. By the time the movie is over and I'm lying on my back as Sean's soft snores compete with the soft whir of the ceiling fan, my mind wanders to Odessa.

In the final moments before I pass out, the dark kaleidoscope of unanswered questions leaves me haunted.

26

Cate

"I'VE DONE SOMETHING TERRIBLE," Odessa's voice is a breathy whisper in the voicemail she left me at five AM this morning. She speaks so quickly her words almost jumble together. *"Meet me at the café on Broadmoor at eight. Please, please be there. I need you."*

I listen to her voicemail for the sixth time, glancing around the empty cafe on Broadmoor—a glamorous if not arguable hole-in-the-wall in a part of the city I never knew existed. Outside, Monday rush hour is in full effect.

I shouldn't be here.

Not only did I spend the weekend writing Odessa DuVernay off for good and swearing up, down, and sideways to Sean that I meant it this time ... but I'm expected to open Smith + Rose in two hours.

Forty-five minutes crawl past. Not a text. Not a call. Not any kind of message saying she's running a few minutes late.

I try to call her phone once more, but it goes straight to voicemail.

Again.

As it has all morning.

"Would you like another cappuccino while you wait?" The server approaches my table, her hooded gaze gliding toward the second empty place setting across from me. The soft tinkle of silver on china marries with the classical piano tune playing from hidden speakers in the ceiling as the scent of fresh coffee and warm pastries fills the air. Warm light rains down from the chandelier above, giving the place settings sparkle and life on an otherwise gray day.

I nibble my nail to the quick, a disgusting habit I once kicked but now seems to be back in full force, and I shake my head. The crystal-clean window next to my table provides an unobstructed view of the sidewalk, and the dark outline of a woman in a dress and heels appears through the fog, a ghost-like apparition. My heartrate quickens, and I grow restless in my tufted velvet dining chair.

But it isn't her.

The woman outside continues on her way, disappearing into another blanket of low-lying clouds.

"I'm so sorry. I need to leave," I say before rising and collecting my things—a stunning Tournesol bag she gifted me two months ago, and my outdated smart phone with its cracked screen. I place a ten-dollar bill on the table to cover my coffee and a tip, and I zigzag through overcrowded tables toward the door.

My stomach is knotted, queasy. The coffee in my belly mixes with a cocktail of nerves as I drive across town to Artemis Cove, the luxe gated community Odessa calls home.

She wouldn't do this.

She wouldn't ask me to meet her, shut off her phone, and then not show up.

The traffic light ahead switches from green to yellow, and I grip the steering wheel, fully prepared to gun the engine and soar through the intersection before it turns red, but the car ahead of me has other plans, cruising to a patient stop.

Exhaling, I check my phone again—in vain.

Nothing.

The light turns green and I stomp on the gas pedal, maneuvering around the silver Mercedes in front of me, flying through the next intersection, my palms sweaty against the steering wheel, when I steal a glance at the clock on my dash.

I'm supposed to open the shop in less than an hour.

Turning off at the next light, I make a right toward the entrance to Artemis Cove, tearing past the manicured hedges, swaying palm trees, and tropical flora, and coming to a hard stop outside the security booth. Up ahead, the neighborhood is covered in a quilt of fog so thick it obscures each and every last multi-million-dollar estate.

A moment later, a guard in a blue-gray uniform steps out of the tiny space and lowers himself to my window, clipboard in hand.

"Good morning, ma'am. Can I get your name?" He gives me a slow, friendly smile.

"Cate Cabot. But I'm not on the list. I'm here to see Odessa DuVernay." I wipe my damp palms against my thighs as the man peruses the list on the clipboard.

The man nods. "One second."

He returns inside the fancy white shack and pages through a slim three-ring binder. Two cars pull up behind me, with a third turning into the entrance.

"I'm sorry, there's a line here, can we hurry it up, please?" I ask.

The man peeks out of his enclosure, examining the line behind me though not saying a word. He disappears inside the booth and another endless minute passes before I see him again. Approaching my car, his hands press against my open window frame, and he leans in.

His expression apologizes before he does. "Sorry, ma'am. You're not on any of my lists, I can't let you in. No exceptions."

Shaking my head, I say, "I know. I told you she isn't expecting me, but it's an emergency. I think she's in danger."

His gray-brown brows knit. "I'm sorry. My hands are tied here. And if you think your friend's in danger, I suggest you call the police. Now, if you don't mind, you're holding up the line. I'm going to have to ask you to leave."

I check my rearview to find a portly man in a black SUV behind me, appearing to mutter a few words under his breath while smacking his leather-wrapped steering wheel.

"You don't understand," I say. "I think something happened. Would you mind calling her house, see if you can get an answer? Her phone is off."

"Ma'am, like I said, if you think your friend is in danger, you should call the police. Now will you kindly pull ahead and turn yourself around so I can help the next guest?"

I peer beyond my dash. In order to turn around, he's going to have to lift the security arm and I'll have to drive around the backside of his booth to get through the exit.

I've always been a law-abiding citizen, but desperate times and all of that.

"Fine." An oversized lump forms in my throat. I couldn't swallow if I tried.

He reaches into the shack and presses a button. The security arm lifts. With my hands white-knuckling the steering wheel and my right foot hovering above the gas pedal, I squeeze my eyes for a second and coast ahead.

Only I don't stop.

I drive straight, disappearing into the hazy thicket.

With my window still down, I hear the guard yelling after me to stop, to come back. I don't see him, but I can only imagine he's running into his booth to call the Palm Shores Police Department.

It'll take ten, maybe fifteen minutes for them to get here, which is more than enough time for me to find Odessa's house and see if she's okay. Once I find her, she'll vouch for me.

I'm careful not to speed too fast through these unfamiliar streets. I'm already trespassing … no need to hit a parked Maserati while I'm at it.

A red stop sign appears through the half-cleared mist ahead, and I bring my Honda to a hard stop, checking the bright green street sign above.

Laguna Terrace.

Hoping my memory is serving me right, I take a left and climb the winding hill to the house at the end, pulling into her circle drive and stopping next to the bubbling limestone fountain. Shifting into park, I climb out, sprint for the front door, and press the doorbell twice.

My heart pounds in my chest before climbing to my ears and reaching the tips of my fingers. My skin is livewire, my thoughts racing in every direction with every endless, passing second.

I glance up, searching for signs of life behind the stucco walls of the massive estate. Twenty-one windows, I count.

Spotless, streak-free glass. Shades drawn. It's as if the inside is cut off from the outside world.

And then I see something—or at least, I think I do.

Squinting, I stare harder at the rightmost second-floor window ... there it is again. The flutter of a curtain, a hint of fingers, drawing back the thick fabric.

I ring the doorbell once more.

The hand disappears from the curtain panel as if it was never there.

Did I imagine that?

"Excuse me," a man's voice behind me sends a shock down my spine. I turn, expecting to find the guard, the police, someone ready to drag me out of here, but he is none of those things. "Can I help you?"

His face is tan, leathery, and he adjusts his baseball cap, dark blue with the words Tampico Garden and Landscapes across the front. His jeans are tattered and stained with earth, and his white t-shirt nearly glows in the foggy atmosphere that envelops us.

"I'm looking for my friend," I say.

"I don't think they're home, miss," he says, resting his hand on the top of a rake.

I point to the second story. "I just saw someone inside."

He shrugs. "I've been here all morning, haven't seen a soul."

"My friend ... Odessa ... she lives here and she called me this morning," I say. "I think something happened to her. I can't get through to her now. You don't happen to have her husband's number, do you?"

The man studies me with a blank expression. Whether he's going to be helpful or a hindrance is anyone's guess.

"What'd you say your friend's name was?" he asks.

"Odessa," I say. "Odessa DuVernay."

He sniffs. "This isn't the DuVernay residence, I can tell you that much. Must have the wrong address."

I hear his words, but they don't absorb. Not at first.

I was just here not too long ago.

I know I was.

I didn't imagine that.

She drove us here, ran inside to drop something off for her assistant. I watched her punch the code into the garage entry door. She disappeared for two minutes. Came out empty-handed. We went on our way.

"No," I say. "That doesn't make any sense."

"Been landscaping this house for three years, at least," he says, gazing up at a gray sky. "No *DuVernays* live here. Last name is Saint Vincent."

I turn toward the house again, my gaze immediately landing on the number 422 which is chiseled in stone above the ornate, iron-wrapped double front doors. I remember staring at them, studying them while I waited in the front seat of Odessa's Range Rover while she ran in.

"I'm so confused ..." My voice tapers to nothing as my thoughts get lost.

"You should probably go, miss," he says a few seconds later, pointing behind him where a woman with frizzed blonde hair and an unbreakable glare the color of steel climbs off a golf cart and toddles in this direction with short, brisk strides. She's wearing the same uniform the gate guard wore, gray and blue with a white nametag I can't read from here.

"Ma'am, I'm going to have to escort you from the premises," she says once she's closer than shouting distance.

I exhale, frustrated to have reached a dead end but relieved that the man at the gate didn't call the police on me.

"This isn't what it looks like," I say, "I'm just checking on my friend. She lives here and she called me this morning … said she had something important to tell me, wanted me to meet her, and then she never showed up. And now …"

"I'm sorry, but my colleague already told you you're not on the guest list, so you can't be in here. No exceptions." She speaks to me with the slow and careful tone one might use with an unstable maniac as her eyes drift to my hands. "So again, we're going to have to ask you to leave. Please don't make this situation any more difficult than it needs to be. It's nothing personal—our residents value their safety here, and we have rules set in place to protect that safety at all times."

I make my way back to my idling car. Climbing into the driver's seat, I stare ahead at the stunning Mediterranean manor awash in mist and early morning light.

The female guard climbs into her four-seater golf cart, surveilling me. I give her a nod, an attempt to reassure her that I'll be on my way in a moment.

I linger in my idling car, staring at the beautiful fog-blanketed estate ahead until the decorative lights that pepper its exquisite exterior spot my vision.

Several yards past the hood of my car, the blonde guard exits her cart and stalks toward me. I imagine she's coming to tell me to leave once again—this time with the threat of calling law enforcement.

Shifting into drive before she has a chance to take this to the next level, I give my steering wheel a hard crank to the left and turn myself around, motoring carefully through foggy streets, back toward the security gate to show myself out.

None of this makes sense.

I head to Smith + Rose to open up for the day—and on

the way, I intend to call the police to report a missing person. Only the moment I turn the corner, returning to the main road outside Artemis Cove, a caravan of police cars with soundless, flashing lights pull into the gated community. My stomach freefalls.

I watch from my rearview until they're swallowed by the fog, hoping for the best but fearing the worst.

27

CATE

I LIGHT another cigarette and pace my living room, waiting for the six o'clock news to come on. Any minute Sean's going to walk in that door and I'm going to have to explain how all the promises I made over the weekend about moving forward and leaving the past in the past and not wasting time caring about people who don't care about me went to shit in a matter of minutes, all because Odessa DuVernay left me a voicemail this morning.

Sean is an understanding man—but this is going to require a big sell.

I don't know if I have the energy for that.

The Channel Six news logo fills the TV screen, and I lunge for the remote to turn up the volume. A preview of tonight's stories flash by, one by one, not a single one mentioning anything about a woman in Palm Shores.

Collapsing on my sofa, I reach for an ash tray, keeping my gaze glued to the news report in hopes that maybe, just maybe there'll be a breaking news story. Then again, wishing for that would be like wishing something bad had happened to Odessa. And I don't. I hope she's fine. I just want answers. I need answers.

My apartment door swings open the instant the weather report comes on, and Sean struts in wearing a smile, running his hand through his messy hair and mumbling something about grabbing a quick shower.

He's halfway to the hallway when he stops in his tracks.

"Cate," he says. "You okay?"

The weather report morphs into the day's headlines, and I wave him off with the swipe of my hand and a harried, "*Shhhh...*"

"What's ..." he begins to ask a question and then stops himself. Studying me, he rests his hands on his narrow hips and waits for the commercial.

"I have to tell you something," I say, mentally calculating that I have at least three minutes before the news returns. "Please, please don't be mad."

"Okay."

Starting from the top, I tell him about the voicemail. I tell him about going to the café at eight AM, about my escapade through Artemis Cove, about spotting the police cars on my way out. I tell him about her phone being off all day, about Googling her name and refreshing local news reports over and over every chance I got at work today and coming up empty-handed.

When I'm finished, he's quiet.

"Say something." I cup my hands together.

His lips are flat. "I, uh ... I don't know what to say. I thought you were past all this."

"I thought I was too," I say. "And then she left that voicemail. She reached out to me, Sean. She asked for my help. She begged me to meet her ... what would you have done?"

He mulls his answer for a moment too long. The news comes back on. My attention is straddled—half of it on Sean, the other half on a chipper blonde reporting on a Cuban art festival.

"I don't know what to say." He shrugs, letting his hands fall limp at his sides, as if he doesn't know what to do with me. "I wish you could let go, I guess. This isn't healthy."

His gaze snaps to the filled ash tray on my coffee table. My small apartment is officially clouded in disappointment and secondhand smoke.

"I think I'm going to go to the Palm Shores police station tonight," I say. "Maybe talk to somebody, see if I can fill out a Missing Persons report."

"Missing Persons report? Seriously, Cate? The woman's got a husband. I'm sure if she were truly missing—"

"—but what if he did something to her?" I ask. "And nobody knows she's missing except me?"

He sniffs, half laughing. "You watch way too much TV."

"She left me a voicemail, Sean," I repeat myself. "She said she did something terrible. Her words. She did something terrible and she asked me to meet her. Begged me to meet her. Then she didn't show up. You don't think I should go to the police with that?"

His chin falls to his chest and within seconds, he nods. "Yeah. Damn it. Yeah, you should go. Let them listen to that and let them do the checking around. I don't need you going down for trespassing. And I'm going with you."

"You don't have to go."

"You're not doing this alone," he says. "Just let me grab a shower first."

"WELL," Detective Moreno plops into his rolling desk chair and scoots in. "I can tell you we don't have a missing person report on file for an Odessa DuVernay at this time."

"Okay, so can we file one?" I spent the last ten minutes filling him in on everything and he played the voicemail not once, not twice, but three times.

"You said you only know this woman casually, is that right?"

"Yes."

"And you don't even know her husband's name, is that right?"

I nod, less confident in the direction this conversation is headed.

"You also said you don't know her birth date," he continues. "And I can tell you the address you gave me ... 422 Laguna Terrace ... is not associated with anyone matching the name you gave me. All you have is a voicemail and an acquaintance that stood you up for coffee. That terrible thing she claimed she did ... there's no way of knowing what it was or if it places her or anyone else in danger. For all we know, she yelled at the paper boy. I hate to be that guy and I know you're genuinely concerned for this woman, but unfortunately there's just not enough for me to file a report."

Sean rubs circles into the small of my back as I search for a proper response to all of this. Detective Moreno's just doing his job, but something's not right.

"I'll dig up an address for this woman, have my guys do a welfare check," he says, leaning back in his chair, like he wants to wrap this up. "That's about all I can do. In the meantime, you're just going to have to wait for her to call you again."

Moreno hands us his card as he walks us out.

"I have to say, that voicemail's got me scratching my head." He hooks his fingers on his belt. "You keep me posted, all right? And I'll let you know if there's anything else I need."

His words are nothing more than a formality, a sliver of false hope in a hopeless situation.

We drive home in silence, both of us unsettled, though probably for different reasons.

I imagine he wants me to let this go.

I would if I could.

28

CATE

I SCRUB the nicotine scent from my hands in the staff bathroom Tuesday morning. Two hours down, two to go until Amada shows up and I can get the hell out of here. Three smoke breaks I've taken already today, and I can't seem to remember my gloves or PVC jacket. My mind is anywhere but here.

Drying my hands, I reach for a community bottle of Gold Clover perfume from a marble tray next to the faucet, and I spritz enough to cover the clinging smoke scent before heading out to unlock the front door.

This place has been dead all day thanks to a morning monsoon. I heard the vice president is in town, speaking at some fundraiser. Maybe that's where they are. Either way, I'm grateful for the silence because it gives me more time to think.

Leaning against the glass counter next to the register, I

retrieve my phone and pull up a search engine for the millionth time today. An hour ago, I learned there are eight DuVernays in Palm Shores proper. There's a Margaret. Age ninety. A Thayer. Age nineteen. There's also a Brynn, a Serena, a Peter, and an Oscar, though from what I gather they're seasonal residents from Connecticut. I was also able to find an "A", aged 47, and a Charles, aged 48—the married couple from whom Odessa stole the watch.

I decide to home in on them.

A quick search of "Charles DuVernay Palm Shores Florida" leads me to the website of his drop ship operation out of Jupiter first. I click on the "About Us" page, scrolling through a handful of headshots and short bios that accompany the photos. I click on his picture, and half the screen is filled with an image of a salt-and-pepper-haired man with a reserved, close-mouthed smile and a generic black suit.

Charles DuVernay is the founder and CEO of DuVernay Drop Ship. He resides in Palm Shores, Florida with his wife and daughter.

That's it?

I page back to the main search results and click on a sponsored result that promises to give me his full address, email, and phone number for the bargain basement price of $59.99.

At this point, the headache and hassle that sixty bucks would save me would be worth it.

I trot to the break room to grab my debit card from my wallet.

Three minutes later, I'm the proud owner of Charles C. DuVernay's mailing address and phone number. According to this, he lives at 2220 Frangipani Way in Palm Shores.

I screenshot my bounty as a backup before scribbling it

down on the back of a shop business card, and then I run a search for Palm Shores County's assessor website to verify that the man still lives at this address.

It takes all of two minutes to confirm that he does, indeed, reside at this address, along with Aviva.

When I'm finished, I type the address into my Maps app and press the icon to get directions. I'm forgoing the visit I'd had planned with my mother today. After everything that came to light last weekend, I don't think heading over there today would be a good idea. I'm not quite sure what I want to say to her yet or how I'm going to bring it up. As of now, I think my afternoon will be better spent trying to find this Charles guy. Could be that their last names are nothing more than a coincidence—or he could be the ticket to locating Odessa.

According to Google Maps, 2220 Frangipani Way is nine minutes east of here—which should put them right on the ocean if I'm not mistaken. I run another query on the address and click on an old real estate listing, one that claims the house was purchased nine years ago for five point eight million dollars—chump change for the average local. I scan the description, absorbing words like "ample yacht dockage" and "custom Calcutta grotto" and "24/7 concierge" ... and I stop when I get to line about Artemis Cove.

This house is nestled in the ultra-exclusive gated waterfront community of Artemis Cove! Showings by appointment only.

What are the odds that Charles and Aviva DuVernay live in Artemis Cove? Where Odessa claimed to live? I scroll up, studying the exterior photos of the home. This one looks nothing like the one on Laguna Terrace. Laguna

Terrace was golden, ornate, and Italianate. This one is more Mediterranean with its white exterior, Greek-style columns and iron balconies.

Not that I'm surprised, but none of this makes sense ...

I distinctly recall the way the Artemis Cove security gate opened the instant she drove up, which tells me she has unrestricted access to this neighborhood, which explains how she was able to steal from Aviva ... but why would she pretend to live at 422 Laguna Terrace?

None of this makes sense.

Unease prickles beneath my skin and my fingers twitch, a silent plea for another smoke, but instead I place my phone down and pace the store. A quick check of the time tells me I've still got another ninety minutes until Amada shows, and that's assuming she's on time today.

I'm not sure what I'm going to do when I leave here, seeing as how I won't be able to swing past Charles DuVernay's house. I'm sure there's a note at the security checkpoint, letting anyone on duty know not to allow the crazy lady in the Honda through for any reason.

Returning to his information, I feast my eyes on his phone number—my best bet.

I decide to call from the shop phone, hoping he'd be more likely to answer a call coming from a local business than some random person calling with a West Palm Shores area code—only the line is disconnected.

Of course it is.

I pace the shop floor, passing a collection of designer candles in opaque milk-glass jars, stopping to inhale some aged lavender and vanilla, hoping for an ounce of calm.

I could try to reach out to Charles at his office in Jupiter.

Sure it's uncouth to bother someone at their place of employment, but this is an urgent matter.

Sprinting across the shop, I nearly drop my phone the second it's in my shaking hands, and within thirty seconds the line is ringing.

"DuVernay Drop Ship, Yvonne speaking, how may I help you?" a middle-aged woman asks on the other end.

"Yes. Hi. Charles DuVernay, please. It's urgent."

I expect a canned "one moment" or "please hold," but what I get is silence.

"Hello?" I ask.

"I'm sorry, is this a personal matter?" she asks.

"It is."

"Then I'm afraid you'll have to call him on his cell. He isn't in the office this morning."

Shit.

"You wouldn't happen to have that number for me, would you?" I infuse as much casual niceness as possible into my tone, considering I'm asking a woman to give a stranger her boss' personal number.

"I'm not allowed to give that out," she says without pause. "But surely if this is a personal matter, you would already have that number."

I start to speak, ready to offer an excuse about losing my phone and contacts, but then I stop myself. She sounds like a woman who'd see through that in a heartbeat.

"Do you know when you expect him in?" I ask. If I have to stop in to see this man, so be it.

Yvonne hesitates. "His schedule is ... a little crazy this week. I'm not sure when I'll be expecting him next. I'd be happy to give you his voicemail?"

His schedule is crazy? His own assistant doesn't know

when he'll be in next? Is that because he's dealing with a personal issue? One somehow related to Odessa?

"Yes, thank you," I say.

A moment later, Charles DuVernay's voice plays in my ear, strong, cordial, educated, and professional.

"Hi, Charles," I say after the tone. "My name is Cate. I'm a friend of Odessa's. I'm having a hard time getting a hold of her ... if you could give me a call?"

I prattle off my number not once but twice before hanging up. I cross my fingers in hopes that I'll hear something back. A dozen scenarios could stem from this, all of them playing out in my head.

Maybe he'll tell me she's a cousin or niece of his, that she's doing well but crazy busy lately. Or maybe he'll tell me he knows of her but hasn't heard from her in a while, in which case I'd be willing to share with him what I know in hopes that he'd do the same. He can't tell me he's never heard of her—if he does, I'll know he's lying ... which will only beget more questions.

The bells on the front door jingle as a leggy blonde in a Ram Piazzo caftan and strappy sandals, an oversized pair of tortoiseshell sunglasses hiding a quarter of her face, and a white cell phone pressed to her ear strolls in.

"Hi, welcome to Smith + Rose," I say.

Removing the sunglasses, she gives me a slight acknowledgement in the form of a nod before making a beeline to a display of vintage clutches in the back. She's chatting with someone about grabbing a quick birthday gift for someone before meeting them for brunch.

It isn't Odessa.

It isn't anyone I've seen before.

I rap my fingers against the glass to keep from biting them, though there isn't much left to gnaw on. I've already chewed my nails to the quick over the past twenty-four hours.

I check my phone when the customer isn't looking, unreasonably expecting to have heard back from Charles—but there's nothing. Not a text or missed call. The stupid thing might as well be dead.

I only hope Odessa, too, isn't dead.

29

Cate

"HI, SWEETHEART ..." I place my mother's voicemail on speakerphone Thursday evening after work. "You didn't stop over Tuesday, and I haven't heard from you ... just wanted to make sure everything's all right. Also wanted to see if you and Sean want to stop by for dinner this weekend. Call me back. Kisses."

It ends as Sean walks in the door. The smile fades from his face when he takes me in.

In his defense, the last time he saw me was Monday night, after accompanying me to the Palm Shores police station.

"Jesus. Cate." He kicks off his shoes but remains planted on my seagrass rug, as if he's unsure if he should come any closer. His gaze fixes on the empty bottle of wine in front of me. "What happened?"

"You're going to have to be more specific." I blink, my voice monotone. He could be referring to the overfilled ashtray in front of me, the thick cloud of secondhand smoke hazing the small living room, or the fact that my hair is pulled into a messy, greasy bun. The only reason I'm wearing a speck of makeup today is because I worked an eight-hour shift at the shop. If it weren't for the industrial-strength concealer under my eyes, I'd probably look like I'm sporting a couple of shiners.

"You just ... you look like you're ... really going through something." He's treading lightly with his words.

"I haven't been sleeping much." If my mind wasn't so foggy, I could probably calculate the hours of sleep I've had over the past few nights on one hand, maybe two. But I'm too tired to think. Seems like all the energy I have lately has gone into refreshing internet searches and scanning local news stations. I spent three hours circling Palm Shores yesterday, driving the same streets over and over, hoping I might catch a blonde in a Range Rover.

I caught several.

None were her.

"I don't understand." He's still planted by the door.

"You don't need to." I stare past the empty wine bottle at a muted television screen on the other side of the room. I thought the wine would help me relax, but dizzy with a side of nausea is all it accomplished.

"You barely knew her."

"I knew her enough," my words snap back at him.

He shifts on his feet, one hand on his hip, the other rubbing his tired eyes. He's had a long day, and the last thing he probably wanted was to come home to a drunk, semi-catatonic girlfriend with oily roots and yellow-stained fingertips.

"You don't have to stay if you don't want to." I give him an out.

"What are you talking about?"

"You're bothered by this. By me. You don't have to be. If you want to leave, I won't stop you."

He squints. Or maybe he's wincing. "You don't mean that. You're drunk."

"I'm serious. Your family hates me. It took me five years to get comfortable with the idea of you staying the night at my place. You're everybody's favorite person, and I'm your personal wet blanket. I don't know why you stay, Sean. I don't. But I'm giving you an out—maybe you should take it."

"You don't know why I stay?" He scratches at his temple. "You ... don't know why I ... stay."

I laugh even though I shouldn't. It's just that seeing Sean so serious feels unnatural, comedic almost, and in my inebriated state, I'm finding it inappropriately amusing.

"I love you, Cate," he says.

"Why?" I ask, reaching for my wine glass before realizing it's empty.

"Didn't realize I needed a reason."

"You honestly expect me to believe that you love me for no reason?"

Sean exhales, jaw setting. "You're obsessed with this woman because, in a way, you feel rejected, and that's kind of been the theme of your life, Cate, hasn't it? But I'm realizing now ... that you push people. You push them away before they can reject you, and then you pin that rejection on them."

I swirl the burgundy remnants in my empty glass, letting his words sink in, mentally rewinding memories of old friendships gone sour, examining the intricacies in order to determine if it was I who pulled away first. I suppose if I'm honest with myself, the answer would be yes.

"I'm not going to let you push me away." His hand is on the door knob.

"Where are you going?"

"Sleeping at my place tonight. Think we should cool off before one of us says something we're going to regret."

I remain seated on my lumpy sofa, the room spinning a little less than it did when he walked in the door.

"Take a shower, Cate." His head is tilted and his eyes fill with a cocktail of sympathy and frustration. "Drink some water. Wash your face. Get some sleep. This isn't you."

My chest squeezes the second he's out the door and the peculiar sensation in my stomach sends me tripping over myself to get to the bathroom. The toilet bowl is stained mulberry by the time I'm done. I wipe my wet mouth on a hand towel, hunched over the sink, refusing to catch the tiniest glimpse of the woman in the mirror.

I let Sean's words play on a loop in my head, mentally revisiting old friendships as my empty stomach lurches in vain.

Sean was right.

The instant I feel rejection on the horizon, I pull away until the self-fulfilling inevitable happens.

But I didn't do that to Odessa. I didn't pull away—she vanished.

And just when I think she's back in my life, she disappears again.

How can Sean expect me not to wonder? Not to look for her? Not to care?

I stumble to the shower and crank the water as hot as it'll go before peeling out of my sweats. Climbing inside, I sit on the acrylic floor. Alone with my thoughts. Alone with the realization that the only way to make this stop ... is to let her go.

30

CATE

I CLIMB the stairs to my apartment just past seven o'clock on Friday night, hand slicked against the railing, bag heavy on my shoulder. I haven't heard from Sean since our fight last night. I'm not sure if he's taking the space he needs or giving me the space he thinks I need, but as soon as I strip out of my work clothes and get settled, I'll give him a call.

I took his advice last night. I showered. I drank some water. I got some sleep. And I promised myself I'd let Odessa go ... and this time I mean it.

I haven't Googled her once today nor have I checked my phone for missed calls. I didn't squeeze in a fruitless, frenetic drive through the side streets of Palm Shores after work.

Rounding the corner to my hall on the second floor, I stop in my tracks and nearly choke on my breath when I spot a nondescript figure leaning against my door. There are no windows in this hallway, only a flickering fluorescent light every few feet that paints everything in the kind of garish shadows that make up nightmares.

Is it a man or a woman? From here, it's all baggy clothes and a baseball cap.

Slow and nonchalant, I dip my hand into my bag to retrieve my keys and my phone—just in case. We get all kinds of crazies and solicitors in this area, but, over the years, I've learned the trick is to walk with your head up and your shoulders back. Alert, self-assured. You're less likely to get messed with that way.

I'm halfway to my door when the stranger's gaze floats to mine. "Cate?"

A second later Odessa is running to me, arms open wide, eyes damp. She meets me with a hug—one so tight it renders me unable to breathe for a moment—and she smells like earth, like grass and fresh air, flowers and soil—the way a person would smell had they been camping ... or sleeping on park benches. Her lithe figure practically swims in the oversized sweats, and her blonde hair is tucked tight into her hat, save for a handful of messy tendrils that have escaped. She's almost unrecognizable dressed like this, and the bare face with thin blonde lashes and dark, sleepless circles beneath her eyes and gaunt hollows of her cheeks don't help.

There are millions of questions I want to ask in this moment, but I start with, "Where have you been?"

Her gaze shifts past my shoulders before returning to mine, and then she grimaces. "I'm scared, Cate ... can I come in?"

Half of me screams to tell her no, to turn her away. She's clearly in trouble and nothing good can come of involving myself in that—not to mention I can only imagine what Sean's going to say.

But the other half of me knows this could be my only opportunity for answers, for closure.

Against my better judgement, I let curiosity win the moment. Jamming my key into the lock, I wave for her to follow me, and I let her in.

31

Zsofia

"FEEL BETTER?" Cate asks when I emerge from her steamy bathroom wearing the change of clothes she gave me, my hair damp from the shower. Twenty minutes ago, I showed up at her door, and like the good person she is, she let me in without an ounce of hesitation. Before I had a chance to explain anything, she asked if I wanted a shower and a change of clothes.

Her place is quaint, her décor collected and eclectic. In a strange way it almost feels like home, but for now it's a refuge.

"I do. Thank you." I head for the kitchen table where she's prepared a bowl of chicken soup for me. The lip of the olive-green bowl is chipped and the spoon bears a water spot. A folded paper towel serves as a napkin.

"Thought maybe you could use a hot meal." She points to the place setting.

"You didn't have to do that ..."

"It's canned. Don't give me too much credit." She gives me a cautious smile, examining me the way a person might study one of those frenzied, hidden image pictures—like she's waiting for something obvious to jump out at her. "Here."

She pulls out a chair for me before sitting in the one next to it, and she lets me take a few sips of the salty velvet broth before gathering a breath and straightening her posture.

"I—I've been so worried." Her hands move from the top of the table to her thighs and back, like she doesn't know what to do with them or how to get comfortable in front of me. "You left me that voicemail, and then I went to the café and you never showed ..."

I rest the spoon, metal clinking against ceramic. "I have a lot to tell you."

"I went to your house." There's a hint of quavering in her voice. "I was told you don't live there, that you never did."

Ah, yes. The Saint Vincent residence. On rare occasions, I would run errands for Mrs. Saint Vincent—an elderly neighbor of the DuVernays, and on that particular day, I'd forgotten to drop off the gift she sent me out for that morning, so I had to hurry back to Artemis Cove before our lunch date. I hadn't wanted to overexplain, fearing that it would only lead to questions—questions I wasn't ready to answer.

I take another sip from my spoon. Canned soup has never tasted so delicious.

"I'm sorry. I should let you finish," she says, elbow propped on the table and head resting on her hand. "It's just that I have so many questions."

"I'll tell you anything you want to know." I dab the

corners of my mouth with my paper towel. "I only ask that you reserve your judgement until after they've all been answered."

Her brunette brows meet in the middle, lifting in compassion—a good sign. "Of course."

I take another sip before my stomach grows queasy. Nerves, not hunger, are to blame. "What I'm about to tell you, I've never told a soul."

Cate is statue-still, unblinking.

"I don't really know where to begin, so I'll start here: my name isn't Odessa DuVernay." I attempt to swallow the lump in my throat, only to have it return. "It's Zsofia Ivanov."

"What?"

"When I was a baby, my mother came here from Russia, in search of a job, a better life for the two of us." My words quaver. "Since she wasn't here legally, she had to take what she could get—and at the time, it was doing domestic work for Charles and Aviva DuVernay."

Cate leans back in her chair, her dusty stare glued to me.

"About twenty-five years ago, my mother ... left me ... with the DuVernays. At first, they raised me as if I were their own, spoiling me rotten and giving me the kind of fairy-tale childhood every girl dreams of. As soon as my teenage years hit, things changed. I grew more opinionated, started asking all the wrong questions. The clothes and gifts stopped. They moved me out of my bedroom and into an apartment above their garage. Started giving me chores, which then turned into a never-ending housework to-do list. By the time I was fifteen, I was doing all the cooking, all the laundry ... and it was all beginning to make sense ... why they never allowed me to go to school, never taught me to read, always sent me to my room whenever company was over. They never wanted a daughter, they wanted a slave."

Cate's hand slowly clamps over her mouth. "My God."

"Aviana ... their daughter ... she's actually mine," I continue. I pause, eyes squeezed tight, and then I tell her about one of the darkest periods in my life. When I finish, she's dabbing a few tears against the back of her hand. "I'd wanted to leave that house so many times before, but I could never bring myself to leave my daughter. But lately things have gotten worse. Mrs. DuVernay had a falling out with all of her friends, and it made her more cruelhearted than ever—and I was taking the brunt of it. I wasn't sure how much more I could take, so I started planning a way out."

"Is that why you sold the compact? And returned the opal ring? And stole the watch?"

I nod, gaze averted onto the now-tepid bowl of chicken soup. "I had around five grand until the watch incident. I had no idea those things were registered." Shuddering, I continue. "I wish I could forget the look on her face when she confronted me ... she took my phone, my car keys, the money ... and she locked everything in her safe. From then on, she had me working sixty, seventy hours a week doing physically-intense chores around the house. On top of that, she had more security cameras added. It was her way of sending a message—that I could never leave."

"Nobody knows about this? You've lived in that house for decades and not a single person has questioned anything?"

I shake my head. "If anyone asks, I'm the live-in help. But no one asks, no one questions anything. In our neighborhood, that sort of thing is normal. Everyone has help."

"And you never thought to slip a note to a delivery person or anything?"

"The DuVernays assured me that if I were to ever involve the police in anything, that I would be deported by the time it was all said and done."

Cate reaches across the table, her hand covering mine. "Odessa—*Zsofia*, you are a victim here. You've done nothing wrong. You were a child when you were brought to this country and the DuVernays enslaved you. What they did is illegal. There are laws and attorneys and statutes in place to protect people like you."

Without warning, Cate flies up, rushing to the kitchen counter and grabbing her phone.

"What are you doing?" I'm paralyzed in my chair, molten-hot panic searing through my veins.

"Sean's brother-in-law is an immigration lawyer." She thumbs through her contacts.

"No, no. I don't want to get you involved in this."

Cate stops scrolling. Glances up. "You kind of already have ..."

"Please, Cate, sit down. I'm not finished. There's something else."

She returns to my side, phone still in hand, and I take a deep breath. "I—I killed Mrs. DuVernay. *I killed Mrs. DuVernay.*"

I close my eyes, bracing for impact, fully expecting her to scream in my face and send me on my way ...

... but she doesn't.

"What— what do you mean you killed her?" An eerie calm is instilled in her tone.

Hands trembling beneath the table, I tell her everything.

About the fight by the pool. Mrs. DuVernay's confession. The shove. Her tripping and falling into the water. And the fact that I can't swim. I tell her each and every painful second that followed, right up until the moment I called her.

It was five AM that Sunday morning, and I hadn't slept in over twenty-four hours. I'd ditched my car by an abandoned factory the second I got to West Palm Shores, and spent most of that Saturday wandering from city park to city park. That first night I'd slept in an alley because I couldn't find a hotel in the area willing to accept a cash reservation with no card on file. I had my debit card, but using it was too risky—it would lead them straight to me.

I was desperate, delirious, and out of my mind. As soon as I called Cate, I realized how stupid that was in case the police were looking for me. I tossed my phone in the trash and bought a burner for emergencies. Didn't even know I'd forgotten to transfer her number until it was too late.

"So where have you been staying all week?" Cate asks.

"I found this woman in Clydesdale Park. She's got this big house and she rents rooms for forty dollars a night. I stayed there the first few nights ... until someone stole the rest of my money." I shake my head. "I kept it on me at all times ... except when I slept. I stuck it in my pillow, thinking if anyone tried to take it, I'd wake up. But I woke up Thursday morning and sure enough, it was gone. Every last dollar."

"So what did you do?"

I drag in a ragged breath. "I asked the woman who owned the house if she could help me figure out who took it, but she just laughed at me. And then she had someone give me a ride to a homeless shelter—the one on Fifth Avenue. I got a little bit of food and a change of clothes ... and then I spent the night at a park ... slept inside one of those plastic-covered slides so no one would see me and call the police."

Cate chews the inside of her lip, wincing. I imagine she's trying to put herself in my shoes, but it's the kind of thing that's impossible to understand unless you've lived it.

"How did you find my address?" Cate asks after a quiet beat.

"There was this kid at the park. Ten, maybe eleven. I convinced him to let me use his phone so I could look you up. Very sweet boy, but in the end, I think he agreed mostly because he was afraid of me ... I mean, you saw how I looked tonight."

"How did you get here?"

I'm beginning to think her questions aren't stemming from curiosity as much as they're stemming from a place of incredulous disbelief.

"I walked." How else?

Cate's lips part, another question on the horizon I'm sure, when out of nowhere her apartment door swings open and a sandy-haired man in a dirty t-shirt walks in.

"Sean." Cate stands. "I didn't know you were coming over ..."

He looks to her, then to me, and the silence between them is strained, palpable.

"I'm sorry." She places her hand on my shoulder. "Will you excuse us for a second?"

With that, the two of them disappear into her bedroom.

The door closes.

They whisper.

I wait.

32

Cate

"THE HELL, CATE?" Sean drags his hands through his hair before making a fist. "Why is that crazy woman in your apartment?"

"Keep your voice down," I whisper, swatting the air before pointing at the door. "And she just showed up. She was waiting for me when I got home from work. I had no idea she was going to be here. And you're not going to believe what happened."

"Yeah, I'm sure you're right."

I pull him into my walk-in closet, placing a little more drywall and an extra door between us and the kitchen, so I can fill him in. Then I tell him everything I know. When I'm finished, he shakes his head, arms crossed, refusing to look at me.

"Say something." I nudge his arm.

"I don't know what you want me to say, Cate. That

story sounds insane. That woman is insane. And you're insane for housing a murderer—if her story's even true."

"Why would someone lie about killing someone?"

"Don't you think that if some rich woman in Palm Shores was offed by her employee that it might make the six o'clock news? Or that maybe that detective would've connected the dots when you showed up with that voice-mail the other day?"

His points are valid.

And fair.

"And you really believe her that she's been living on the streets?" He points in her general direction, though she's rooms away.

"She looked pretty rough."

"How can you believe a word this woman says after everything she did? Everything she lied about?"

"She had explanations for everything."

His eyes roll. "Show me a liar who doesn't."

"I think we should call Rob," I say, referring to his attorney brother-in-law.

"What?" Sean doesn't whisper, instead he laughs, but it's an incredulous sort of laugh. "I'm not involving my family in any of this. I don't even want *you* involved in this."

"Yeah, well, that's not up to you."

"So what, you're just going to take her in? Let her stay with you indefinitely? What's your plan here, Cate?" He fists another handful of hair before tossing his hands in the air.

"*I don't know.*" My words are choppy and terse. "All I know is she literally has nothing and no one, and I can't just turn her out onto the streets."

"You realize harboring a fugitive is illegal, right? I mean, assuming she is an actual murderer and not some crazy chick."

"Can you keep your voice down?" I envision a scenario in which Zsofia is hearing every word we say, bolting out the door, and disappearing into thin air all over again. I don't have the number to her burner phone and I wouldn't have the slightest idea how to reach her so she can get the help she needs, legal or otherwise. "I'm not going to keep her here forever, Sean. I promise you that. And believe me, I'm well aware that there are holes in her story, things that don't make sense. I was actually in the middle of asking questions when you walked in ..."

His expression softens.

"I really think reaching out to Rob would be the next move here," I say. "She needs to hear it from someone else that she's a victim, that she's not going to be deported. And if what she's saying is true, I can't see why she wouldn't want to talk to him."

Sean's jaw flexes.

"I know you want me to walk away from this, to let it go—"

"—it's not that, Cate. I just want you to be safe. That's what this is about. Your safety. Your *sanity*."

"I'm going to help her ... with or without your blessing."

"I know you are." Without another word, Sean pulls me into his arms and kisses the top of my head. His breath is heavy, much like his mood. As soon as this is over, we can be us again, but until then, I have to help this woman.

I'm all she has.

"I should get back out there." I begin to pull away. "She has to know we're talking about her. Don't want to be rude."

Sean lets me go, catching his hand on mine. "My handgun's in the left nightstand."

"Now you're overreacting."

"Maybe. Maybe not." He lets me go, and I leave the bedroom, fingers crossed that she's where I left her.

"Zsofia," I say when I find her on the sofa, paging through last month's Vogue. A quick glance at the missing soup bowl and place setting at the kitchen table tells me we were in the next room long enough for her to finish her dinner—and pick up after herself.

"I don't want to cause problems for you." She sits straighter, folding the magazine and placing it neatly on the coffee table, next to my emptied ash tray. Did she do that? Upon further inspection, I realize my living room has been tidied. Blankets folded. Pillows fluffed. Reading material stacked. Perhaps these kinds of things are so ingrained into her that she can't help herself.

"Don't even worry about that ... I just needed to fill him in on what was going on. After that voicemail you left, he kind of got invested in your situation," I tell a white lie for the greater good before taking a seat next to her. "I think you should meet with Sean's brother-in-law, maybe figure out how we can use the legal system to protect and not punish you."

Zsofia's complexion turns a sickening shade of ash as she rubs her palms against the tops of her thighs.

"I'm sure you're terrified right now." I'd put my hand on hers, but I'm not a touchy-feely person, at least not with anyone but Sean. "But it's going to be okay. Rob's good at what he does—one of the best in his field—he reminds us of that every Thanksgiving." I offer a chuckle to lighten the mood, though I'm sure it'll take more than an inside joke to carry that burden. "You're not the monster in any of this ... *they* are."

She turns to me, her wide blue eyes clouded in thick

tears, and she throws her arms around my shoulders. I accept an embrace from a stranger wearing my clothes, scented with my body wash.

This woman is nothing like the one I thought I knew.

Nothing.

Then again, that woman never existed—she was merely a costume.

An avatar.

"Thank you, Cate," she whispers. "I don't know what I'd do without you. You're truly an amazing friend."

I wish I could say the same, but I don't know Zsofia in that way ... at least not yet.

"This is going to sound random ... but do you want to watch a movie or anything?" It's a strange thing for me to offer her, but it's barely eight o'clock and she's not in a position to be able to leave the apartment. I imagine it could be a good distraction for her—and for me as well. A little something light to take us away from this strange, heavy world in which we live.

Two hours later, we finish *Splendor in the Grass*—one of my favorite classics, and I shuffle to the hall closet to retrieve a pillow and clean blankets since she'll be sleeping on the couch.

When I finally retire to my bedroom for the night, Sean is perched on the edge of my bed, my laptop cracked open in his lap. The glow of the screen paints his face in cool blue light. He startles when his eyes meet mine.

"What are you doing?" I shut the door behind me with a soft click.

His lips purse, and he shrugs, clicking the mouse. "Just a little research."

I take the spot next to him, resting my chin on his shoulder. He scrolls through a list of local news articles on

Channel Six's website. I don't have to ask him for an explanation—he's doing what anyone would do after having heard Zsofia's larger-than-life story.

In fact, from the instant I put on the movie tonight, I could hardly concentrate, obsessing over and memorizing all the searches I was going to perform as soon as she goes to bed.

"No DuVernay has been murdered in Palm Shores, I can tell you that." Sean hands me the blazing hot laptop. He must have been on this thing all night. "Not this week, not ever. If that isn't a hole in her story, I don't know what is."

33

ZSOFIA

I'M up at six Saturday morning, but the apartment is void of any signs of life and their bedroom door is still closed. I'm sure the two of them are still sleeping, so I tiptoe around the apartment, quiet as a mouse. I manage to find a plastic tote of cleaning supplies under Cate's kitchen sink, so I do some light cleaning.

By the time I'm finished, it's almost eight. Her bathroom is sparkling and her kitchen appears as if it belongs in a model unit.

Cate mentioned last night that Sean has to go to work today, and that she was scheduled to cover Amada's shift from nine-thirty to two, so she should be up any minute.

I'm already growing restless in this apartment—I can't imagine what I'm going to do to keep myself busy. That movie Cate had us watch last night was awful, but I didn't tell her that. She kept saying it was one of her favorites, that no one could compare to the inimitable Natalie Wood, but I thought the ending was trite and depressing, and I hated that the parents institutionalized Natalie's character ... I've always thought psychiatric hospitals were a kind of prison, one for the body *and* mind.

I take a seat on the sofa and reach for one of Cate's magazines. A minute later, the bedroom door opens, followed by a shuffle of feet too heavy to belong to her.

"Morning," I say when Sean comes around the corner.

He says nothing, squinting against the light, and then he gives me a wave.

"Coffee's fresh," I tell him. Old habit, I suppose ...

"Sweet," he says. The sound of clinking coffee mugs and slamming cabinet doors wafts from the kitchen a moment later.

"Hey, good morning," Cate emerges from the hallway, hair sticking up in every direction and pajamas wrinkled.

Sean hands her a cup of coffee, which she graciously accepts.

"Don't thank me, thank our guest," Sean says.

"What?" Cate turns to me. "You didn't have to do that."

"Looks like she cleaned the kitchen while she was at it," he adds. "Don't think I've ever seen it so ... shiny."

"Zsofia, please ... you don't have to clean for us," Cate says.

I shrug. "I was up early. It gave me something to do."

"I can't believe we slept through all of that," she says to Sean.

When Sean doesn't answer, she rushes to fill the void. "Oh, good news. Sean's brother-in-law said he'd meet with you today. It's a Saturday, so he wants to meet at the coffee shop by his house in Cerulean Heights around one."

I'm sure the expression on my face speaks before I do, but I can't risk being seen in public.

"I thought I'd order you an Uber," Cate adds. "Then I could just pick you up on my way home from work."

"I hate to ask this, but is there somewhere more private we could meet?" I flinch from the guilt of having to make such a request when they're being so generous already.

"Um ... I can talk to him and see," Cate offers before she exchanges a look with Sean.

"I should jump in the shower," Cate says, sipping her coffee before turning on her heel and disappearing into the bathroom in the hall.

Sean drinks from his mug on the other side of the kitchen island.

I don't like the way he watches me.

Cate always made him sound so gregarious, so sweet and kind, but his piercing stare sends a torrent of ice water through my veins.

"Busy day today?" I ask, hoping small talk might put us at ease.

"Yep." He takes another drink before dumping the remains in the sink and heading down the hall. "Thanks for the coffee."

"You're welcome," I call out, though I'm not sure if he heard me.

Returning to the sofa, I page through another one of Cate's magazines, unhurried as I pore over each and every painstakingly dull article—anything to kill some time.

The morning commotion from the bathroom dies down after a half hour, and then fifteen minutes after that, the two of them emerge in tandem. Sean wears faded jeans and a t-shirt bearing the name of some electrical company, and Cate is dressed for a day behind the counter at Smith + Rose.

"I really hate to leave you like this," Cate says as she

gathers her things. "I'll write my number down for you in case you need me. Otherwise, I'll plan on picking you up from the coffee shop after two. There's a spare key by the door, if you could lock up when you leave and then slide it under, that'd be great."

She must have forgotten to ask the brother-in-law about relocating our meeting ...

"Help yourself to whatever," she says, stepping into a pair of patent leather ballet flats by the door. "Food, drinks, Netflix ... anything. Just make yourself at home."

"I appreciate that."

A minute later, the two of them are out the door. Three seconds later, the tumbler slides into position. I'm not locked in, I could easily disengage it from this side, but the sound sends a start to my heart just the same.

Going to the window that overlooks the parking lot, I watch from a slit in Cate's vinyl blinds as the two of them walk to their cars, stopping in front of her Honda to chat for a while. Sean points toward the apartment for a second, Cate bats his arm down.

They're talking about me.

I turn away, unable to subject myself to another second.

I have no control over whether or not they believe me.

Making my way to the kitchen to appease the rumble in my stomach, I stop when I pass a black cell phone plugged into a charger on the counter. Cate's phone is white with a rose gold Ana Tucci case. This must be Sean's. Tapping the screen, it comes to life without so much as requesting a passcode.

Rookie mistake.

I abandon the phone and my urges to snoop (old habits die hard), and head to the couch for some bad daytime television, certain that any moment now, Sean will come strutting back home in search of his phone. Honestly, I wouldn't put it past him to have left it on purpose so he'd have a reason to come back unannounced, a reason to try to catch me in the act of doing God knows what.

He doesn't like me, doesn't trust me.

That much he's made clear.

I settle in and flip the channels when I remember that today is Saturday and daytime talk shows don't run on the weekends. Logging into Cate's Netflix next, I spend an hour surfing for the perfect show to watch before settling on some documentary on travel tourism—something to broaden my horizons.

Another hour passes.

And then another.

I head to the kitchen, checking out the contents of the refrigerator out of sheer boredom. Nothing but bottled water, condiments, and chilled cans of RC Cola rest lifeless on the inside. On my way out, I pass Sean's fully-charged phone once more, half-tempted to tap the screen and maybe scan an email or two. It isn't right, I know. But Cate seems to fawn over him all the time, and I'm sorry, but no man is *that* perfect.

Taking a deep breath, I talk myself out of it. The clock on the microwave tells me I have two more hours until I'm supposed to meet with Sean's brother-in-law. Grabbing the slip of paper where Cate left her number, I call her from my burner phone, but she doesn't answer. I'm two seconds from leaving a voicemail when I chicken out. A voicemail can be just as damning as a text message. I'm sure she'll see the missed call and ring me back when she gets a chance.

I fix myself a cup of tea if only for the sake of killing another five minutes before I have to get in the shower—I have no idea what I'm going to wear. I'm slightly taller than

Cate, but I imagine I could find something in her closet if I get creative.

Tiptoeing down the hall, I press my fingertips against her bedroom door, which swings open with a slow creak, and then I show myself to her walk-in closet. It takes all of three minutes for me to choose something—a modest sheath dress and a pair of forgiving heels a size too small. I'm on my way out when I pass what must be her laptop, considering the cover is faux pink marble.

I have to admit, I've been curious to know what the media is saying about me, how intense the search is.

Placing the dress and heels aside, I take a seat on the edge of the bed and pull the computer onto my lap. Dragging my finger across the trackpad, I breathe a sigh of relief when the screen wakes without prompting for a password.

Pulling up a search engine, I begin to run a search for Odessa DuVernay—the name I've been forced to go by almost my entire life, the name that would be plastered in the news should anyone be searching for me ...

... only the search bar auto-populates.

Odessa DuVernay Palm Shores
Odessa DuVernay fugitive
Zsofia Ivanov Palm Shores
Aviva DuVernay death
Charles and Aviva DuVernay
Palm Shores crimes
Palm Shores murder
Palm Shores local news
Charles DuVernay Drop Ship Jupiter, FL
2220 Frangipani Way

Pulling up the complete search history, I see that a

significant portion of these searches were performed last night, after Cate claimed she was going to bed.

I knew Sean didn't believe me—now I know that Cate doesn't either.

I slam the laptop lid closed and struggle to keep my breath. I can't meet Sean's brother-in-law today. I can't be seen in public. They're setting me up.

I imagine arriving at that café at one o'clock to meet with the immigration attorney, only to find myself face to face with Charles.

Heart banging in my chest, I grab a pair of leggings and a t-shirt from one of Cate's dresser drawers, steal a quick shower, and get the hell out of here.

I refuse to be locked up ever again.

34

CATE

I DIDN'T WANT to leave her at my house this morning, but given the short notice, finding someone to cover the shift I was already covering for Amada was out of the question, and Margaret and Elinor are on another finding spree, hitting up a string of Connecticut estate sales this weekend.

The shop's been buzzing all morning, tourists and locals flitting in and out in their sunny garb, bellies full from brunch at LeFabio's up the street.

It's a quarter past noon when I take my first break. Locking the front door, I head to the back, steal a sip of my cola, slip on my gloves, and grab my purse. A minute later, a Newport is pinched between my lips as I light the tip and inhale. My phone buzzes in my pocket. I've been running around so much this morning I haven't had time to check it.

Sliding it out, I'm met with a couple of missed calls and a recent voicemail.

Shit.

I forgot to ask Rob if he could meet Zsofia somewhere else. I had every intention of calling him on my drive in this morning, but then Sean stopped me outside my car in the parking lot and told me Rob wasn't too thrilled about taking on a pro bono case (typical Rob ...) and I spent the majority of my commute stewing over his predictable-yet-ironic lack of compassion.

Pulling up my Uber app, I order her ride. I'm two seconds from calling the number I'm assuming is her burner phone when a call comes in from a blocked number.

Taking a quick drag, I exhale through my nostrils before answering. "Hello?"

"Yes, is this Cate Cabot?" the man on the other end asks.

"This is ..."

"Detective Moreno returning your call."

Oh, thank God. I called him a few minutes before the shop opened this morning, asking him if there had been any recent murders in Palm Shores.

"Yeah, so there were no murders in the past week in Palm Shores," he says. "In fact, last murder was about seventeen months ago. Your question has to do with that DuVernay woman you came in asking about the other day?"

I'm tempted to say yes, but until I figure out what's going on here, I'm better off keeping my mouth shut.

"You ever find her?" he adds.

"No," I say.

"Yeah, well, as far as I know she's still alive." He offers a sniff of a laugh from the other side, like he thinks it's cute that I'm trying to do his job.

"Thanks for your time," I say before hanging up.

I take one last drag before stubbing out my cigarette and tossing it in the trash. Heading in, I snap off my gloves, pop a stick of peppermint gum, and spritz a few sprays of perfume from the staff bathroom into my hair before unlocking the front door where three women greet me with expressions that would indicate they've been waiting for hours.

"I'm so sorry. Come on in, welcome." I usher them inside and return to my post behind the front register.

The women are in and out in fifteen minutes without buying a thing, and I use the opportunity to check my phone again. Moreno confirmed there have been no murders in Palm Shores, but Zsofia seemed reluctant to be seen in public—clearly she did something awful. Or she believes she did.

Pulling up that screenshot from earlier in the week, I check out Charles DuVernay's contact information, the half-accurate information that cost me a whopping sixty dollars. And it's then that I see a second number listed below the first—how I missed it earlier I haven't a clue, but there it is. Plain as day.

Grabbing a nearby notepad and pen, I copy down the second number, checking it three times before typing the digits into my phone and tapping the green button.

Two seconds later, it rings.

Four rings later, a man answers, "Hello?"

My heartbeat pulses in my ears and my mouth runs dry. "Hi, yes, is this Charles DuVernay?"

He hesitates. "Yes. Who's this?"

"My name is Cate Cabot ... I left you a message at work earlier this week—"

"—I haven't been in the office this week," he interrupts. "If this is a work matter, I'll have Jared give you a call first thing Monday—"

"—this is in regards to a personal matter," it's my turn to

cut him off. "One regarding Odessa DuVernay ... or rather, Zsofia Ivanov."

The other end is silent for a couple of beats before Charles exhales into the receiver. "Jesus."

"Would you have time to meet with me this afternoon?" I'm supposed to pick Zsofia up from the coffee shop after two, but Sean gets off at one today. I'm willing to wager that I could convince him to do it for me if I tell him I'm checking into her story. "Maybe around two fifteen?"

"What'd you say your name was?"

"Cate Cabot," I say. Not that it matters, not that he'll remember it.

"Do you know where she is?" he asks. The desperation in his tone is ripe, pathetic. He reminds me of a man with everything to lose and just enough money to make his biggest problems disappear—except this one.

"Even if I did, why would I tell you that?"

I envision that smug headshot from his website, how benign if not boring he looked. All the horrid things his wife did to Zsofia, and this sorry excuse for a man looked the other way. He's just as evil as she is.

"Please, I don't know who you are or what you want, but we've been searching for her all week," he says. "We're worried sick. We need to know if she's safe."

My first instinct is to believe this is nothing more than some D-level acting ... and then I realize he said, "We..."

"Who needs to know if she's safe?" I ask.

"My wife and I," he says without hesitation.

"Your wife ... Aviva?"

"Yes," he says, "If you know where our daughter is, please. If she's in some kind of trouble—"

"Your *daughter*?" I ask.

"She told you her name was Zsofia?" he asks.

"She told me everything," I clarify.

Charles releases an exhausted groan from the other end, and I imagine a wearied man crumpling into an overstuffed chair.

"I don't know what she's told you," he says, "but none of it is true."

"Convenient."

I think back to Sean's words last night. Liars are always quick to offer explanations. With a secret this heavy, the DuVernays have probably honed and polished their lies to perfection over the years.

"Miss, please. I don't know where this hostility is coming from, but we've been worried sick about Odessa all week and we're willing to do anything to have her home again," he says.

Of course ...

"I really want to believe you, Mr. DuVernay. I want to believe that people like you don't exist in this world, but—"

A woman's voice is muffled in the background, but I can't make out the words—Charles must have the receiver covered.

"Hello?" the woman comes on the line. "This is Aviva DuVernay. Do you have our daughter?"

I bury my forehead against my palm.

"I think we need to meet in person, clear some things up." Charles is back on the line.

Standing straight, I clear my throat. "I completely agree. Two fifteen today work for you?"

"Is that the soonest you can get here?"

"It is."

"Twenty-two-twenty Frangipani Way," he says. "We're in Artemis Cove. I'll add your name to the security list. Cate Cabot, you said it was?"

"Yes," I say. "I'll see you then."

The instant I hang up, I call Sean, my trembling hands barely able to maintain a hold on my phone. He doesn't answer, and the man never checks his voicemail, so I hang up and shoot him a text: **JUST SPOKE TO CHARLES DUVERNAY. STORY STILL NOT ADDING UP. I'M GOING TO MEET WITH HIM AND HIS VERY MUCH ALIVE WIFE AT 2:15 ... CAN YOU PICK UP ZSOFIA FROM HER MEETING WITH ROB?**

The message shows as delivered, so I put my phone away and greet the crimson-haired woman swaggering into the shop with a pair of thousand-dollar sunglasses resting on top of her head.

Two o'clock can't come soon enough today.

The wait is killing me.

35

CATE

THE DUVERNAY HOUSE looks exactly as it did in the real estate listing photos, save for bigger trees and fuller bushes. I park my Honda in the circle drive and tap out a quick text to Sean, letting him know that I'm here. My last message to him shows as "read," so I can only assume he begrudgingly picked Zsofia up from her meeting with Rob. Maybe the three of them are chatting or maybe he and Zsofia are en route to the apartment. Regardless, we're going to have a lot to discuss when we reconvene after all of this.

Tucking my phone away and snatching my keys from the ignition, I exit my car and trot up the front walk away to ring the bell. The door opens within seconds—answered by the man of the house.

"You must be Cate," he says. "Thank you so much for meeting with us. Please, come on in."

He's dressed in navy linen shorts and a white polo. A pair of wire-framed glasses rest on the bridge of his nose. He isn't exactly the smug bastard in the headshot that I expected.

"Aviva is in the living room," he says as I step inside the two-story foyer and he shuts the door behind me. "I'm afraid you'll have to excuse the mess ... we've not been ourselves this week."

Or their "housekeeper" has been away ...

I glance around and spot a crystal vase filled with drooping flowers and a random pair of shearling-lined house slippers sitting askew by the front rug—nothing that I would remotely describe as a "mess," but to each their own.

He leads me through the foyer, down two small steps, and into another two-story room, this one complete with floor-to-ceiling windows and a breathtaking view of the Atlantic just past the pool area.

"You must be Cate," the blonde woman—Aviva—rises to greet me. "Thank you so much for coming."

The woman standing before me wears not an ounce of makeup. Her eyes are baggy and swollen, as if she's been crying or not sleeping—or maybe both, and her hair is pulled back into a low bun, a hint of oil beginning to darken her otherwise pale roots.

"Please, have a seat." Charles motions toward an over-sized wingback chair. He and his wife take the sofa across from me and he reaches for her hand, giving it a squeeze.

The entire drive here, I rehearsed the things I wanted to say to them. In my mind, they were monsters, inhuman, the worst of the worst, and I intended to make it clear that I was well aware of their transgressions.

But sitting here, I can't help but feel like I'm sitting across from a grieving mom and dad worried sick about their child.

Only Odessa isn't a child, and she's hardly young enough to be their child.

But if there's anything I've learned, it's that looks can be deceiving.

"Where is she?" Aviva's brilliant blue eyes plead with mine. "Where's Odessa? Is she okay? Is she eating?"

"Can we just ... can we stop with the act?" I ask. "She told me everything. *Zsofia* told me everything. I know about the enslavement. The torture. The abuse."

I know now that Zsofia lied about killing Aviva—or perhaps she truly believed she did—but the reason isn't important. Abuse victims have to do whatever it takes to survive ... and I want to believe that's what she was trying to do—survive. Perhaps believing she killed her employer gave her the courage, the push she needed to finally run.

Aviva buries her head in her hands and Charles lifts his arm around her, pulling her close and shooting me a look as if I'm the cause of all of this.

"I'm afraid you have it all wrong," he says, rubbing her back. "Odessa ... and that is her name ... Odessa—*not* Zsofia—is our adopted daughter. She's our niece biologically, Aviva's sister's daughter. Her mother had issues with drug abuse and mental health and unfortunately she took her own life when Odessa was just shy of thirteen. Rather than having her put in the system, we decided to take her in, adopt her, give her the kind of stability she'd never known. We had good intentions, we did. But as Odessa got older, we realized she'd inherited a few of her mother's ... *issues*, and we also learned she'd been through some trauma in her childhood. Things we weren't aware of. Things that were never addressed or dealt with. I guess what I'm getting at here is that one of the things Odessa struggles with is what doctors haven't quite been able to diagnose, but it's somewhere in the spectrum of Dissociative Identity Disorder. She has a few distinct personalities ... one of which is Zsofia. She makes up these elaborate fictitious ... stories? I guess you could call them? Imaginary exchanges?"

"I should have known." Aviva lifts her head, staring at a vase on the coffee table, her gaze lifeless. "She left coffee out last week, on a tray by our bedroom door. I should have known."

"You can't blame yourself," Charles say to her, his intonation soft and low, like a good husband attempting to comfort his grief-stricken wife.

Sean's words play in my head again. This could all be an elaborate façade, a well-rehearsed lie. A prominent Palm Shores family going to prison for domestic slavery would be ruinous and scandalous, the kind of secret someone would do whatever it took to protect, no matter how ridiculous it be.

"I have adoption papers." Charles rises from his seat. "I have files upon files of her medical records."

"With all due respect, those things can be easily faked," I say. I hate to be rude, but I also have to state the obvious.

The DuVernays exchange looks, lingering in unreadable contemplation for a moment, before he disappears down the hall and she returns her attention to her lap, picking at a chipped manicure.

When Charles returns with thick stacks of file folders tucked under his tanned arms, he places them one by one on the coffee table before turning them toward me.

I scan the labels on the sides: *Odessa Adoption, Odessa Medical, Odessa Psychiatric* ...

"She may be our adopted daughter, but we love her as if she were our own," Aviva says.

"What about your other daughter?" I ask, suddenly

recalling Zsofia's tearful retelling of birthing a beautiful baby girl, only to hand her over to Mrs. DuVernay without so much as a chance to hold her first.

Aviva's gaze snaps toward the ocean view windows.

Charles forms a peak with his fingers.

"You must be referring to Aviana," he says.

"Yes, Aviana."

"Aviana was our stillborn daughter." Charles takes his wife's hand. "Odessa was about fifteen when it happened, and it was quite upsetting for her. It was devastating for all of us, of course, but I don't think she knew how to process it."

"I'm so sorry," I say.

"I don't suppose you'd like to see her death certificate too?" His question is curt, deservedly so if he is, indeed, telling the truth.

Reaching for the *Odessa Psychiatric* file, I flip to the first page and scan the text of one of her earliest evaluations. Everything matches what Charles has shared, but I stand by my conviction that these kinds of things can easily be faked.

"We tried to go to the police last weekend to file a Missing Persons report," Charles says. "But we were told because she's an adult and she left willingly and doesn't appear to be in danger to herself or to others, that it didn't meet the criteria. Guess it wasn't enough that the location tracker on her phone was off or that West Palm Shores police found her car abandoned at a city park ..."

"She told me she killed you," I say to Aviva.

"What?" Her eyes are bloodshot and she looks to her husband before returning her confused gaze my way. "Why would she say that?"

"She told me you had a fight by the pool Friday night,

that she shoved you and you fell in, hitting your head on the concrete on the way. She thought you drowned ..."

Charles drags a hand along his bristled jaw. "My God."

"That explains it," Aviva says to him.

"Explains what?" I ask.

Aviva rises from the sofa, making her way to the sweeping east-facing windows. "Our pool has been drained since last month. There's a crack that needs to be repaired, and they can't send anyone out until the thirtieth."

"Here." Charles hands me his phone. The top of the screen is filled with the blue and orange Belgrove Security logo, and beneath it are a series of black and white videos. "This is the security footage from the night she left."

I press play on the first one, the time stamp designating it as a 11:48 PM Friday night. The video is dark, slightly grainy, but there isn't a doubt in my mind that the woman pacing the perimeter of the pool, appearing to have an argument with no one, is Zsofia.

Three minutes pass when Zsofia stops pacing, stands perfectly still at the edge of the pool, and then crouches, as if she's examining something. A moment later she sprints to the pool house, tugging on the locked doors before dashing inside.

I press play on the next video, this one stamped at 12:01 AM Saturday—a simple video of Zsofia backing out of the DuVernay driveway in her Range Rover.

Handing the phone back, I'm at a complete loss for words.

"As you can see, this is what we've been dealing with this week," he says.

"Please tell us where she is," Aviva says, teary-eyed. "She needs help. She needs her medication. She needs to come home."

My heart is tight, and my response gets stuck on the way up.

"All we've done this week is drive around the city looking for her," Charles says. "Every night we wait by our phones. My wife isn't sleeping, isn't eating. Odessa has put us through quite a bit over the years, but she's never run away, and we're afraid something terrible could happen to her if she finds herself in the wrong company."

"She's safe," I say.

"Oh, thank God." Aviva clutches at her chest, exhaling the longest, slowest breath, and then she buries her head against Charles' shoulder. "Where is she?"

"She's at my apartment," I say. "She came by last night. I gave her some clean clothes, she took a shower, had some soup. Said she'd been living on the streets this week but she's okay."

Aviva smears a tear from her cheek. "I have to say, as upsetting as this misunderstanding has been, it's comforting to know she has a friend. She hasn't had a lot of those over the years. I'm sure you can understand why."

"Cate, I know you have good intentions," Charles says, "but we need to get her back home. You should know that without her medications, her behavior can sometimes be ... erratic ... unpredictable."

A chill rushes through my veins.

She's with Sean.

"Perhaps you consider Odessa to be your friend, but believe me when I say that helping her could put you at risk. Her delusions can sometimes be ... dangerous," he adds.

"Where is she, Cate?" Aviva asks.

"She's at my apartment right now," I say. "Or at least she should be. 4489 Hawthorne Court, 2C."

The two of them rise from the sofa, nearly bumping into

one another as they head for the kitchen, grabbing shoes and keys and bags and phones. Aviva hands me a pen and paper and has me scribble down the address for them.

Gathering my things, I follow them out the garage door. They climb into a black Bentley, and I make a mad dash for my car. It's only when I climb inside that I remember Zsofia —Odessa—claiming she was forced to live in a small apartment above the garage. Glancing up at the Mediterranean estate before me, I realize the roof above the garage is perfectly flat.

There is no apartment.

Everything she told me was a lie.

Everything.

The DuVernays are already gone, en route to my apartment. They haven't wasted a second.

I start my engine and floor the accelerator, fumbling for my phone so I can call Sean to give him a heads' up, only the second I get to the first stop sign, I find a text from my brother-in-law: **YOUR FRIEND NEVER SHOWED. THANKS FOR WASTING MY TIME …**

What?

Why wouldn't Sean have told me? Surely he would've sent me a text, especially since I asked him to pick her up.

The car behind me honks—a red Mercedes. I slam my foot into the gas pedal. Racing through the winding palm-tree-lined streets of Artemis Cove, I don't stop until I'm past the security gate and caught at the next red light.

With shaking hands, I call Sean—only to be sent to his voicemail in the middle of the second ring.

Sean never sends me to voicemail.

The light turns green and I gun the engine. It isn't until I'm speeding through the next yellow light when a text comes through—from Sean.

Coordinates.

It makes sense now. He must be in danger, unable to answer a call or send a text, so he sent me his location.

If Odessa hurts him, so help me ...

I tap the coordinates and slam my finger on the "directions" icon, waiting several endless seconds until the route is calculated.

Twelve miles to my destination, an estimated seventeen-minute trip.

With a death grip on the steering wheel, I drive to the industrial side of West Palm Shores, unable to assume anything but the worst.

36

Cate

I COME to a stop outside a gray warehouse when my phone alerts me that I've arrived at my destination. The sun-faded remnants of an old factory logo tattoo the north side of the building, and below that a steel door is propped open with a lone cinderblock.

The only vehicle in the parking lot is mine.

If Sean is here with Odessa, where's his truck?

I shift into park as another text comes through from Sean: **HURRY**.

Charles' words play in my head ... Odessa could be dangerous, unpredictable. Climbing out of my car, I leave my bag on the passenger seat and my keys in the ignition in case we need a quick getaway. Reaching in, I retrieve my phone and pop the trunk. A tire iron is the closest thing I have to a weapon, a means of defense.

Heading in through the open door, my heart in my teeth, I press 9-1-1 into my phone—if I can't talk to them, at least they'll be able to trace my call, get a location, and send an officer to respond.

One step and I'm engulfed in darkness.

"Hello?" I call out, only to be met with echoes. "Sean?"

I know better than to call for her. I know better than to clue her in on the fact that I'm aware of her mental instability.

"Everything okay?" I ask, trying to play dumb despite the obvious rattle in my voice.

I try to scan my surroundings, only I can't see a thing. The sliver of afternoon sun coming from the door behind me hardly illuminates more than a handful of steps beyond its steel frame.

Raising my phone, I wake the screen. The light stings my vision. Through squinted eyes, I tap the flashlight icon—only to be met with a fully-illuminated woman with wild eyes and a gun in her hands—Sean's gun.

Startled, I drop my phone into the dark abyss, the feeble flashlight pointing up enough to provide an eerie, under-cast glow on Odessa.

Hand over my ricocheting heart, it takes everything I have to tamp my fight-or-flight response. I imagine a scenario in which I lunge at her, the two of us wrestling in the dark to obtain control over the firearm, and the gun accidentally going off ... hurting one of us in the process —or worse.

"I don't understand." I lift my palms to show her that I'm willing to cooperate. "What is this about, Zsofia?"

I use her fake name in hopes to keep her as unruffled as possible. And I don't ask about Sean because he's my Achilles heel. If she knows he's my main—and only—concern, who knows how she'll use that against me.

"Can you please put the gun down so we can talk?" I ask, offering a tepid, wavy smile.

Odessa readjusts her hold on the grip. Her eyes narrow, glinting in the dark.

"Rob said you didn't show up to the appointment ... I know you were worried, but you're going to get through this. Whatever's going on, whatever this is about ... I'm here for you," I say.

"Spare the bullshit, Cate. You don't care. You're just as fake as everyone else. You're one of them."

"*Zsofia, I care about you,*" I say with as much conviction as a woman with a gun pointed at her can offer. "And I'm nothing like them."

"And you would know that how?" she asks, head tilted. "Or would you like me to answer that question for you?"

My mouth turns dry. Paralyzed, I hesitate to swallow, to make so much as a move, a sound.

"I know you went to see Charles today," she says. "I know you don't believe me."

"It's not that simple."

"No, I think it is. I confided in you, Cate. I went to you for help and you took care of me, made me promises, you were going to make everything better, you were going to keep me safe," she says, tears building in her crazed stare. "But I saw your search history. Some friend you are."

I try not to flinch, try not to react at the thought of her going into my bedroom, helping herself to my computer, to Sean's side of the bed where his handgun was kept in the top nightstand drawer.

What were her plans? What was she searching for to begin with?

"Your parents—"

"—my parents? Is that what he told you?" Odessa interrupts me, this time waving the gun as she gestures. "Please tell me you didn't buy that."

"There's no apartment above the garage," I say. "The roof is flat, there's no way—"

"Were you even at the right house?" Her tone is so convincing I almost believe it. "They own multiple properties."

"They're worried about you," I say.

"Who?" Her nose is wrinkled.

"Your *parents*."

Her hands fall to her sides, the gun remaining in her grip. "You're a smart woman, Cate. I don't know how it is you can't see through their lies."

I agree with her—I consider myself more attuned than the average person.

And I don't know how it was that I couldn't see through hers.

"If I believe you, will that change anything?" I ask, gaze darting to the gun and back. She doesn't answer and her lips are pressed flat. "I know you're angry with me, I assume you lured me out here so you could hurt me. But I'm willing to hear you out. Maybe we could go somewhere and talk? Compare notes?"

"You must really think I'm dense."

"Where is Sean?" I ask the million-dollar question, seeing as how she's proving to be a difficult one to assuage. "Do you have his phone? It was you texting me, wasn't it?"

"No idea what you're talking about," she answers without an ounce of emotion in her tone. My stomach caves, drops. She doesn't want me to know if he's okay ... or if he isn't.

"Please, Zsofia. Leave him out of this. This is between us."

"He isn't here. But you'll find him. Eventually ..."

She could be bluffing, trying to scare me.

Or she could be telling the truth.

It's impossible to know.

My open palms turn into clenched fists for a moment, and hot tears blind my vision. I picture myself returning to my apartment, finding Sean dead from a gunshot wound to the heart. Perhaps he came home looking for her, after she stood up his brother-in-law, only to find himself staring down the barrel of his own gun.

"You don't have to do this," I tell her. "If you were upset with me, you could have just left. You could have walked out of my life and not looked back."

It's what most people seem to do ...

"Kind of hard to leave when you don't have a dollar to your name," she says, lifting the gun and examining it. "I was actually looking around your place for some cash when I found this. Originally planned to pawn it or sell it on the street, but something small like this isn't worth more than a couple hundred dollars, and God forbid I try to sell it to a plainclothes cop."

"So you thought this would be the better alternative?" I ask.

"I didn't do what I did only to trade one prison for another." The assertion in her tone leads me to believe she is fully Zsofia in this moment, living out a situation she believes to be real.

And what makes you think I didn't call the police before I came in?

Now that I think about it, I don't remember pressing the green button to send the call through.

I tapped the three numbers ...

I walked inside the pitch-black warehouse ...

Everything from that moment until my phone tumbled out of my grasp is lost in an anxious haze. I'm not sure how long I've been here, but I imagine the police would've come by now had I pressed send.

"Zsofia, please," I say, hands clasped in front of my chest. "If you put the gun down now, if you disappear, we can pretend this never happened. We can go our separate ways, and I won't tell a soul about any of this."

"You actually expect me to believe that? You sat there and listened to my story. You gave me clothes and food and a shower. We watched a movie together, and then you went back to your room and searched on your computer for proof that I'm a liar. Why would I make this up?" A thick tear slides down her cheek but she brushes it away with the back of her hand, lowering the gun in the process. "Do you have any idea how it feels to be betrayed by the one person you thought you could trust?"

If she only knew ...

"I do, actually. I know exactly how that feels."

Her expression softens in the dark, or maybe I'm imagining it, maybe I'm searching for hope in places hope could never belong—until the wail of sirens sound in the distance.

"You called the police," she says, voice quavering. "Why would you do that? They're going to take me away ... they're going to put me in prison or send me back and—"

"—you didn't kill Aviva DuVernay," I say. "You're not going to prison. You're not a murderer."

"I saw her," Odessa says. "I watched her fall into the pool. There was *blood*. You're just saying that. You're lying to me."

Dragging in a rugged breath, I shake my head. "I saw the security footage. You were pacing around an empty pool. It looked like you were having a heated argument with someone ... but there wasn't anyone else. Aviva DuVernay? She's alive. I spoke with her today. And she's very concerned for your safety. They want you to come home."

The sirens in the distance are louder now, closer.

If she truly lured me out here to kill me, she has mere seconds to get the job done.

"Put the gun down," I say. "This is your final chance to keep this situation from becoming a hundred times worse."

"No," she says, two hands gripping the handle. "You don't understand. You don't believe me. Nobody ever believes me."

Without warning, Odessa presses the gun against the underside of her jaw, a woman who wholeheartedly believes she has no other way out.

"You have no idea how loved you are," I tell her. "Don't do this."

She presses the nose of the revolver deeper into her flesh, eyes locked with mine as her lips tremble.

I've watched far too many crime shows over the years to know that if the police walk in and see her with a gun, they have a fraction of a second to determine if she's an immediate threat, a fraction of a second to determine if they need to use lethal force.

The sirens blare on the other side of the factory walls. Red and blue lights flash through the sliver of propped door.

"*Please*," I plead. "Put the gun down!"

Our eyes hold for a single, never-ending second—until the door behind me swings open, banging against the wall. In an instant, I'm on the ground, curled, head tucked against my knees and eyes squeezed tight as the police announce their presence, screaming at Odessa to drop her weapon.

The gunshot that follows reverberates through every part of me.

My ears ring.

I don't want to look up.

I don't want to know ...

A moment later, a hand loops into my elbow, pulling me up, dragging me out of the abandoned building and through the steel door where a caravan of squad cars are parked, lights flashing and doors left open.

"Cate!"

Someone says my name. Or maybe I'm imagining it. My ears still hum from the gunshot and with overwhelmed senses, processing everything around me seems like an insurmountable task at the moment.

"Cate, oh God." Somebody wraps me in their arms, though I hardly feel it I'm so numb. "You're safe, I've got you."

It's Sean.

I cling to him until my arms ache.

"Where is she?" A woman asks, rushing toward the building before an officer stops her. A few paces back, Charles trots to keep up with Aviva. I can't make out what the cop is saying to her, but I can only assume the worst when she lifts her hand to her mouth before burying her head against her husband's chest.

A million thoughts flood my mind all at once, rivers of conflicting emotions trickling in every direction.

I turn away, unable to watch for another moment—until I hear a shriek.

Glancing back, I realize I had it all wrong. As per usual, I assumed the worst ...

Emerging in handcuffs, two officers flanking her sides, is a very-much-alive Odessa DuVernay. Charles and Aviva rush to her side, their flagrant show of emotion a stark contrast against the void of hers.

The gunshot I heard must have been an accidental discharge.

Sean pulls me tighter against him. "I forgot my phone today. Left it at the apartment. When I got home from work around two, it was gone. I knew right away she'd taken it, so I hopped on your computer and logged into my mobile account so I could locate it ... was going to wait for you to get home so we could find it together—but then the DuVernays showed up at our place. They said you were right behind them. We waited a little bit, but you never came. That's when I knew something wasn't right. I called the police, gave them the coordinates to my phone, and came as fast as I could. Longest drive of my life."

He hugs me again, kissing the top of my head.

"She saw the search history on my computer," I say. "And if you left your phone ... she must have seen the texts I sent earlier—telling you I was meeting with the DuVernays. She also took your gun."

He exhales a hard, warm breath. "Jesus. I didn't even think to check—everything happened so fast. I just wanted to get to you. What was she planning on doing?"

"I don't know," I say as the police load her in the back of one of the cars. I imagine she'll be looking at firearm-related charges. If only she'd listened to me. "I don't even think she knew."

A curtain of ragged blonde hair obscures the side of Odessa's face as she sits in the backseat of the police car, chin tucked against her chest.

Odessa is carted away, and the DuVernays head toward their daughter, only to be directed away. A tear-stricken Aviva says something to the officer, arms flailing. Charles soothes her, tries to direct her back to their Bentley. I imagine she simply wants to speak to her, ensure she's okay.

An officer approaches me, a pen and a pocket-sized notepad in hand. He has questions, I'm sure.

We all do.

The car hauling Odessa pulls away. The DuVernays follow close behind.

It didn't have to be this way, but at least her parents can rest easy knowing she isn't sleeping on the streets—and that she'll get the help she so desperately needs.

37

CATE

MY FIRST DAY back at the shop after a week off is dream-like, as if I've stepped into a parallel universe. Everything looks the same, smells the same, sounds the same—and yet everything feels different. Or maybe it's just me. I don't think a person could go through what I went through and not come out different on the other side.

Sean took the past week off too, refusing to leave my side for more than a minute at a time. It was overwhelming at first, but then I embraced it, reminding myself of those gut-wrenching moments I was certain I'd never see him again.

Over the span of a week, things between us have shifted, leveled-up. I don't take him for granted. I don't resent him for loving me anymore. I allow myself to need him, and I don't punish myself for it either.

No one knows what the future holds, but as long as mine holds him, that's all that matters.

The sun gleams a little brighter, a little hotter today. Not a cloud in the sky, not a rain drop to be found. Another Palm Shores summer is on the horizon, one filled with brightly-dressed tourists and the usual assortment of transient residents.

I told Sean over the weekend that I think it's time for a change ... be it job, apartment, or last name—and not surprisingly, he offered his full support.

I don't think it'd be the worst thing to never to set foot in Palm Shores ever again. Over the years, I've always associated it with my Cabot roots, quietly living vicariously through the well-to-do locals, imagining an alternate universe in which I was raised with that Cabot silver spoon, dining at the nicest restaurants in the most exclusive yacht clubs, a fortunate woman with a bona fide connection to Golden Age legends.

My fantasies were only ever an escape, a way to fill in the blanks.

Now that I know I'm not a Cabot, I'd like to set my sights on figuring out who I am, unlocking a part of me I never knew existed. I've already placed an order for one of those mail-order DNA tests that help you find your relatives and ancestors. Given my mother's history and the sliver of information John Cabot shared, more than likely my biological father is a random man who paid for one fateful night with my mother. I doubt he knows I exist and for that reason alone, it's impossible to be bitter about it.

I've yet to confront my mother—one thing at a time.

I'm sure the whole John Cabot story was just a way for her to give me answers, an identity instead of a giant question mark. My mother is far from perfect, but she hasn't a malevolent bone in her body. She was simply doing what she thought was best for her fatherless daughter.

The bells on the door jangle and the morning's first customer waltzes in, a pleasantly plump woman in a white shift dress, lips the color of pomegranate and auburn hair cut into a glossy, jaw-length bob.

"Welcome to Smith + Rose," I say, standing behind the glass counter. Tugging on my sleeve to ensure it covers the nicotine patch on my arm, I steal a glance at the time. It's been hours since my last smoke. I don't give myself too much credit though seeing how this is merely day one. "Looking for anything in particular?"

Her coffee-hued gaze darts around the shop, the familiar look of a woman overwhelmed by options.

"I need to get a gift for a friend ..." she says in a thick Southern drawl. "Preferably something small enough to stick in a carry-on. Going up to Stone Mountain for the weekend and God forbid you show up to Suzanne McConnell's country house empty-handed. You ever see a Southern conniption fit?"

I chuckle. "No, I'm afraid I haven't."

The woman's brows lift and she whistles through her bright lips. "Well, it ain't pretty, I'll tell you that much."

Sauntering around the shop, she examines silk scarves, vintage tea cups, and candles before heading to the glass counters that house our fine and costume jewelry.

Hovering above the ring case, she leans in closer before tapping her punch-pink fingernail against the class three times. "Oh, that's a pretty one. The opal with the diamonds. She'd love something like that."

"Good choice," I say, wrangling the key from the chain on my wrist and unlocking the display. A moment later, I place the ring on a square of velvet, standing back as she admires it from all angles.

"Have half a mind to keep this for myself," she says,

working it over the last knuckle on her right ring finger. "But my mama always said it's bad luck to buy yourself an opal ..." The woman examines and inspects the shimmering bauble before tugging it off her finger. "All right, fine. I'll buy it ... *for my friend.*"

I place my hand out, palm-side up, ready to settle the transaction. "Lucky girl."

38

Odessa

"YOU JUST HAD to go making a mess of things again, didn't you?" Aviva's words play on a loop in my head.

I shuffle across the linoleum floor in my rubber-soled shoes, sliding a wrinkled dollar bill into a vending machine. Every soda, every bottled water costs a perfect one dollar. God forbid they have change in this place. That could get dangerous. Can't hurt yourself with a dollar bill—I mean, technically you could if you tried to eat it or choke on it, but the human body has mechanisms in place to prevent that sort of thing.

But coinage!

My word, you can do all sorts of nefarious things with quarters and dimes and nickels.

Or at least that's what my new friend, Scarlett, told me.

We had a lengthy discussion yesterday on the dangers of loose change and all the reasons why they're considered contraband at Glenn Ridge Psychiatric.

Scanning the endless array of sugary drink choices and two selections of sold-out water, my finger hovers over the second to last button from the bottom. A quick push is followed by a clunk and a thump, and just like that, an icy-cold bottle of Royal Crown cola waits for me in all its safe, plastic glory.

I retrieve my prize, give it a moment for the fizz to settle, and amble toward a sofa that faces a barred window, taking a seat beside a girl who can't be much older than eighteen. Her features are sunken, hollow, and her body is drowning in her pale pink extra-small sweatsuit. Eating disorder if I had to guess, though I've been wrong before.

"You're new here." I slump into the seat beside her, uncapping my soda and taking a quick pull. Kicking my feet up, I use the wall as a footrest before I dig my hand into my imaginary pocket and retrieve an imaginary cigarette. I imagine the way it would feel sandwiched between my index and middle fingers, envision the gray wisps curling from the cherry red tip, and then I bring it to my lips, dragging in a breath before letting it go. It's mind-blowing how soothing the simple act of breathing can be. *In. Out. In. Out.* Just like that. "Name's Cate, by the way. Cate Cabot. What's yours?"

Sitting up, I pretend to toss my cigarette on the floor before grinding it into the milky linoleum with the rubber sole of my left Ked.

Without saying a word, the bone-thin girl gets up and walks away.

They tell me my name is Odessa, that I have multiple personalities, and that I'm here to "get better." What they don't know is that the joke's on them. I know exactly who I am, which is why I'd much rather be someone else—*anyone* else.

Today I feel like being Cate.

If only she knew how fortunate she is to have avoided the fate I'd planned for her that day—unlike the real Zsofia Ivanov.

The way I look at it, I did that poor woman a favor by pushing her off my parents' boat in the middle of the Atlantic last summer. Charles and Aviva were never going to come clean about what they did to her mother, and they were never going to let her leave. Too much of a liability. Death was the only way to end it, to put them all out of their misery.

Someday they'll thank me.

But for now, I'm here.

I take a generous gulp, letting the sugary bubbles bounce on my tongue before they tickle my throat on the way down. In the corner of the room, a man sits at a table, sketching into his notebook with a charcoal pencil. His sandy hair is long, swooping over his forehead, partially obscuring his twenty-something baby face.

Rising from my spot by the window, RC cola in hand, I make my way over to introduce myself.

He's no Sean, but he'll do.

Available Now!

Dove

It's been three hours since you died. Well, more like five. It was five hours ago when they found you cold and lifeless in the birch grove outside my apartment. But it was three hours ago when they knocked on my door and asked me when I'd last spoken to you.

I type my password into my work computer—one-zero-one-four.

October fourteenth.

Today's date.

What should have been our fifth wedding anniversary.

The screen flickers to life and plays its joyful chime as a picture of us populates the desktop wallpaper pixel by pixel. We were baby-faced in this one, both of us just having finished our junior years at Holbrook College and venturing on a cross-country road trip to celebrate. We stopped at some hole-in-the-wall ski town east of Telluride. Neither of us had ever skied before, but we loved the idea of being skiers someday.

We were staring down the barrel of forever back then, weren't we?

"What are you doing here?" Noah—Dr. Benoit—stands in the doorway of my office in his white dental coat, a paper mask hanging from his neck and a file under his left arm, and I'm ejected from my melancholic trance. His brows come together and his thin mouth is agape.

"Sorry I'm late." I double-click on the insurance soft-ware icon: a smiling tooth against a sky-blue background.

"I didn't think you were coming in today." He speaks with the kind of carefulness one might exercise when handling a delicate china tea cup.

"How'd you find out?" I'm not in the mood to explain something he couldn't begin to understand, so I deflect with a question.

"The clerk at the gas station was talking about it," he says. "Did you get my text?"

"Yeah," I say. Now that I think about it, he did text about an hour ago to check on me. But the last few hours have been a hazy blur. "Thank you for that."

If good news travels fast, bad news travels faster, especially in Lambs Grove, Kansas, where nothing tragic ever happens.

We always used to joke that there was some kind of magnetic force field surrounding our hometown, an invisible blanket that shielded us from things like natural disasters, mass shootings, and scandal—political, professional, or otherwise. But sometime between midnight and four AM, the protective force field was shattered when you were left to die in the birch grove outside my apartment.

Noah examines me with his dark hooded eyes and an unreadable expression on his boyish face, and I imagine he's wondering why I'm not crying.

I would if I could.

Numbness, disbelief, and a cocktail of mood stabilizers will do that to a person.

"I thought maybe you'd want some time to ... process everything," he says, his cadence like a gentle tap dance as he avoids weightier words like death and grief and murder and loss.

"These insurance claims aren't going to file themselves." I manage a flicker of a half-smile before my gaze moves toward the name plate on the edge of my desk. *Dove Damiani.* I never changed my last name back to Jensen, and I never intended to because you were going to come back for me. "Oh. And here's your almond milk hazelnut latte. No sugar. Extra foam. The balance on your card is getting low. FYI."

I slide the coffee toward the edge of my desk. He hesitates before retrieving it.

"If you change your mind ... if you want to go home later ... if you want to take a couple of days," he says, "we can handle things around here."

"I'll be fine." *Home* is a sorry excuse for an apartment on the north side of town—4.7 miles from the cozy brick ranch we used to share—and today it's the last place I want to be. Five-hundred square feet of contractor-beige, assemble-yourself furniture, and clearance-bin candles to cover the cat urine-scented carpet. I never bothered to feather this nest because it was only supposed to be temporary.

I gather the stack of encounter forms from the top tray

of my desk—last Friday's appointments that I wasn't able to file since the system was down for maintenance that day.

Noah lingers. I'd be annoyed at him if he wasn't coming from a good place. It's a shame you two never got to meet. I think you would've been friends.

"Pretty sure you're booked solid this morning," I remind him as I type in the name of the first patient and press enter. The machine whirs and the software 'thinks' as it tries to process my request. I reach for my coffee, taking a sip out of my glittery, rose gold-colored reusable mug—the French Press Café gives a thirty-cent discount when you bring your own.

"Right," Noah says, pressing his lips into a flat frown until his dimples show. They make me think of your dimples, the ones I'll never get to see again, the ones that gave you a youthful, playful sort of look and made waitresses, sales clerks, and strangers on the street do double-takes.

My desk phone rings—a transfer from the receptionist.

"We'll chat later," I tell him before spinning in my chair until my back is toward him. Lifting the receiver, I cradle it on my shoulder. "Benoit Dental. This is Dove."

"Is this the office manager?" a woman asks. Her piercing voice sends a shock of pain to my eardrum.

I tap the volume down several notches. "Yes it is. How may I assist you today?"

"My daughter was just there for a cleaning last week and when she got home, she realized some *jackass* slipped a card in her goodie bag," she says. "Some referral for some shrink or something? I want to file a complaint against the hygienist. You're a damn dentist office. You clean teeth. You're not qualified to tell people they need mental help."

A torrent of cold bursts beneath my skin and my middle tightens.

I don't tell her that the "jackass" was me, I don't tell her how I consoled the crying young woman in the hallway for a solid twenty minutes, nor do I tell her the enamel of her twenty-one-year-old daughter's teeth is destroyed from years of the bulimia she kept secret from her hypercritical mother.

It was I, not her hygienist, who slipped the card for Dr. Deborah Schermerhorn into the bag.

"I'm so sorry to hear about that," I say. "I'd be happy to share your concern with Dr. Benoit on your behalf."

"That won't be necessary. I want to talk to him myself."

"I understand, but he's scheduled with back-to-back patients this week and as the clinic manager, I handle these matters." I speak quickly, before she has a chance to talk over me. "I can assure you I'll address the responsible staff member as soon as possible, but please know that we're terribly sorry for upsetting you and your daughter."

It's a lie. I'm not sorry.

Sometimes people aren't capable of acting in their own best interests, sometimes they need a gentle nudge—or a good hard push—in the right direction.

It's times like these that I think about you and your students, Ian. All those instances you went above and beyond, staying long after the final school bell rang to hold study sessions or volunteering to take the history club to Washington, D.C. for a week every summer and paying for your expenses from your own pocket so there would be extra money in the budget for more sightseeing.

Remember when you donated your clothes to that family with all the boys when their house burned down?

And how could I forget all the times you'd give school

rides to neighbor kids when they missed the bus after their parents had left for work?

There's a reason you won the prestigious Greenleaf-Montblanc Education Association's *Teacher of the Year* award your first year at Lambs Grove High. You were an angel, Ian. A saint of an educator. And you left a legacy no one will ever be able to outshine.

It's funny how people expected me to hate you after the divorce. They assumed I was bitter, told me I had every right to be angry with you, to curse your name and air your dirty laundry. But it was going to take a lot more than a piece of paper and a naked ring finger to make me fall out of love with the man who'd made the last twenty years of my life the best ones I'd ever known—frighteningly perfect.

I glance at your vintage LeCoultre aviator timepiece on my left wrist—the one I snuck into a small box of mementos when I moved out six months ago. The second hand is motionless, the time stuck at 1:43. It needs a battery and a tune-up, but the idea of parting with it for a week doesn't appeal to me, not now.

You treasured this watch, and it was one of your favorites—a gift from Grandpa Damiani before he passed. But as soon as it stopped working, you placed it in your top dresser drawer for safe-keeping and never got around to getting it fixed. I took it when I left, planning to get it serviced and give it back to you when the time was right.

But the time was never right.

And then you requested all communication be handled directly through our lawyers—which was right before you started dating my then-friend, Kirsten Best.

You weren't yourself this year, Ian, but I loved you too much to hold that against you. I knew you too well to take it personally. It was a phase. A whim. A funk. You were going to come back to me.

Returning to my screen, I finish e-filing the first of Friday's claims. The scent of your citron and vetiver cologne wafting off the collar of my blouse fills the air with a subtle transporting softness. I'd taken one of your travel-sized bottles from the bathroom the day I moved out, thinking it might help to spray it every once in a while when I was feeling particularly blue and nostalgic. It only took a month for me to use it up and I ended up opening a charge card at the department store so I could buy a new bottle. When the woman behind the counter told me it was a limited edition, that they were going to stop carrying it soon, I bought two of the larger bottles.

I still can't believe you're gone but I swear to you—I'm going to find out who did this.

You have to believe me.

Dove

"Kirsten did it." Ariadne points a splintered chopstick at Noah from her side of my kitchenette table after work Monday. "My money's on her."

"And you know this how?" Noah counters.

Ari lifts a shoulder before readying a bite of sesame chicken. "She was the closest person to him. And nine times out of ten, it's the significant other. Maybe he pissed her off? Maybe he cheated on her and she snapped? Women snap all the time. That's why there's that show about it ... what's it called? Oh, yeah. S*napped.*"

Noah exhales, mouth pressed flat, as he considers Ari's theory. "They hadn't been together that long. You have to have more invested in a relationship to snap like that."

"Unless you're crazy," she says without pause. "And someone who steals their friend's ex-husband the second he's single ..."

"Doesn't make them crazy," Noah cuts her off. "Self-serving? Yes. Coldhearted? Absolutely. Insecure? Very much so. But crazy? I disagree with you there."

My kitchen table is a panorama of opened wine bottles and paper boxes of savory Chinese takeout, but my hunger has yet to show its face.

During my lunch break earlier today, I grabbed a deli salad out of habit, sat in my car with the box in my lap, and didn't take a single bite. Ninety minutes went by before I realized I'd been sitting there, dazed, and I hurried back to the office, sneaking in the back door before anyone realized I was late.

"Fine, *Detective Benoit*, what are your theories?" Ari angles her body toward him, her elbow resting on the table.

"He knew something," he says. "And someone wanted to keep him quiet."

Ari rolls her eyes. "So you're basically saying he was a mafia informant. In Kansas. Who moonlighted as a history teacher."

"No. I'm not saying that at all," Noah says.

I glance behind me toward the muted TV in my living room, only to find them reporting on the upcoming pumpkin festival.

"Maybe he was making meth? Like that chemistry teacher in that Breaking Bad show?" Ari's mocking him now, her lips wrestling a smirk.

Noah ignores her sarcasm. "I'm just saying he probably knew something about someone, something really awful, and that someone wanted to make sure their secret was safe. Forever."

"You guys," I interrupt them. "He was a small-town high school history teacher, not an FBI informant or a drug dealer or a mob rat."

"Maybe we shouldn't be talking about this right now?" Noah's elbows settle on the table as he studies me. He's been doing this all day, looking at me like I'm two seconds from falling apart.

I almost left work early today because I'd finished my claims for the day, but also because Noah wouldn't stop checking on me.

And I get it.

To the outside world, it looks strange that my ex-husband was murdered in the middle of the night and I went into work like it was any other day, but it's not like there's a manual on this sort of thing.

All I knew was sitting at home in isolation, pacing my apartment wasn't going to find your killer.

When I got home tonight around a quarter past five, they still had the birch grove girdled in yellow tape, and an officer in a squad car had taken up residency outside the entrance to the hiking trail, keeping people from stepping foot inside. The scene was night and day from this morning when the parking lot was packed full of police and DCI and news vans.

Locals have been coming out in droves. I watched them from my car for a few minutes when I pulled in. Everything from rusty conversion vans to shiny white BMWs crawled and creeped through the parking lot, trying to steal a glimpse of ... well, there isn't much to see anymore.

By the time I parked in my assigned spot, I noticed a sunny-blonde newscaster from Channel Seven standing in front of the birch thicket as a heavy-set camera man filmed her giving a report. I don't know what she could possibly be reporting on. Seems like all they do now is recycle the same information fifty different ways until it almost sounds new again.

Anything to sell ads, right?

You always said the news was in the business of spinning tragedies as entertainment to make a few bucks, and you weren't wrong.

"You doing okay, Dove?" Ariadne places her hand over mine, pulling me out of my thoughts. "You're quiet."

"She's always quiet." Noah winks at me from across the table.

"You know what I mean," Ari snaps at him. She reaches for her wine glass, throwing back a liberal swig. "This whole thing is wild. I mean ... stuff like this never happens here, and then for it to happen to someone we know?" She glances down. "*Knew*."

Noah says nothing.

He doesn't know you and he never knew you, only the version he gleaned from stories. I painted you in the best light I could, but Ari couldn't resist getting her digs in when the opportunity arose. You weren't her favorite person to begin with, and you didn't do yourself any favors by breaking my heart. I'm sure Noah sees through it though. He's good at reading between the lines.

You were too.

"Anyway, are there *any* leads?" Ari asks, changing the subject.

I sigh, releasing a lungful of tension. "I wouldn't know. I kind of want to call his parents, but I don't want to overstep."

Ari scoffs. "You were married to the man for almost five years and you've known him since you were fourteen. You have every right to call and ask what's going on. Screw what they think."

If only it were that easy.

I have nothing but love for your parents despite no longer being in touch. I'll reach out at some point to offer my sympathies, but not today. I imagine they're raw, and the last person they want to hear from is their former daughter-in-law.

"I just had a thought," Ari says. "Remember a couple of years ago when Ian volunteered to chaperone his AP History class on a trip to St. Louis? And you wanted to tag along and he said you couldn't because they had enough volunteers?"

"Someone needed to stay back with Lucy," I say.

"Is that what he said?" she asks.

"Kennels are expensive, and we'd just replaced the alternator in my car."

"But he had money for a hotel room ..." she says. "He paid for it from his own pocket, right? Because he wanted to make sure the kids could go to some extra museum or something?"

"He split the cost with a couple of the other teachers," I say.

"Didn't one of them back out at the last minute?" she asks, brows lifted. "I swear you told me that."

"Jeannie McNamara's mother was in hospice," I say. "She had no choice. By the way, what are you trying to imply?"

"That maybe if you stop making excuses for him for two seconds, you might realize that the signs were there all along." Ari crosses her arms in her lap, shoulders squared with me.

"Signs for what?" I ask.

"That he was up to something," she says. "That maybe he wasn't as perfect as you always thought? That maybe he wasn't always giving you the full story? That there might have been more going on than you realized?"

"I think I'd know my own husband," I say. I resist the urge to scoff and remind her we were together for twenty years.

"And what about all those grad courses he was taking? All those night classes semester after semester, with no degree to show for it?" she asks.

I don't need to explain to her that you took a few terms off here or there and that graduate degrees take years to finish when you're chipping away at them one class at a time.

"The man is dead. Are you really going to criticize his academic shortcomings?" My voice is higher, louder than I intended.

We trade a hard stare for a moment, a silent standoff.

"It's tragic," Noah finally speaks, his gaze secured on me as he cuts through the tension with his placid attempt to moderate. "Regardless of the fanfare and excitement coming from our end of the table, I hope you don't think we're making light of any of this."

He reaches across the table, navigating through white boxes of fried rice and chicken, and he places his hand—which is soft like the powdery insides of a latex glove—over mine.

Sometimes I think he *likes* me, but as my boss and a new dentist with a budding reputation to protect, he's never once acted on it—thank goodness. I never wanted to have to explain that I was waiting for you to come around.

He's too pragmatic to understand.

"Speak for yourself," Ari says, getting up from the table

to take her dish to the sink. She swats her hand at him. "Ian was a selfish prick. Maybe now you can finally start moving on."

The small space is engulfed in a quietude so heavy it sinks into my shoulders, rendering me motionless as I lean back in my seat.

"What is wrong with me?" she asks with a self-directed sneer. "That was a shitty and insensitive thing to say. I just mean, maybe now you can find someone who will treat you better. Someone who'll actually appreciate you."

Ari peers at the empty plate in her hands.

"I'm horrible at this kind of thing ... death," she adds. "I never know the right thing to say. Sorry if I'm all over the place."

I don't fault her for any of it.

She's the kind of person who laughs at funerals and cracks jokes in uncomfortable situations. You always thought she was excessively sardonic and coldhearted, but I've been around her long enough to see that that side of her is nothing more than a coat of emotional armor.

On the inside, she's as vulnerable and sensitive and full of heart as anyone else. It's too bad you never got to experience that side of her, but it was always easier for me to keep the two of you separate.

"It's okay." I lean across the table and top off her wine glass to show her there are no hard feelings.

"Shoot," she says as she watches me. "I can't stay, babe. I have to let my mom's dog out. She's on her fifth cruise of the year. The woman can sail all over the world on luxury cruise liners but God forbid she opens her Givenchy pocketbook for a proper pet sitter."

"No worries," I tell her.

She leans in, giving me a quick side hug. "Call me if you

need anything, okay? I mean it. I don't care what time it is. My phone's always on for you."

"I know," I say. "Thank you."

She heads toward the door, stepping into her neon cross trainers before snatching her bag off the console table. Ari's a vision in blue, still dressed in her dental hygienist scrubs. It means the world that she came straight here after work, not bothering to stop at home for a quick change.

Before she leaves, she turns back and offers an apologetic wave, lips pursed.

"Everything's going to be okay," she says. It's rare for Ariadne to offer any sentimental (if not cliché) words of advice. She isn't the world's most optimistic woman, as you know. "We'll get you through this."

Her attention moves to Noah, then back to me, and with that, she's gone.

The door closes with a firm click, and I look to Noah, who's dabbing the corners of his mouth with a paper napkin, so polite.

You were always proper like that. Overdressed and well-mannered was the unspoken Damiani family motto. In all our years together, I think I saw your father in jeans all of three or four times.

I miss your parents.

Your mother reached out once, after the divorce papers had been filed, and I ran into your father with a few of his golfing buddies at the Mexican restaurant in town a few months ago. I think it was more awkward for them than for me. You were their son, their loyalty naturally belonged to you. But they also loved me like a daughter and love—in any form—doesn't just go away, it doesn't dissolve into thin air.

Your mother didn't say this explicitly, but I think she disagreed with your decision. Your father, if you're curious, offered nothing but avoided eye contact and small talk about the weather as we'd had a massive heatwave that day. He's always been one to deflect and change subjects that are too uncomfortable for him. I was glad he didn't ignore me or look through me the way you look at a former acquaintance who has since become a stranger. That would've stung.

Before we parted ways, I never had a chance to tell them what they meant to me, and I regret that. If it weren't for them, I might never have known what a lasting, functional marriage looked like or how a "normal" family environment operates.

That was one of the things I loved most about you, Ian.

Everything about your life was ordinary in the best of ways.

Your parents didn't fight. Your house was always clean and smelled permanently of cinnamon potpourri. You had a dog and a cat and an older sister who didn't make your life a living hell. Your parents had stable, white-collar jobs and your mom drove a Chrysler minivan until you left for college. You never smelled of second-hand smoke and your clothes were always wrinkle-free and dryer-fresh. You were amazing at baseball and soccer and your parents never missed a game, whether it was home or hours away.

You had the perfect family, and I was blessed to be a part of it. I'd never experienced so much love and inclusivity. The Damiani home became *my* home.

Even during our college years, when everyone was homesick for their childhood bedrooms, I was homesick for your mother's chicken cacciatore and your father's dry sense of humor and the way the hall by the laundry room smelled after your mother had just switched a load of white towels into the dryer—Downy April Fresh with a hint of chlorine bleach.

But I digress.

From where you are now, I'm sure you know these things.

"You need to eat something," Noah says as he clears the table.

"Not hungry." My stomach is as hard as a rock, braced to reject anything I might attempt to offer it.

He pours what's left of one of the wine bottles down the sink, his back to me. I shouldn't be drinking with my meds anyway. It could cause seizures and black outs. It says so right there on the labels, in neon yellow stickers with bold print.

"I can't imagine what's going through your mind. I wish I had some sage advice for you, but I've never lost anyone close to me before."

"It's enough that you're here," I say. If he wasn't, I'd probably be poring over old photo albums of us while our wedding video played on the TV screen in the background.

Remember our wedding dance and how we practiced every night for an hour the month leading up to the big day? You wanted it to be perfect.

And it was.

Every choreographed step, every camera flash, every grin plastered on the faces of our friends and family as they watched you twirl me and toss me while the live band performed a medley of swing songs.

I rise from the table and place what's left of the food cartons into the fridge where they'll likely remain untouched. It was kind of Noah to spring for dinner like that, and I don't want to come off unappreciative.

"You want to take a walk? Maybe get some air?" Noah asks when we're finished cleaning up a few minutes later. It doesn't take long to clean a kitchen so compact it could fit in an RV. It's not like the kitchen we used to share in our house on Blue Jay Lane. There's no island, no stainless-steel hood vent. No oversized side-by-side refrigerator humming between built-in cupboards and cabinets, ready to spit crushed ice with the press of a button. "It's kind of chilly, but I've got a jacket in my car I could throw on."

In many ways, it's like someone else's kitchen and I'm just borrowing it for now ...only "now" has turned into an indefinite and non-specified amount of time.

I contemplate his offer for all of three seconds before saying, "I think I'm going to stay in tonight."

Noah lifts a dark brow. "Are you sure?"

You were never a worrier, Ian. I loved that about you. You were a doer. A restless soul. A fearless embracer of change, taking on every plot twist life threw at you as if it were an adventure. That was the Sagittarius in you.

Noah yawns, covering his mouth with the back of his hand.

"You should go home," I say. "Get some rest."

Noah lingers in front of the kitchen sink for a moment before dragging a hand through his short, dark hair.

"Yeah, all right," he says. His eyes lift to mine. "I'll have my phone on all night if you need anything. And if you want tomorrow off—or the rest of the week—take it. Take all the time you need."

"Appreciate it," I say, leaving it at that. As of now, I fully intend to be at work in the morning, but I'm not psychic. I'm not sure what tomorrow will bring.

None of this feels real yet, and honestly I'm still waiting for reality to sink its teeth deeper into me, all the way to my marrow.

I escort Noah the full five steps to the door, standing back as he slips on his shoes and checks his pockets for his phone and keys. He's an organized type and there's something deliberate about this, like he doesn't want to go yet, and I wish he would because if he asks me if I'm okay one more time …

"Thanks for dinner," I say, arms folded as I lean against the wall. "And thanks for coming by."

"Dove, of course," he says, eyes squinted almost as though my show of gratitude offends him.

We exchange wordless goodbyes as he leaves, and I lock up behind him.

It's funny—growing up in Lambs Grove, no one ever locked their doors at night, but ever since moving to this apartment and living alone for the first time in my life, I've made a quick habit of it.

Making my way to my room, I take a seat on the floor beside the bed and fish the wooden memento box from beneath the box springs. It's the mahogany one you made in your high school wood-shop class with Mr. Pierson, the one with your initials cauterized into the bottom. A minute later, I'm flicking through stacks of old photos of us as a myriad of your things surround me on the floor.

Faded shirts.

Ties.

Your lucky keychain.

Ticket stubs.

A dried prom boutonniere.

Grabbing the empty bottle of your cologne next to my left ankle, I lift the nozzle to my nose and inhale your scent, dragging it into my lungs again and again until I can no longer smell it.

The fact that someone wanted to kill you is one that I can't wrap my head around. You were smart and kind and educated, involved in your community and your parents' church. You went above and beyond for your students, put in long hours without so much as a single complaint. You never forgot a birthday and always made sure to equally divide Mother's Day amongst your mother, my mother, and all the grandmothers. Your best friends were the same ones you'd had since childhood, and I've always thought that said a lot about the kind of person you were—loyal, nostalgic, dependable, and reliable.

I can't imagine anyone feeling such animosity toward you that it would drive them to take your life.

It had to be random ... that's the *only* logical explanation.

This had to have been the work of an opportunist— maybe the kind of opportunist who swoops in like a vulture to feed on the remains of her best friend's marriage?

Rising, I fish my car keys from the bowl by the door.

I'm going for a drive.

Dove

She saw me.

But in my defense, I wasn't trying to be inconspicuous. I wasn't trying to sneak by unnoticed. It's not illegal. I wasn't harassing her. I would never do those things.

This isn't about me getting revenge, this is about you getting justice by any means necessary.

I slowed to a crawl when I got to the house, trying to grab a quick mental snapshot before speeding off. But all I gleaned was that she was home—evidently alone—and she was peering out the living room window, her body poorly masqueraded behind a curtain panel.

Hands gripping the wheel, I turn off Blue Jay Lane and

head back to my side of town, the window half rolled down and the radio tuned to some Top 40 station.

I find it interesting that your parents aren't there to console her—or to be consoled by her.

If we were still together, your parents and I would've been inseparable from the second news broke.

It makes me wonder what they think of her, if they find it odd that you spent twenty years with me and the instant you bring someone new into the picture, you're mysteriously murdered. Of course Michael and Lori are too kind-hearted to make their opinions known to anyone but themselves, but I can imagine the connection they're drawing and I can imagine it matches the one I'm drawing myself.

In less than ten minutes, I'm back home.

I strip out of the day's clothes and wash up before crawling beneath the chilled covers of my lumpy used mattress. My thoughts go to her. To Kirsten. The way she peered out from behind the curtain as if the backlit living room wouldn't give her silhouette away. It's like a cat that thinks it's hiding beneath a chair, tail sticking out to give it away.

I stare at the ceiling for several endless minutes, mind spinning, before I relent and grab my phone off my night-stand. The screen flashes to life and I wince as I dial down the brightness and tap in my code. A second later, I type your name into a search engine to see if there are any new developments. The top result in an article on CNN, but the timestamp shows it was posted earlier this morning. No updates. I check the articles on the three local news stations in the area, but the information is stale and recycled.

They still don't know who killed you and they haven't released an official cause of death.

I can only pray it was quick.

I don't like to think about you suffering.

A yawn hits me out of nowhere and the phone turns to dead weight in my hands. Looks like I might get some sleep tonight after all.

In the seconds before retiring for the night, I decide to perform one last search ...

... on Kirsten.

Why I never thought to do it before is beyond me. Then again, I've always taken people at face value.

The first time we met was when she came to deliver some mail of mine at my paint-n-sip and introduced herself as my business neighbor, the owner of Best Life Yoga. Everything about her was Zen and graceful and centered, the way a yoga instructor should be. We met again after that at a mixer for local business owners. She ran up to me, excited to see a familiar face, and we talked all night like two people who'd known each other their whole lives.

Our close friendship spanned two years, and not once did I ever think she would do what she did.

Not once.

You think you know someone, Ian ...

She duped us both, I'm afraid.

I type "Kirsten Best" into the search bar and the results assume I'm searching for "Kirsten Dunst." Sighing, I type in "Kirsten Best Detroit, Michigan" and try again. Results populate the screen in seconds, and I start at the top with an unused LinkedIn account, before continuing to an article about a legal aid under scrutiny for embezzling—the photo does not match.

The third result is a memorial.

I click on the headline.

A black and white photo of a good-looking man with

dark hair and dimples, unquestionably too young for an obituary, takes the upper left-hand corner. I scroll down and find his name—Adam Nicholas Meade. And then his age—twenty-seven. His obituary is brief, mentioning that he grew up in Detroit, worked as a welder, and passed unexpectedly.

There's no mention of parents or siblings, just that he had a lot of friends ...

... and that he is survived by his *fiancée*, Kirsten Best, of Detroit, Michigan.

END OF SAMPLE.

AVAILABLE NOW!

ABOUT THE AUTHOR

Sunday Tomassetti is the pseudonym of a Wall Street Journal, Washington Post, Amazon Charts and #1 Amazon bestselling author (Winter Renshaw/Minka Kent) who wanted an outlet for her passion projects. A thirty-something married mother of three, she resides in the Midwest where you can always find her hard at work on her next novel. She is represented by Jill Marsal of Marsal Lyon Literary Agency.

For more information, please visit www.sundaytomassetti.com or sign up for her newsletter here.

Don't forget to follow her on Instagram and like her on Facebook!

Made in the USA
San Bernardino, CA
07 March 2020

65423244R00178